The HAUNTING of CRIMSHAW MANOR

THE
HAUNTING
OF CRIMSHAW MANOR

MARK E. DROTOS

bhc
press™

LIVONIA, MICHIGAN

Edited by Stephanie Bennett
Proofread by Caron Oty

THE HAUNTING OF CRIMSHAW MANOR

Copyright © 2022 Mark E. Drotos

This book is a work of fiction. The characters, incidents, and dialogue are drawn from the author's imagination and are not to be construed as real. Any resemblance to actual events or persons, living or dead, is entirely coincidental.

Published by BHC Press

Library of Congress Control Number:
2020940647

ISBN: 978-1-64397-245-9 (Hardcover)
ISBN: 978-1-64397-246-6 (Softcover)
ISBN: 978-1-64397-247-3 (Ebook)

For information, write:
BHC Press
885 Penniman #5505
Plymouth, MI 48170

Visit the publisher:
www.bhcpress.com

To Mary, my wife, my love.
I cannot fathom taking on this journey without you.
Thank you for putting up with my strangeness.

To Elizabeth, Nicholas, Emily and Andrew,
my children whom I love.
I hope I am a good example of how
to never give up on a dream.

And to the readers who have decided to
open this book and explore the paranormal with
a touch of mystery, suspense and of course, humor.
I hope you enjoy it and look forward
to future investigations.

The HAUNTING of CRIMSHAW MANOR

1

E ver since he was a child, strange things seemed to follow Stephen. After graduating from high school, most teens wanted to leave home and go to out-of-state schools or the military. Not Stephen. Strathmore University beaconed to him like a lighthouse, and when he found out a program was being introduced in paranormal studies, there was no doubt that he was going to attend Strathmore University.

After earning his bachelor's degree, he applied and was accepted to Strathmore's graduate school. He worked hard in a field that was seen as odd or strange, but Stephen was used to those labels. It had even earned him the nickname "Stephen Strange." That was fine with him; Doctor Strange was a cool comic book hero in his mind.

What made Stephen strange was not his behavior. It wasn't his talk or mannerisms. He wasn't a geek or freak. In fact, standing at six feet tall with a slim body toned from rock climbing and dark features, he was seen as mysterious. He enjoyed playing up the stereotype of a college professor and sported a trimmed mustache and goatee. There really wasn't anything that stuck out as strange about him, but Stephen had *odd* things happen to him and around him. It had always been a part of his life, and what was strange to some people just *was* for him.

"Are you going to come in, Stephen, or just stand there?" a voice said from the other side of the door. Stephen opened the door and entered Dr. Marcus's office. It was not his first time here, but things were different now.

Dr. Mark Marcus was the Dean of Paranormal Studies at Strathmore University. He had an interesting career as a college professor and had written several books about the occult and the paranormal. During Stephen's undergraduate studies, Dr. Marcus had guided him along. Eventually, Dr. Marcus became his mentor during graduate school, and he sent Stephen a letter offering him a position as an adjunct professor. The letter was like a beam of light from the Strathmore lighthouse.

"Come in, Stephen, come in. Have a seat," said Dr. Marcus, offering his hand as he came around his desk. "Can I get you some coffee or something to drink?"

"No, I'm fine, Dr. Marcus. It's good to see you again."

"Please, call me Mark. We are colleagues now, after all."

Stephen smiled at that. He did not see himself as an equal to Dr. Marcus; this would take some getting used to. Stephen sat down in an old chair in front of Dr. Marcus's desk. He looked around at the office. Nothing had changed in the year he had been gone. Stacks of books and even taller stacks of papers fought for space upon Dr. Marcus's large desk. Bookcases lined every bit of wall space and contained not only the best books on the occult and paranormal but strange artifacts, trinkets and oddities. It was a comfortable place for Stephen.

"I have to laugh at this turn of events and must make a confession of sorts." Dr. Marcus chuckled. "I have selfish motives for hiring you."

"Is that so?" Stephen was intrigued.

"Yes, yes. After all, you of all my students have had the most promise of bringing credibility to our field. Your gifts, and yes they are gifts, make you truly stand out among our peers," Dr. Marcus said.

"Thank you, sir. I have always enjoyed researching and studying. Your offer was a godsend, but you did seem a little vague about what my exact duties would be."

"I did? That's because there will be plenty of time to discuss everything. School starts in about two weeks and as you can imagine the school waits until the last moment for wishful requests that cost money. You were mine. I need someone to teach some of the intro classes, and you would be a perfect fit."

"That sounds great. How many classes?"

"Three classes for the upcoming Fall Semester. Two on Monday, Wednesday, and Friday; one on Tuesday and Thursday. The program has really had a lot of interest due to the popular shows on cable over the past several years."

Stephen cringed at that comment. A lot of students who took classes in Paranormal Studies were weird, freaks or, quite honestly… strange. Most took the class as a joke or figured it would be an easy elective. In reality it was a lot more difficult than most believed— research, documentation, scientific experiments. Hopefully the word had gotten out that these classes were not an easy A.

Dr. Marcus looked like most professors: early fifties, salt-and-pepper beard, glasses. As he sat behind his desk Stephen couldn't help but think he looked guilty of something.

"There is one other duty that comes with this position," Dr. Marcus said slowly.

"What might that be?"

"The school has been requested to recognize a student organization and has agreed to do so. The group needs a faculty advisor. That…would be you."

Okay, not a deal breaker, thought Stephen. "That's fine. I wouldn't mind it at all."

"Good, very good then." Dr. Marcus got up from his desk. "I will get you set up in an office down the hall, and we can go over classes, schedule, paperwork, and everything else tomorrow. Get yourself settled, and we can meet first thing in the morning."

Stephen stood and the two walked to the door. Dr. Marcus shook his hand. "I am looking forward to you being here."

"I'm looking forward to being here as well. I can hardly wait to get started. I have so many ideas."

"That's what I was hoping for." Dr. Marcus smiled and thought that hiring Stephen Davenport fell into his plans perfectly.

◆ ◆ ◆ ◆ ◆

Walking out of Mercer Hall, Stephen was ecstatic about how things had turned out. Having graduated a year ago, he did not have many prospects for his future. He had stayed in Strathmore, living with his mother and younger sister. It had been his childhood home—heck his only home—and like most unemployed, well-educated twenty-four-year-olds he needed a place to live while he was figuring out what to do.

Stephen took a deep breath, enjoying the late summer day. *Yes, life was good*, he thought. He looked about his surroundings with a fresh outlook. It was as if everything on campus had changed and to some extent it had. Strathmore had taken on a whole new atmosphere. He was not only looking at his hometown and university, but he was now seeing it through the eyes of an accomplished adult.

Strathmore was a typical Virginia town located near the western border of the state. Blue-collar workers and middle-class professionals filled the town, and farms were scattered along the outskirts. Strathmore had a long history and many secrets to go with it.

The town was situated along the Amangamet River between two ranges. It had originally been built to facilitate trade going into Wardensville, West Virginia and Harrisonburg, Virginia. The river unofficially separated East Strathmore from West Strathmore.

East Strathmore contained the old downtown, the majority of homes, plazas and older farm properties. West Strathmore was where the university had been built. Newer homes, apartments, college bars and restaurants had been and continued to be built to accommodate the school. The bridge that connected the two halves was the sentinel.

Stephen grew up in East Strathmore. His mother and sister still lived in their family home on Grove Avenue. Stephen had wanted to move out, to feel more like an adult, but it just didn't make sense since his meager part-time jobs barely kept gas in his car. His mother worked at the nearby elementary school, while his twenty-one-year-old sister worked at Sheetz, at least this month.

His father had died of a heart attack when Stephen was only fourteen years old. Stephen's father had seemed too young to have died, but he was a smoker and drank excessively. Despite these flaws David Davenport was a good man who made sure his family was taken care of. While the investments and savings he had stashed away during his thirty years of working for the railroad didn't make the Davenports rich, it had provided them with a comfortable life. Stephen had been able to go to college; the family took nice vacations. All in all, they had lived the American dream.

Stephen thought about his father. It had been roughly a year after David Davenport's death that Stephen had experienced his first "strange" event. He had been sleeping fitfully when he awoke around 3:00 a.m., and for whatever reason he had gotten out of bed and had wandered into the family room as if drawn to it.

It had been very cold, he remembered, like it usually was in the dead of winter when the electricity goes out. Wondering if something was wrong with the furnace, Stephen was headed to the basement when he was met by a most unusual sight. Sitting in the old La-Z-Boy recliner with a newspaper in his hands was his deceased father. A strange feeling entered Stephen as he gazed upon him, not fear but curiosity.

"Dad?" Stephen croaked out, still wondering if he was asleep.

The figure lowered the paper, and with a shocked expression on his face looked at his son. He seemed to realize that Stephen could see him as well. He stood and with silent words said, "*I love you.*" And with that he faded.

◆ ◆ ◆ ◆ ◆

Stephen blinked his eyes, still standing on the steps of Mercer Hall. While it had been ten years ago, it felt like it had just occurred. What had made him think about that? He never did see his father again, but he did see other things. Many things. At the age of fifteen many changes took place within young Stephen. Among the many normal changes of a teenager something else had happened. Stephen began to see those who had died. *Yes, I see dead people*, he thought. Not as a medium, or at least not what he believed a medium was, but Stephen could see and interact with the dead. This is what people felt was strange about him. An aura of death surrounded him. For Stephen this is what had been literally haunting him for the past ten years, and he believed it would continue for the rest of his life.

The decision to study Paranormal Studies seemed only natural. Stephen was fascinated with the field of paranormal research and quite honestly wanted answers as to why he had these "gifts" and what their purpose was.

"I guess this is my path, Dad," Stephen said to himself as he walked down the steps. It was still a fine day and plans had to be made. After all, it was the first day of the rest of his life.

2

E velynn Dumavastra was sore. Sore and dirty. Having just finished ballet practice, she wasn't in the mood to think about the upcoming semester at Strathmore. She wiped the sweat from her face and neck, packed up her ballet slippers, water bottle, towel and other items and prepared to exit the dance hall as soon as possible.

"Thank you, girls. Please be on time next week," Mrs. Bresser said.

Evelynn frowned at that. Next week was going to be hectic as it was. She was not sure she would be able to attend the practice, let alone be on time. She mentally went over her to-do list. Start school, organize the club, prepare for the fall recital, begin writing her paper, take the dog to the vet, get her hair cut… The list went on.

Mrs. Bresser, however, was helping her, and being on time was the respectful thing to do. Having a dance scholarship placed large demands on Evelynn's time, and juggling everything took effort. She appreciated the extra private lessons that Mrs. Bresser offered outside of class.

Evelynn was in her senior year at Strathmore University. Majoring in dance was not something she craved, but she could not afford to pass up the scholarship offered to her. Paranormal Studies was her dream. She was good at ballet, having done it most of her life, and if doing so allowed her a reduced cost on tuition, all the better. Several people thought it would be too much for her to keep up with her studies and performances. Not Evelynn; after all, it's not hard to do something you enjoy. And dance and the paranormal were her two greatest loves.

Exiting the dance hall, Evelynn walked across campus in the early evening. It was cool and the air felt good. It was nice this time of year. The days were warm, the evenings cool and not many people were on campus yet.

She shared a condo with another girl off campus which was close enough but not too close to the hectic noise and distractions of dorm life. Still, it was students who lived there, and while they were mostly juniors and seniors, they were still college coeds.

Evelynn had taken summer school classes due to her workload and desire to be at Strathmore, so she had the condo to herself. Her roommate, Christine, was due to arrive in a few days. Her sabbatical, as she thought of it, would then be over.

As she entered the two-bedroom condo on the second floor, she thought about how much she would miss the quietness and privacy she had enjoyed these past couple months. She entered her room peeling off the dance skins she had been wearing. Throwing the dirty clothing to an ever-increasing pile surrounding a basket in the corner, she smiled. "I'm going to have to fix that bad habit," she said to herself. Christine was a clean freak.

Evelynn walked out of her room and into the living area stark naked. *Something else I'll have to stop doing*, she thought as she grabbed a water bottle and yogurt before sitting on the couch. Being on the second floor and with the campus being practically a ghost town during the summer, Evelynn was not fearful of being seen.

At twenty years old Evelynn had a dancer's body. Firm and muscular, she preferred to be free of the tight-fitting clothing she seemed to constantly wear for practices and recitals. Standing at five foot nine with long legs and a mane of long black hair, Evelynn had turned the heads of many young men. For a variety of reasons, however, her dating escapades did not seem to last very long.

Most of the boys, and that's what they were, were either only interested in getting into a physical relationship with her or were just too immature. Any real conversation quickly demonstrated no common interests and, combined with her cautious approach to sex, ended with no further dates and the occasional guy spreading lies that she was either a lesbian or an ice bitch. The first she knew wasn't true, but the second she wondered about.

Evelynn wasn't an ice bitch; she was just distant. It wasn't on purpose. Since she was a teenager, whenever she got emotionally attached to someone or something, she would dream about them. Not the fantastical dreams of most teenage girls but other dreams. Dark dreams.

The dreams would be interwoven among her normal ones, but after a while Evelynn discovered that while they were only dreams, they tended to portray possible events yet to come or vague things that had happened in the past. Over the years she discovered that with some discipline and practice she could somewhat interact with and recall the dreams. Through her studies at the university she had discovered that she possessed a sort of precognition ability that apparently manifested itself while she was in a dream state.

At first the novelty of being able to occasionally mystify her friends with her insight was neat; she soon discovered a darker side to this ability. Evelynn's high school friends thought she had great intuition based on her ability to know who liked who or if so-and-so was going to be asked to the dance. It didn't always happen, however, and it only seemed to happen with those she had a close relationship with.

Her family riddled her dreams often, and at the age of sixteen she had a disturbing dream of her father touching and kissing his secretary. Rather than going to school that morning, she went to his office and confronted him directly about Ms. Flynn.

Her father acted shocked and denied any type of indiscretion between his secretary and himself. Evelynn could tell that he was embarrassed and must have been at least thinking about the young, attractive woman. A week later Ms. Flynn was transferred to another department, and her dad began to spend more time at home. Coincidence? Perhaps. But other dreams that she had did come to pass, if not exactly, then close enough.

It was her senior year in high school, and the Spring Formal was the next day. She was planning on going with her three best friends and their dates in a rented limo. They wanted to really make a night of it.

That night, however, she had a dark and disturbing dream that involved her friends. It was strange and bizarre, but the dream ended with her friends driving in Becky's dad's Lexus along the interstate. A terrible accident occurred, and her friends' bodies were strewn along the highway. Waking in distress the next morning, she felt drained and bothered by the dream and went to school late.

By the end of the school day Evelynn was still bothered by the dream. When she tried to explain it to her friends, they only mocked her. They were going in a rented limo, not Becky's dad's Lexus. When the limo came to pick her up, she was relieved. She danced and socialized at the formal, but a lingering feeling of dread loomed around her.

The dance ended around eleven, and Evelynn was dropped off at home. She was exhausted and drained from the prior night's disturbing sleep and the current night's anxious activity. She shortly thereafter went to bed and fell into a deep sleep.

The next day she was awakened by her mother and father whose faces were solemn and pale. They explained to Evelynn that there had been an accident late last night. Evelynn's friends, Maureen, Lisa and her best friend Becky, had been in a terrible accident on the interstate. All three girls had died when their Lexus went off the road and struck a tree.

In shock and disbelief Evelynn searched for her cell phone to call her friends. Finding it on the kitchen counter where she had left it the night before, she saw a text message from Becky. *Going to an after-*

party. Want to come? It was sent at 11:30 p.m., only ten minutes after Evelynn had come home and gone to bed.

Evelynn still felt the pain of that loss three years later. Guilt filled her. It didn't matter if it was simply survivor's guilt; it still stuck with her. She even felt a sense of negligence that she had known that it would happen and hadn't done enough to stop it. The counseling she had afterward did little to ease her pain. The incident left a cold spot upon her soul. Distance protected her or so it seemed.

Evelynn turned on the TV to watch *Wheel of Fortune*, collected the mail and sat back on the couch, eating her yogurt. After solving the puzzle "There's No Place Like Home," she went through the mail. Seeing an envelope from Strathmore University's Dean of Students made her frown. Nothing good seemed to come from the dean. The letter read:

Ms. Dumavastra,

After locating a suitable academic advisor for the Strathmore University Paranormal Investigations, your request for sanctioned university club status has been granted.

The academic advisor is a new hire to the university in the Paranormal Studies Department and should be of great help with the stated goals of your club. His name is Professor Stephen Davenport, and his contact information is below. We regret the short notice but if you are able to participate in the club fair, please contact us so we may have a table available for your use. Because you are the founder and temporary President of the Strathmore University Paranormal Investigations, we will send you additional information regarding the use of university space and participation in the Student Council. If you have any other questions, please feel free to contact...

The letter was a surprise to Evelynn. She had been trying for over a year to organize a sanctioned university organization that actually did paranormal investigations. This was unexpected to say the least, but what was more unexpected was the academic advisor, Stephen Davenport.

Evelynn's heart skipped a beat. She knew Stephen, actually liked him and went out with him when he was in graduate school. Stephen was different. She smiled. They had gone out toward the end of his final grad year, but she had pushed him away because that was her natural reaction when someone got close to her. She regretted that.

"Stephen Davenport," Evelynn said, a wicked grin on her face. It would be interesting dealing with him again. Hopefully he wasn't mad at her. She didn't think he would be, but he was a mysterious one. Tall and dark, with an athletic build. A stirring began within her. She remembered their time together and smiled again.

Amid Evelynn's happy thoughts, she remembered the rest of the letter. The Club Fair! It was an opportunity for all the clubs to compete for new members, and it was only a week away. She had a million things to do in a short period of time. Grabbing some sweats, she headed for the door, making a mental checklist of what needed to be done.

3

S tephen grabbed the mail sitting on the table in the foyer. Thumb-
ing through it he saw a few bills, a letter from the Dean of Students,
a large envelope from Strathmore University's Human Resources,
junk mail from various politicians and a letter from his old friend Ted
Rexpen. He took the mail with him as he walked to the living room.

A lot had happened in the last few months. After graduation
Stephen had taken a vacation out West to climb and camp. He had
recently purchased a used Jeep Wrangler, and he wanted to get away
and relax. For Stephen the best place to relax was the outdoors.

He brought two friends camping with him: John Davis and Ted
Rexpen. John had been Stephen's roommate at Strathmore. John had
graduated with a degree in Computer Science and quickly got a job
after graduating. Ted was another story.

Theodore Lasitor Rexpen was a story in and of itself. Born into
the world of old traditions and even older fortunes in the South, Ted
went to Strathmore University because that was the thing to do after
high school. He was to be educated and work for the family business.
What exactly that business was nobody really knew. Something in the
import/export industry Ted always said. He graduated with a liberal
studies degree and after graduation went back to the South to work in
the family business.

Ted was a tall, slender, fair-haired guy who brought the idea of a
Tolkien elf to mind. His intellect, sense of humor and interest in "the

strange," made a tight friendship between Ted and Stephen. Stephen had kept in contact with him after graduation but had seen him rarely since then. Getting a letter from Ted seemed a little odd especially in the modern days of email and cell phones.

Stephen opened up the envelope and slid out the handwritten letter. It read:

Dear Stephen,

How are you? It has been a while since we have spoken, but I have been out of the country on business and didn't have a good internet connection. I heard that you were back at Strathmore and are working as an adjunct at the university. Congratulations! I know that is something you really wanted to do and you will excel in it.

I will make this short, sweet and to the point. I have a job proposition for you that will not interfere with your duties at the university, will be a great source of supplemental income, and will be an opportunity for you to get out of your Mom's house. How's that sound? Meet me at DeMaine's on Saturday at noon. I'll even buy lunch! - Ted

How bizarre was that, thought Stephen. How did Ted know about his university position? It had only been a few weeks since he himself had been notified. Stephen looked at the envelope and noticed no postage upon it. Strange.

Ted always assumed you would do whatever he asked. It wasn't meant to be insulting or demeaning as one might think; it was simply Ted's way. Similar to a child believing that if he wanted something it would be given to him, regardless of what other people would say or how they would react.

DeMaine's was what really caught his interest. He knew that somebody had bought that property and had been working on it for some time now. The mystery was that nobody knew what was being done with it. DeMaine's, the mere mention of it, gave him the creeps and for good reason. As a child he remembered it as an old funeral home that had always just *been*. It had been around for over a hundred years and was actually listed as a historic site. It wasn't till his father's death and funeral that he had actually been in the place, and those memories weren't exactly pleasant ones.

It was about a year after his father's funeral at DeMaine's that they closed their doors for good. It didn't really make sense that a funeral home would close, but it was a business and sometimes businesses failed. The windows were boarded up and the doors locked, and there it sat for years and years until about eight months ago.

Growing up the stories of DeMaine's were numerous. Most were some variation of it being haunted, and with the stories came the infamous teenage dare. The dare was, of course, to spend the night inside the creepy old funeral home. Stephen was about seventeen when the dare was first presented, and it didn't seem like a big deal to sneak into the closed building. He had always had difficulty making friends, and after his father's death he just wasn't concerned with popularity, sports or much of anything. He just wanted to finish school and move on with his life.

He was smart enough to realize that he was at a critical point in his life. He could withdraw from the world or partake in it. He chose the latter and eventually made some friends in high school through a gaming club.

It was late summer before his senior year. The group of four had convinced their respective parents that they were going to camp out in a nearby wooded area on a friend's property. They actually did set up a tent and campsite, but as the sun went down, the group threaded their way back to Strathmore and downtown toward DeMaine's.

DeMaine's was old and large. It had been opened in the mid-1800s as a furniture and cabinet factory. DeMaine's became a funeral home in the 1870s due to death being a more profitable business than furniture.

The huge building had been built to last and that is what it had done. The three stories and a basement level took up the corner lot of Artman Street and had been quite the institution before it closed.

Everyone in Strathmore had been inside DeMaine's either for a service or as a client.

Stephen and his friends arrived near sundown and went to the rear parking lot away from the main streets. The sun was beginning to cast long shadows upon the town and while some of its dying rays still bathed the upper story of the building, Stephen thought it looked like a fortress of sorts. The structure was made of huge square stones, and the three stories above ground had at one time held several stained glass windows. Most of them were boarded up now, but several of the windows had lost their boarding and reminded him of missing teeth. Only blackness and the birds and animals that had entered the old place were beyond.

"We can enter through the back side area," said Jimmy. "I found a window board on the ground level that is loose."

Spencer, Kevin and Stephen only nodded and followed in silence as they worked their way closer to the back side of the darkening fortress. The group stood in front of the window Jimmy had indicated and began to move an old crate underneath it. Jimmy began to pull on a corner of the loose board while the others looked on.

"Don't just stand there, asswipes." Jimmy grunted and his face was red and puffy. Kevin, Jimmy's brother, went to him and lent him a hand. The board groaned in defiance as the nails slowly began to give way. Stephen looked on feeling oddly strange and watched as the final sunbeams left the top of the building. The last nail popped out and Kevin and Jimmy flew off the crate and landed in a heap.

Stephen stifled his laughter but Spencer did not. As Jimmy slowly got up off the ground he said, "Shut up, ass." Jimmy had a gash in his arm from where a nail had inflicted some damage, and he wiped the blood on to his shirt. "Thanks for all your help," Jimmy grumbled as he repositioned the crate in front of the window. Jimmy grabbed both sides of the window frame and lifted himself up. "Let's find us some ghosts," Jimmy said in a hushed tone as he pushed through the dark opening and disappeared into the darkness.

Stephen followed him through the window and landed inside close to where Jimmy was. He could barely make him out given the setting sun and boarded-up windows. But he could definitely smell him. Jimmy must have been sweating up a storm. Spencer and Kevin came in close behind Stephen, and a light clicked on behind him. Kevin shined the flashlight about the room.

They found themselves in one of the old viewing rooms. It still had some chairs stacked along the wall. Not much else was there, which made sense since the building had been closed for some time. "Cool," muttered Jimmy as he started walking further into the room. The trio followed. Looking back at the room they were leaving, Stephen could only see a lighter square of darkness from the window they had crawled through.

"Give me that light, Kev," Jimmy said as he took their only means of illumination from his brother's hands. They walked out to the main hallway; floorboards creaked from not being used for such a long time. The front door was ahead and several other viewing rooms were to either side. Offices and bathrooms also occupied the main floor along with a staircase that went upstairs from the main hall.

"So, this place is haunted?" asked Spencer, a thin, gangly, messy-haired boy with wide eyes.

"Has to be with all the dead people that came through here," said Kevin.

"Shit!" Jimmy said. "I don't believe in any of that stuff. It's just stupid stories to keep people out."

"I don't know," Spencer continued. "Some of the girls at school said they have seen lights, shadows moving past windows and stuff like that."

Jimmy let out a laugh. "What do those girls know? Have they ever come in here before? They just say stuff to make you think they know something. They don't know shit." Jimmy had moved into the office area and began to go through the desk drawers.

Stephen closed his eyes and turned his back to Jimmy who was waving their only flashlight erratically. Ever since they tore the boards off the window Stephen had felt odd. He felt as if they had intruded in this area. Well, they *were* intruders, but it felt different, like they were invading someone's home as opposed to just trespassing in an abandoned structure. Stephen felt as if somebody were here, and that somebody did not want them there. It made him feel watched, guilty and uncomfortable.

As he opened his eyes for the briefest of moments, Stephen thought he saw a shadow pass into one of the viewing rooms. A darker shape in the darkness. It could have just been Jimmy's light casting a shadow of one of them, but it gave Stephen a chill all the same.

"Jimmy, can you stop swinging that light around?" Stephen asked, staring hard at the viewing room's doorway.

"Sure thing, Stephen. Besides, this looks like a good place to set up," Jimmy said.

Stephen turned around to see Jimmy sitting behind the desk with his feet propped upon it and his hands behind his head. The flashlight sat upon the table balanced upright casting the beam onto the ceiling.

"Set up what?" Stephen asked.

"Set up our shit to have a good time, Steve-o." Jimmy moved his legs and caused the light to fall over. Setting it upright again, Jimmy reached into his pocket and brought out some candles, matches and cigars. Spencer opened up his backpack and pulled out a mason jar of black liquid. Stephen cringed. Spencer's "oil cans" were a concoction of every liquor in his dad's liquor cabinet mixed together. Spencer took just enough to not be noticeable by his dad. The collection of eight to twelve different liquors made a dark oil-like substance that was foul to drink but would mess you up very quickly. Kevin produced a Parker Brother's Ouija board, and Stephen pulled his contribution from his backpack, two bags of Doritos chips. With the mood of excitement in the air, the small group began to enjoy themselves.

◆ ◆ ◆ ◆ ◆

Thirty minutes had passed and the edginess of being in the abandoned funeral home had lessened.

"What about when you fell off the electric box and broke your arm while peeping into her window?" Kevin laughed and passed the "oil can" to Spencer.

"Yeah, well…well… Shit," Spencer slurred out, taking another sip of his potion.

The small group sat in the office around the desk that Jimmy had commandeered. They took turns sipping the alcohol from the mason jar. Strong as it was and young as they were, the effects quickly became noticeable to Stephen. After one nasty burning sip, he decided he wanted his wits about him that night.

They had only been in DeMaine's about two and a half hours, and Stephen was beginning to feel very paranoid and anxious. Every so often out of the corner of his eyes he thought he saw something move past the doorway of the office. After one such sighting, he jumped up and grabbed the flashlight to see what it was. Finding nothing but ridicule and name-calling from his friends, Stephen now kept his observations to himself.

It was during Jimmy's impression of Charlton Heston's *Planet of the Apes* speech that Stephen heard the sound. At first, he thought it was just the building making noise, but the faint creaking of the wooden floorboards had taken on a consistent pattern. He realized that the noise was footsteps coming from the floor above. As he gazed up to the ceiling, he realized that Jimmy had stopped blathering, and everyone else was looking up as well. They all heard it. The floorboards *creaked, creaked, creaked*, then stopped. *Creaked, creaked, creaked*, and then stopped.

"Somebody's upstairs," whispered Kevin.

Nobody said a word, but they all looked at the ceiling as the floorboards creaked, creaked, and then faintly creaked away as if a person had left the room above them.

"Nobody's here. Jimmy, nobody's here, right?" Spencer asked, quickly trying to regain focus.

Jimmy grabbed the flashlight from the desk. "Nobody is here. Just us. And before you girls start saying it's the ghost, we will just go and check it out." Jimmy headed for the hallway taking the illumination with him. Kevin and Spencer leaped to follow him as if magnetically drawn to his bulky presence. Stephen hesitated.

"Steve-o. You coming?" Jimmy asked. Stephen wanted to say no, but instead he got up and followed the light out into the hallway.

Jimmy was a bulky teen. In fact, he was fat. This weight advantage seemed to give him a false sense of being the leader. Stephen had seen several occasions where Jimmy would make a decision to do something with no real knowledge of what was actually going on and without thinking of the consequences. This decision to go look for the source of the noise felt like the same thing.

Jimmy walked up the steps at a cautious pace with Kevin and Spencer right behind him. Stephen followed an arm's length behind the two of them, so if something happened to them, he would have time to react. As Jimmy got to the landing that led up to the second floor, Stephen glanced back toward the office where a few of Jimmy's candles were lit. Stephen continued walking up the steps and could see the glow of the candle flames piercing the pitch blackness of the first floor. He was thinking that they could accidentally start a fire in this old building when he heard it.

A voice, or at least he thought it was a voice, spoke so close to his ear that he could feel the single word on his cheek as it said, "*Hear.*" Stephen jumped. He was so startled that he caught his foot on the last step and fell upwards to the second floor. Kevin and Spencer likewise jumped and cursed as Stephen lay upon the floor. Jimmy, swinging the flashlight around and blinding Stephen, loudly whispered, "Stop screwing around dumbass."

"I thought I heard something," Stephen said as he got up off the floor.

"Like what?" Spencer asked nervously.

Stephen replied quietly, "Like a voice…saying 'hear' or something like that." He was not sure if he had heard anything anymore.

Jimmy had moved on past the stairs that went up to the third floor and stopped. "This is the room that is over the one we were in." He motioned to the closed door.

The second floor reminded Stephen of an old house. An old, haunted house. The broken windows were boarded up, but there were a few windows where the glass was mostly intact. Light from the outside streets pierced the dark hallway and gave some relief from the unknown darkness.

Kevin and Spencer were so close to Jimmy that they looked as if they were one giant blob in the hallway. Stephen stood by the staircase and wondered what they were doing. He could hear a low whispering that he thought was coming from the three of them. Were they actually discussing something?

"Guys?" Stephen said lowly.

"What?" Jimmy replied. His reply was quiet but of a volume that indicated that the whispering was not coming from them. Stephen didn't respond.

"What? What do you want?" Jimmy said again.

Stephen could feel something or someone very near his right shoulder. He tensed up looking straight at Jimmy who didn't seem to notice anything. Jimmy shrugged his shoulders with annoyance and turned back toward the closed door.

"Kev. Go to the other side of the door," Jimmy whispered.

The air around Stephen started to cool down rapidly as if an icebox door had been swung open.

"Spencer, on my count you turn the knob and push the door open." Spencer nodded.

The hair on Stephen's arms and neck started to rise as if electrified. An odd sensation like an electric current went up the back of his neck and skull. The words, or sensation of words being forcibly spoken, again sounded so close to his ear. "*Me.*" He tensed up trying to ignore what he had heard.

"*Can,*" the voice, a female voice he believed, said in a forced whisper. "*You.*"

"One." Jimmy raised a finger.

Stephen's jaw was clenched so tightly shut that he thought he was going to break a tooth.

"*Hear.*" The word chilled his ear and neck.

"Two." Another finger went up and Spencer grabbed the doorknob.

"*Me?*" Stephen turned his head to the right. A woman with a blue tinge about her stood a foot away looking at him, imploring him and then slowly faded away.

"Three," Jimmy said. Spencer turned the knob and pushed the door open. Stephen screamed and bolted down the stairs yelling all the way. Kevin and Spencer yelled as well and raced to the stairs leaving Jimmy in front of the open door.

4

Stephen flew down the stairs, falling the last three steps. He landed in the dark hallway, his heart pounding hard. Something was loudly coming down the steps. His first thought was to get out the way they had come in, but looking in that direction he saw only darkness and more darkness. A quick glance toward the office area confirmed that some of Jimmy's candles were still lit, and the faint glow from the room was symbolic of a lighthouse offering safe harbor. Stephen darted toward the office to get away from the something thundering down the steps behind him.

A sense of relief came to Stephen as he came to the sparsely lit room. The relief was short-lived, however, and replaced by confusion. The candles Jimmy lit earlier had been on the desk. Two of the three now laid upon the floor, their flames out. The last candle sat on the desk, its flame flickering as if gasping for air. This alone was not what confused Stephen, but what surrounded the candle did.

He couldn't comprehend at the time what he was looking at, but it appeared to Stephen that a group of shadow figures hung around the flame in a circle. They looked like people but without real form. All were holding what would be their hands toward the flame, the lone flickering flame. It was then that Stephen realized how unnaturally cold the room had become. Suddenly he was struck from behind, and Stephen fell to the floor for a third time that night. Kevin and Spencer stood over him laughing like idiots.

"Get off!" Stephen said, irritated but relieved it was only them. Kevin and Spencer were still laughing, and Spencer jokingly pointed out that Stephen had scared the piss out of them when he had screamed. This was payback.

Stephen chuckled to himself. It was kind of funny. He hadn't meant to yell and run, but the woman...the woman that wasn't there had spoken to him. "*Can you hear me?*" she had said. Screaming and running away had been a natural response. Stephen remembered the shadow figures and looked toward the desk. The candle was burning fine now, and no shadows seemed to be around it. The only shadows left belonged to Kevin, Spencer, and himself. It may have been his imagination, but the room did seem warmer now.

"Man, you screamed like a banshee and then took off." Kevin continued, "I didn't know what the hell happened, so I ran, Spencer yelled and the next thing I know you're falling down the stairs." Kevin could hardly contain his laughter by this point. Spencer laughed too but not as heartily. He twisted off the mason lid and took a drink of liquid fire.

"Shit, I didn't know what the F was happening," Spencer said.

"*oooo...*" A sound faintly floated through the room.

"I know! And then I see Stephen smack into the wall and fall down the bottom steps like a cartoon." Kevin yammered on.

"*oooOOOO...*" The sound was slightly louder and coming from the hallway.

"Shut up. What was that?" Stephen asked.

"What was what?" Spencer replied.

"*ooOOOOOO...OOOOOO...*" The sound was much louder and seemed like it was coming toward the office door.

"That. What is that?" Stephen moved away from the door. Spencer and Kevin likewise moved away from the door and closer to the desk. Something was moving outside of the office, a shape that seemed to float and weave without real form.

"OOOOOOOOOOO…" The shape came within the light that was being cast by the single flame in the room. A white glow materialized within the floating shape.

"Get out. Get…out…" the figure whispered. Kevin, Spencer and Stephen were chilled. They jumped behind the desk as if it were a magical barrier able to stop any supernatural attack. Spencer, wide-eyed and on the verge of tears, grabbed something off the desk and flung it at the figure.

The object, triangular in shape, flew through the air like a frisbee, striking the figure in its glowing head.

"Ugh!" the figure said as it fell to the floor in a heap. Stephen, Kevin and Spencer came around the desk and found Jimmy on the floor tangled up in curtains and rubbing his head.

"Jimmy! You dumbass! What the F?" someone yelled.

Jimmy looked up still massaging his forehead and grabbed the flashlight. "Just messing around. What did you throw at me anyway?" Looking about he found the projectile within the curtain. It was the Ouija board game piece. They all laughed in spite of having been so scared.

The tension had been broken by the near decapitation of Jimmy the "ghost." The four friends laughed again. They retold the tale, lit all the candles, set the flashlight up, sipped the oil and munched on snacks. Even though Stephen had felt a little better and had started rationalizing what he had heard and seen, he still didn't believe half of the explanations he was trying to convince himself of.

He had seen something, and that something had actually spoken to him. "*Can you hear me?*" she had said. That brief interaction on the second floor was burned into his memory and for some odd reason he didn't want to forget it.

He dubbed her the Blue Lady because of the bluish tinge that surrounded her. He figured the blue tinge came from the early twentieth century blue dress she had been wearing. She had asked if he could hear her. Yeah, he had heard her, and that was almost more frightening than seeing her was. Stephen never told anyone about seeing or hearing his dead father several years earlier; he had chalked that up to a dream, but seeing and hearing the Blue Lady could not possibly have been a dream. He had definitely seen her and heard her speak to him.

Stephen hadn't told Jimmy, Kevin or Spencer about the experience. They had believed that he had been screwing around with Jimmy's dramatic countdown when he screamed and ran. His actions had caused Kevin and Spencer to freak out and run away too, which they all thought was funny. Stephen, however, was the only one who had been truly freaked out.

When everyone had left Jimmy at the open door upstairs, he had just stood there and watched the three idiots running and screaming down the stairs.

"I looked into the room and saw this white floating object fluttering about in there," Jimmy said with intense seriousness. Stephen's ears pricked up.

"Really?" Spencer asked.

Jimmy laughed. "Yeah, dumbass. It was a curtain that was hanging over a broken window. That's what I put on to scare you guys till you flung the F-ing Ouija piece at me."

They all laughed. Kevin had the Ouija piece in his hands, having just finished duct taping the piece back together, which had cracked when it had impacted Jimmy's bulbous head.

"I fixed it," Kevin stated, reaching for the Ouija board. "Let's talk to some ghosts."

Stephen ignored Kevin and asked Jimmy, "What else was in the room?"

"Nothing," he replied. "It was empty except for some trash and bird shit."

"What about the noise we heard?" Stephen asked. "We all heard someone walking around up there."

"Uh-uh." Jimmy shrugged. "I didn't check the other rooms or the third floor."

Stephen guessed it didn't matter to Jimmy or the others that they had not found the source of the noise. But Stephen couldn't forget so easily. The noise, combined with hearing and seeing the Blue Lady, was really starting to bother him. And then there was the shadow people he had seen around the candle flame. Was he losing it?

When Stephen had ran into the office, he could have sworn he had seen people or their shadows huddled around the desk where the lone candle had been. Stephen couldn't help but think of the wraiths in *The Lord of the Rings* and shuddered.

Stephen had finally started to calm down after the excitement of the last half hour. He had been pretending to drink Spencer's oil, because he wanted to have his wits about him. When Kevin pulled out the Ouija board, Stephen's anxiety resurfaced again.

The four sat around the board. They had to sit on the floor since there was only one chair. Stephen intentionally sat facing the door.

"Okay," Kevin said. "Everyone has to place their fingertips lightly...*lightly* on the piece and then we can ask questions."

"I'm not lightly...*lightly* placing my fingers on your piece," said Spencer, laughing.

"Shut up," Kevin said. "If you don't want to do this, then don't."

"No, I want to do it," Spencer replied. "Let's talk to a ghost. Maybe they will tell us what your mother is doing."

Realizing that Spencer's comment made no sense, everyone ignored the intoxicated boy and placed their fingertips upon the Ouija piece. The board was flat, smooth and made of wood. It had fanciful artwork around the edges and letters in the middle. Near the top left corner next to a drawing of the sun was the word *Yes* and in the top right corner next to a crescent moon was the word *No*. Across the bottom were the numbers one through nine followed by a zero. Underneath the numbers was the word *Goodbye*.

At first, they joked around and asked stupid questions like "Does Kevin like boys?" and "Will Spencer ever see Christine naked?" and pushed the game piece to the funniest answer. The triangular piece had a clear circle in the center which would show either a letter to spell out a word or the simple one-word answer *yes* or *no*.

"It doesn't work that way," Kevin said after several more stupid questions regarding Principal Gainus and if he was an anus. "You have to be quiet and let the spirits guide the piece through you."

"Like my head," Jimmy muttered.

Everyone snickered and then quieted down. The candles were a third of the way gone and the flashlight still illuminated the ceiling. Kevin asked in a serious tone, "Are there any spirits here with us tonight?" At first nothing happened but then the piece started to move, slowly and erratically. The felt pieces on the bottom of the piece made an odd noise as it moved across the board toward the word *Yes*.

"You're pushing it," Jimmy said to no one in particular. No one replied.

Kevin spoke again. "Are you in this room now?" The question gave Stephen chills. He glanced up toward the door as a shadow seemed to pass by. The Ouija piece didn't move.

"Ask another question," Spencer said to Kevin, who was now the de facto medium.

"How many spirits are here?"

Stephen looked back to the board.

"You guys feel that?" Jimmy asked.

The piece began to move down and rested on the number one. It then moved upwards and over to the number two.

"Two or twelve spirits?" asked Jimmy.

The piece then moved over to the number four, paused, then slid over the rest of the numbers and off the edge.

"What the F?" Jimmy said. "Are you guys pushing it?"

"No," Kevin said. Spencer shook his head no, his eyes wide.

"I guess that means a lot of spirits are here," Stephen said quietly, thinking of the shadows huddled around the candle.

The air had definitely gotten cooler. The candles fluttered as if a breeze was trying to blow them out. Kevin looked nervous but still asked another question. "Can you show yourself to us?" Spencer pulled his hands back.

"What are you doing, asswipe?" Jimmy asked.

"I'm not sure we need to do this anymore," Spencer replied.

"Stop being a little girl and put your hands back on the board."

Spencer did so without much protest. Kevin asked again, "Can you show yourself to us?" All was quiet; everyone seemed to be holding their breath. Then slowly the plastic piece began to skid across, the laminated board squeaking in protest. It slid over to the letter *D*, then continued slowly, still making that awful noise as it slid. It hadn't made noise before, so why now? *O*. It stopped, then jerked left one letter to *N*. Finally, it landed on *T*.

"Donut," said Kevin. "Why Donut?"

"Not donut, Kevin," Stephen said. "Don't."

Everyone slowly removed their hands. Not even Jimmy had anything to say to that. As the boys looked at each other, waiting for someone to either laugh or say something, they heard it. *Knock! Knock! Knock!* The sound came from somewhere in the building. It wasn't fast or overly loud. It just sounded and then stopped.

"I'm not sure if we should be here anymore," Kevin said seriously.

Spencer slowly nodded and looked around, as if he suddenly realized where he was. Jimmy got up and grabbed the light. "You guys are just freaking yourselves out. Ain't nothing here."

Knock! Knock! Knock! The sound came again a little fainter but still noticeable in the eerie silence.

"Jimmy," Kevin said, "let's go back to the campsite. We've been in here long enough."

"No," Jimmy said. "You can go if you want to, but I'm staying."

Stephen was surprised when Kevin got up and started putting stuff into his backpack. Jimmy glared. "What the F are you doing?"

Kevin slid the Ouija board into the backpack and looked at Spencer. "I'm going. You coming?"

Spencer looked at Jimmy's face as it started to turn different shades of red and nodded to Kevin.

"Fine!" Jimmy exclaimed. "Steve-o and I will stay. Go home little bitches!"

Kevin and Spencer got up, entered the hallway and went to the front door. Everything happened so fast that Stephen suddenly found himself alone in the room as Jimmy followed them into the hallway.

"Really, Kevin? You're really leaving?" Jimmy yelled.

Kevin unlocked the front door, turned to face Jimmy and said, "Jimmy, if you don't think something is going on here, then you're stupider than you act. Spencer and I will be at the campsite the rest of the night." And with that he turned and walked out of DeMaine's.

♦ ♦ ♦ ♦ ♦

Jimmy looked like he was in a state of shock. Kevin had never really stood up to his older brother before, always content to let him be the leader. Spencer must have been scared to have left with him since he usually followed Jimmy's lead too. Jimmy turned and looked at Stephen.

"Are you leaving too?" he asked.

Stephen wasn't sure what had just happened. He felt sluggish, as if he was groggy from sleep. Only moments before the group had been sitting together around that stupid Ouija board. Prior to tonight Stephen hadn't been sure if he had believed in its ability to communicate with the dead or not, but after tonight's events, why not?

"No. I'll stay," Stephen said. He didn't know why, but he didn't think he was supposed to leave, not yet anyway.

"Cool. F them little bitches," Jimmy muttered as he came back into the room. Suddenly, it sounded as if a chair was being pushed across the floor above them. Jimmy and Stephen looked up as if answers would be written on the ceiling. Jimmy started to say something when more knocking sounded from somewhere else in the building.

"Somebody is screwing with us," Jimmy said as he grabbed the candle in one hand and the flashlight in the other. "Come on, Steve-o. Let's find this guy."

Stephen had sort of figured that this was going to be the eventual course of action, but he wasn't sure if he had made the right decision or not. He got up and followed Jimmy to the stairs.

Jimmy was pissed off, which meant he would probably act rashly. He stopped at the foot of the stairs and motioned with his hand for Stephen to be quiet. Stephen waited and then heard what sounded like footsteps walking somewhere above them.

Jimmy looked at Stephen and said in a hushed voice, "I think someone is still up there. Let's go." Jimmy moved up the steps slowly. Stephen hesitated, but since Jimmy had the only light source, he decided to follow him so he wouldn't have to wait in the dark. When they got to the second floor, Stephen became nervous. This was where the Blue Lady had spoken to him. He glanced nervously about but didn't see anything to cause alarm.

They walked to the room where Jimmy had found the curtain. Nothing appeared to be within the room. The two of them proceeded to cautiously look through all of the other rooms. They opened the doors and found only emptiness or discarded broken furniture. Jimmy walked back toward the stairs and looked up to the third floor. They hadn't been up there yet, and no light from outside pierced that very dark space.

"Come on," Jimmy said as he placed his foot on the step. Stephen began to follow but glanced back down the stairs. He wasn't sure if it was light from outside or just his eyes playing tricks, but he thought something was moving down the steps to the first floor. His first reaction was to say something, but at this point he figured they would be chasing shadows all night if he did. He remained silent.

Jimmy pointed the flashlight straight ahead. For a moment it seemed like the beam was growing weaker, as if the batteries were getting low. They made it to the third floor without incident and were surprised to find the level open and mostly vacant. Tables and crates occupied one end of the floor and a hallway led to two rooms at the other end. Pitch blackness, due to every window being boarded up tight, gave them both an uneasy feeling. They walked toward the two rooms, and Jimmy quickly opened the doors revealing nothing within.

"Jimmy, maybe the noises were just from the building settling or something."

"Maybe," Jimmy said, looking around. His brow furrowed, as if he was trying to solve an algebra problem. "I have a plan…"

When Jimmy had finished explaining his "plan," Stephen looked at him as if he were insane. The plan was for them to split up in order to cover the rest of the building. They walked down to the basement, which was the only part they hadn't explored yet. The heavy wooden door to the basement resembled the entrance to a dungeon. Not knowing what was down there was scary, but the two of them walked down the curving staircase anyway. They quickly discovered the purpose of the basement at DeMaine's, which creeped them out even more.

The basement was smaller than the floors above. There were no windows to be seen, making the room feel very much like a tomb. Two large metal tables occupied the main portion of the room. Empty shelves and boxes took up space along one wall, and they could see a large double door on another. Nothing much was left in the room. The realization that this was the morgue and preparation room of the funeral home suddenly hit them.

"What's that?" Stephen asked, pointing to two large barn-style doors.

Jimmy walked over and opened the doors. Inside was the largest dumbwaiter they had ever seen. "I guess this is how they got the bodies up to the first floor," Jimmy said peering up the shaft. "Cool."

Stephen didn't think it was cool. A very uneasy feeling began to creep into him. The other doors led to a refrigeration area where the bodies would have sat on ice for preparation. Even though there was no electricity currently on in the room to keep it cool, it still felt colder than the other one.

Going back up to the first floor, Stephen really could not think of a worse plan. Jimmy wanted Stephen to go down into the basement, while Jimmy would go up to the second floor. After half an hour, they would switch.

"I'm not sure I want to be down there," Stephen said, standing at the top of the curving staircase.

"There's nothing down there; we went through it all. You said you wanted to find a ghost, so go down there, be quiet and see what happens."

"It's too dark. I can barely see anything on this floor, and the basement is even darker."

Jimmy looked down at the flashlight and the candle in his hands, then handed the candle and a book of matches to Stephen. "Thanks, Jimmy. Thanks a lot." Stephen held the candle and matches tightly in his hands.

Jimmy picked up a piece of scrap wood nearby. "Look. I'll prop the door open, so it's no big deal." He then pushed the basement door open and jammed the wood underneath. "Thirty minutes and then we switch." Then he turned to go upstairs.

◆ ◆ ◆ ◆ ◆

Stephen lit the candle, noticing that he only had four matches left. Then he went down the stairs to the basement. The basement had a distinct, yet unexplainable feeling about it. While he didn't see any shadow people or the Blue Lady, he did sense an uneasy quietness. He set the candle down on one of the tables in the middle of the room and looked about his surroundings. He could see little evidence of the people who had been down here before him. Not much was left in the room other than the tables and some chairs. A draft made the flame of the candle dance about, which made Stephen think the shadows were moving, but it was easy to tell it was only the candle flame and nothing more. Stephen sat down in one of the chairs to wait.

With the door propped open, he could hear Jimmy lumbering up the stairs. With no one else in the building, it seemed that the structure carried sound easily.

Fine, Stephen thought. *I'll just sit here and wait for Jimmy's stupid thirty minutes to pass and then maybe we can go.* After a few minutes Stephen couldn't hear Jimmy moving around and thought that he was most likely sitting in one of the rooms upstairs. That was when he heard someone walking on the floor right above him. Stephen looked up as the footsteps walked, then stopped. Walked, then stopped again. *What is Jimmy doing? He's supposed to be on the second floor.*

He could imagine stupid Jimmy flashing the light about as he searched the rooms above. Had it been thirty minutes already? The footsteps stopped, replaced by a faint scraping noise. He realized what the scraping noise was when he saw the piece of wood come falling down the steps, followed by the sound of the basement door clicking shut.

"Oh shit!" Stephen got up and moved toward the steps. "No! No! No!" In a semi-panic, Stephen grabbed the candle, being careful not to accidentally put the flame out, and raced up the steps as quickly as he could to try the door. Pushing and pulling, he wasn't sure if it was locked, stuck or blocked, but regardless he was not able to open the door. "Shit, Jimmy! This isn't funny! Open up the door!" Stephen yelled while slamming on the door. There was no response.

Stephen then heard something from upstairs. It sounded like a muffled yell or scream followed by the tremendous noise of something running down the stairs from the upper floors. It had to be Jimmy; no doubt about it. Stephen listened as the steps hit the first floor and then moved toward the front door. "No, no! Jimmy! Get me out of here!" Stephen yelled as he heard the front door open and then slam shut.

Stephen pushed and pulled on the door some more, but nothing was working. He was stuck. Either Jimmy was playing a terrible joke on him, or he had left in a state of panic. Stephen wasn't sure which option was worse. He walked back down the steps and looked for a way out.

The candle didn't illuminate the room as much as he would have liked, which required him to move around the room with the candle in order to see better. As he did so, the candle cast wicked shadows upon the walls, and the darkness seemed to consume the areas the small light couldn't reach. The air felt colder as Stephen set the candle on the metal table and went back to the chair where he had been sitting earlier. Stephen thought it was just his imagination, but when he started to see his breath, a deep fear built in his stomach. It was getting colder; the temperature was dropping quickly. The candle flickered, brightened and then weakened, as if a jar had been placed over it. Stephen got up and headed for the table as the flame went out.

"Shit!" Stephen hissed as he reached for the candle and blackness engulfed him. The air was much colder now, and as he started to strike a match, he heard a low exhale of breath that was not his own. His hands shook as he struck the match too hard, causing the match head to break off. He heard the low exhaling of air again, and it sounded closer than before. Stephen grabbed the candle off the table and backed up till he was against the wall near the steps.

In the darkness he thought he heard the slight noise of a chair being moved. Stephen struck the second match and saw for an instant a darkness darker than any of the shadows standing in the center of the room. Stephen yelled, dropped the match and the candle and tripped on the first step. Pain shot through his knees and shins as he fell. Scrambling to a crouch, he found and struck another match— it broke. Stephen pulled out the last match, consciously slowing his hand down in order to strike it carefully. It lit just as the door at the top of the stairs burst open. A draft from the opening door caused the tiny flame to go out, but not before Stephen saw a large dark thing crouched on the floor moving toward him.

A figure at the door said, "This way, lad." Stephen ran up the steps in a panic. He reached the door and realized the window they had crawled through earlier in the evening was only a few steps away. Without a hint of hesitation, Stephen leaped and dove through the window, smacking his knees on the sill as he tumbled out into the alley behind DeMaine's.

◆ ◆ ◆ ◆ ◆

Stephen looked up from the letter, released from his memories. He had made it home that night after deciding not to go back to the campsite. He had not thought about the incident for some time. While it would be interesting to see Ted again, the thought of going into DeMaine's made him nervous.

5

Evelynn was walking across campus mentally going over her very busy first couple of weeks of the fall semester. The large oak trees were starting to turn color, giving her the full feel of the season. While it was still warm during the day it wouldn't be long till the air would become crisp and the evenings chilly.

Christine had moved all her belongings back into the apartment. After settling in and telling Evelynn about her mission trip to Columbia and a brief romance with a boy who was on the trip, she started arranging knickknacks and cleaning the apartment. Thankfully, Evelynn had tidied up the apartment prior to Christine's arrival. Despite her clean freak obsession and her almost overbearing religious views, Christine was a good person, and she put up with Evelynn and all her weirdness.

The club fair had gone off with only a few hitches, and the turnout was somewhat good. Evelynn had made a sign out of poster board that read *Strathmore University Paranormal Investigations* and a flyer with some basic information for folks to take. She had displayed a few books on hauntings and set out a clipboard for would-be members to sign up and provide contact information.

Evelynn was surprised to see Christine stop by the table and sign the clipboard. When Evelynn had asked her if it was a mercy signing, she laughed and said that she was actually interested in the paranormal but from another angle. A few freshmen read the flyer, asked some questions and signed the clipboard. It was during a conversation with a giggling female that she heard a familiar voice.

"Soupy?" said Robb with a smirk.

If Evelynn was the Strathmore University Paranormal Investigations de facto president, then Robb Winchester was the club's de facto vice president. Smaller in stature, yet stocky and muscular, he had been a wrestler in high school. Robb was a theater major who often reminded Evelynn of an imp due to the way that he seemed to relish misbehaving.

"Hey, Robb," Evelynn said. "What are you talking about?"

"S.U.P.I." He pointed out the letters with his hands. "Strathmore University Paranormal Investigations."

Evelynn had turned her head and stared at him. With all of Robb's antics it made sense that he was interested in the paranormal. When Evelynn had played with the idea of starting a club, he had signed up immediately. She had believed that this redheaded wolverine, who had been seen more than once running down the dorm hallway in his underwear, was just joking around, but he came to the first meeting and had helped her build it from the ground up.

Evelynn pushed aside her thoughts as she walked up the marble stairs and into Mercer Hall. It was one of the original buildings on campus. It was large with old dark wood paneling and housed the Paranormal Studies Department, Social Science Department and other behavioral science disciplines.

She stood in front of a thick wooden door with a frosted window. She could see someone moving behind the newly stenciled words: *Stephen Davenport.* Evelynn tentatively knocked, not sure why she was nervous.

"Come in."

Evelynn turned the knob and entered Stephen's office. He had obviously been in the middle of moving in. Stacks of books sat among boxes and papers. Stephen was casually dressed and seemed taken aback by Evelynn's presence.

"Evie," he said as he walked around his desk. He looked like he wanted to hug her, the emotions of the past not forgotten. She saw him hesitate as he awkwardly opened his arms wide, dropped them and then thrust his hand out.

Evelynn stared at his hand as if he were an alien used car salesman. "Hello, Stephen, ah...Mr. Davenport." She quickly shook his outstretched hand and glanced around his chaotic office.

You can tell a lot about a person from their office. The books they have, photos they display and their mementos scattered about all say something about that person's interests and what they deem important. Stacked on the shelves and desk were books of all sizes. Most seemed to deal with the occult, hauntings, demonology, witchcraft and paranormal investigations, but there were a few books about photography and rock climbing. A map of some unknown mountain range was spread out on the desk and sitting amid all this clutter Evelynn spotted a tiny snow globe with the words *Strathmore University Winter Festival* engraved on it. As she took in his office, she was flooded with unexpected emotions. *It's good to see that Stephen still has some good memories of us.*

Stephen looked uncomfortable. "Mr. Davenport? That seems a bit formal after all we..."

Evelynn cut him off. "I'm happy that you will be our academic advisor, Stephen. The club has really grown, and I have a lot of great ideas. You should come to the first meeting this Sunday."

"Um...yeah, that sounds good." Stephen appeared dumbstruck.

Evelynn moved to the door and opened it. "Okay, it will be at 7:00 p.m. in room 313 here at Mercer. I'll see you then." Evelynn exited the office leaving a confused Stephen standing behind his desk.

Evelynn's heart was beating fast as she skipped down the steps. *Smooth. Real smooth.* She had known it would be strange, but she hadn't expected to really *feel* anything. She'd liked him a lot, but after winter break, they hadn't met up anymore. Thinking back, she had to admit that it was probably her classic "push them away before they get too close" move. Unfortunately for her, he had graduated and left the university after that semester.

She had always been interested in him. He was different, but so was she. He had been a bit slow in his initial approach, but she figured he was just shy, or maybe he was picking up on her "stay back" vibe. She was going to have to work on that. Evelynn was sure she wouldn't be in any of Stephen's classes since he would be teaching the intro courses. She wondered if it would be difficult to reignite what they had started before. With a devilish grin, Evelynn walked about into the fall afternoon sun, thinking of the possibilities.

◆ ◆ ◆ ◆ ◆

Stephen was speechless. He wasn't sure what he had expected to happen when he saw Evelynn again or how he would react, but he definitely hadn't expected this. He liked Evelynn, always had. He had met Evelynn Dumavastra when he was a graduate student. They had shared an interest in the paranormal and went out during the fall semester. When they had come back from winter break, classes were more intense and took more of his time. He hadn't seen much of Evelynn, and the few times he'd tried to contact her had ended with no response. Damn, she looked good. Realizing that the university probably frowned on professors dating students, he forced himself to push those thoughts down.

6

S tephen walked out of Mercer Hall thinking about Evelynn. He had experienced so much within the last couple of months that he felt like a hamster on meth running on the wheel of life. While he was glad to see her again, he knew that working with her as her club's academic advisor was going to be dicey.

Stephen was heading to the next dramatic event in his current production of a life. He was going to downtown Strathmore, or DT according to the locals, to meet Ted Rexpen at DeMaine's. Strathmore was an old town, and back in the day the main industry had been the moving of goods via rail or by boat on the river. The downtown area had gone through a transformation during the past twenty years with old warehouses and factories changing into trendy condos and shops. DeMaine's apparently was part of this trendy conversion, and Ted was its new owner.

An uneasy feeling stirred within Stephen's gut. It was a cross between being kicked in the privates and eating bad Indian food. He had been in DT Strathmore hundreds of times since that incident as a teen at DeMaine's. He had even passed the building several times, not even giving the boarded-up, rundown building a look, but this was different.

As Stephen pulled onto Artman Street, he saw that the dilapidated, old building was no more. It was being transformed into something new, and it was the center of a bustling hive of activity. It had been easy to forget the past when the past was hidden in dreary shadows. Now, the past was being renovated and renewed with a fresh coat of paint.

Stephen parked his Jeep along a side street in order to stay out of the way and walked toward the looming building. He had not walked down Artman Street for some time, and he was amazed at the amount of new construction. The area was being revitalized, and DeMaine's seemed to be at the center of it all. The building retained its original structure of large stone walls, but a few modifications could be observed already.

A temporary fence had been erected around the property to keep out trespassers and thieves. The boarded-up windows no longer kept the outside world out. They had been replaced by fanciful glass that gave the place a mysterious gothic look. A veranda had been added onto the third floor, and a huge green canopy hung over a semi-circular driveway by the front doors.

"Nice, isn't it?" said a familiar voice. Stephen turned around to see his friend Ted.

"Mr. Rexpen." Stephen smiled and shook Ted's hand. "It is good to see you. How have you been?"

"Busy as you can see." Ted spread his hands wide to indicate the construction. "I heard that you landed your dream job. Professor Davenport of Strathmore University. Impressive. I am happy for you."

"Yes, I am happy too," Stephen replied, still pondering how Ted knew about his new job. "What have you been up to? Obviously, you bought the old funeral parlor. But what exactly are you going to do with it? I don't see you as the undertaker type."

"You're right. Too morbid of a career choice for me." They started walking, and Ted continued, "I traveled after school. Father wanted me to get more involved in the family business, but I just wanted to see the world. I ended up in the Middle East poking around ancient ruins and historical sites. I really should have become an archeologist.

I love that stuff. While I was there, I heard that my dad had passed away, and I returned back to the States as soon as I could."

"I'm sorry to hear that."

"Yeah. It was not unexpected; he really didn't take care of himself. At any rate I came back home to settle some things and pay my respects, of course. One of my older brothers took over running the family business." They were nearly to the front doors. "And with the money I inherited, I bought this."

"A funeral home." Stephen chuckled.

"No, no. A piece of history; right here in Strathmore." Ted opened the double doors. "Did you know that DeMaine's has been here since 1746? These walls are made from local quarries. It is a piece of art that was going to be destroyed and replaced with condos. I couldn't let that happen." They entered the foyer and walked into an office on the right. Stephen had a sense of déjà vu. The place was the same, but different. The floors were polished hardwoods, the windows actually allowed natural light in as opposed to shutting it out, and the office where he and his friends had visited so long ago was now refurbished and decorated.

A desk occupied one end of the office. Various papers, blueprints and other odds and ends, including some strange looking gargoyles, sat upon it. In front of the desk were two leather wingback chairs, a low table and a matching couch. Ted sat in one of the chairs, and Stephen chose the couch.

Stephen was a bit awestruck. "Ted, this is beautiful. What do you plan to do with it?" Ted poured Stephen a drink from a decanter on the table.

"My plan is to open this up as one of East Strathmore's most happening nightclubs," Ted said, handing a drink to Stephen.

"Really?" Stephen was surprised. "Another bar in Strathmore?" It sounded more condescending than he wanted it to, but it didn't seem to hinder Ted's excitement at all.

"Not a bar, Stephen. A nightclub. Anyone can go down to Lucky's and get a beer, have their shoes stick to the floors and see the occasional college brawl. I am bringing some class to the area." Ted stood up and motioned to the window. "You saw it, Steve. This place is being rebuilt. Trendy apartments, condos for the yuppies, boutiques, specialty shops, even a Starbucks down the road." It was true; this area was being revitalized.

Ted went into salesman mode. "DeMaine's will be where everyone wants to be." Stephen cringed. "It will be the trendiest club in the area due to its exclusiveness. And…" Ted paused and turned to face Stephen. "I want you to be part of it."

Stephen had just taken a sip of his drink and nearly spit it out. He chuckled nervously. "Yeah, right."

Ted stared at him with a slight smirk and waited.

"You want me to be part of what?" Stephen croaked out as he stood up.

"I want you to be part of DeMaine's or whatever I decide to call it; I want you to manage it."

"Are you nuts? What makes you believe that I could manage a nightclub? Hell, I can hardly manage my own life. Have you lost your mind, Ted? I'm sure you have people who can manage this latest adventure of yours who are much more experienced."

"Whoa, whoa! Easy, Red Leader. Didn't mean to have you go all postal here." Ted motioned him to sit again, taking his own chair.

"Steve, I am envious of you."

That was unexpected. Could this day offer any more surprises?

"Envious…of me?"

"Yes, I am. We've been friends for some time now. You have always had a loving family, while mine only tolerates me. You always knew what you wanted to do and didn't let anyone or anything stop you. I admire that. I value our friendship, and I want to be part of your life."

"Part of my life?" Stephen asked.

"Well, that sounds a little weird…"

Stephen burst out laughing and Ted got up.

"I'm serious, Steve. I want you to manage this club."

Stephen sat his drink down. "Ted, I just took a new job at the university."

"Yep. And the salary is not fantastic. Also, I am sure your mother isn't thrilled about her adult son moving back home."

"The pay will increase… Wait, what?" Stephen asked.

"I've given it a lot of thought, Steve. This is the best of both worlds. I have an investment, some roots finally planted somewhere. However, I can't stay here and run the place—that's not me. I want to go places and see things. You, on the other hand, need a source of income that will allow you to live your life. And the best part is that this job comes with accommodations."

"Accommodations?" Stephen asked, intrigued now.

"Yes. Come on; let me show you the place." Ted ushered Stephen toward the door to begin the grand tour.

They left the office and walked through the foyer to a bar room with a huge television against one wall, a full-length bar against another and several tables for patrons to sit and enjoy. Ted explained that he had wanted to keep as much of the original structure as possible but had to take down one or two walls to suit his grand design.

"I have always heard this place was haunted and wanted to keep that flair alive by going with an English/Gothic design for the décor," Ted remarked.

"It is haunted," Stephen had replied without thinking, gazing at the stairs that he had ran down so long ago.

"That's right. You told me about that experience back in college. It's funny, you know. A few things have spooked the workers. Cold drafts, misplaced items. Who knows? Maybe it is haunted."

Ted took him down the hallway on the first floor and showed him the kitchen.

"It's nothing too fancy, but I do have a kitchen manager and staff that will deal with the food. You wouldn't have to deal with that. Oh, wait. Check this out, Steve. It's a dumbwaiter. I kept it and had it updated. Electronically activated too."

Ted opened the doors and pushed a button. Stephen could hear an electric motor somewhere as they watched the cart rise to the current floor.

"It's huge! I had it redesigned to go from the basement up to the second floor in order to bring up kegs and other stuff. It was a pleasant surprise."

"You do know that they used it to bring the bodies up from the basement when this was a funeral home, don't you?"

Ted looked at it, cocked his head and said, "Well, that makes sense. Let's keep that between us. It's a little morbid to think about drinks and food riding in a corpse elevator."

Ted pointed to the steps leading down to the basement and stated that storage and a huge refrigerator were down there. They didn't go down which was fine with Stephen. The second floor was where Ted had focused most of his efforts. The second floor was going to be the main part of the nightclub; it would be a more exclusive area for patrons and live entertainment. Keeping with the decor below, Ted had installed rich-colored polished wood throughout the entire floor. Booths made from the same polished wood lined the wall, giving the entire second floor a sort of old English pub feel. A large bar occupied a good portion of the room, and a grand piano was placed at the other end of the room. Stephen went to the piano and placed his hands on it.

"Holy crap, Ted. How did you... Where did this come from?"

Ted sat down on the bench and hit a couple of keys. "Well, to answer the second question first, the piano came from my family's old house in Louisiana. Nobody was using it, and when my brothers and sisters find out I *relocated* it, I will deal with that then." He continued, "As for getting it in here... That was a bitch. Had to open a wall, use a crane to lift it up and then repair the wall afterward. This is not going anywhere else. Unless it's in pieces."

The bar was a huge wooden masterpiece. Shelves and mirrors lined the wall behind it where all the liquor would go. A large, framed painting dominated the center of the wall. Stephen laughed. "Is that Count Strahd?"

Ted grinned. "Yes, it is. Only the coolest vampire ever known." Stephen could not believe this.

"Ted. How much did this all cost? How rich are you?"

"A lot. And very," Ted said, standing up. "The family business has done very well over the years, and Father seemed to believe money shouldn't be spent. But wait; there's more!"

They walked to the far side of the room, which Stephen realized was the same room where Jimmy had gotten the white curtain to play his joke on them long ago. Now it was a short hallway with bathrooms on either side. At the far end of the short hallway was the item Ted wanted to show to Stephen. Mounted on the wall in another Gothic-looking frame was a painting of an undead knight riding into battle with mace in hand.

"Ha! That is so funny. You know, Ted, most people probably don't even know who Count Strahd von Zarovich and Lord Soth are." The light in the hallway flickered.

"Yeah, I know," Ted said, "but they do go with the decor and theme of the place." The light flickered again. Then twice more. "Damn, what is up with that?" Ted said. "Hector." Ted motioned to one of the men who had been working on the second floor. "What's up with this light?" It flickered three quick beats but stopped as Hector walked over.

"Not sure, Mr. Ted. I will check the wires again."

"Please do. Don't need an electrical fire." Ted walked to the main room, but Stephen lagged behind. Stephen looked at the painting of Lord Soth and smiled to himself. The light flickered again as Stephen walked away to catch up with Ted.

"This door will be locked so that the guests will not be able to access the two private rooms back here." Ted opened the door to reveal another hallway with a door on both walls. The only illumination was a single overhead light.

Stephen walked into the room on the left with Ted. Floor-to-ceiling built-in bookshelves occupied most of the wall space. Most were empty at the moment, though some shelves contained books and boxes. A table occupied the center of the room with four chairs placed around it. One window allowed the afternoon light in, but the other window looked out into the bar area. Stephen didn't remember seeing a window in the other room—only a mirror. Ted saw him looking out at the club. "One-way mirror," he remarked.

"Paranoid?"

"No, I just thought it would be a nice view."

"I don't get this, Ted." Stephen continued, "You have this nightclub and a library… What is all this?"

Ted walked over to a bookcase and absently withdrew a book from a box. "Steve, you know that I have always been interested in the paranormal. Would have loved to have done what you did, but I had other *obligations*. I now have the means to pursue my dream. I have to admit I have selfish motives and have created this club with them in mind." Ted placed the book on the shelf. "I figure that this nightclub should produce a profit. The family back home will be happy that I am pursuing a business model of sorts. But I was hoping to persuade you into working and living here, so we can continue our relationship with the paranormal."

"You're sounding weird again, Ted."

"You know what I mean." Ted sounded irritated.

"Ted, this is awesome. All of this. But I don't know if I will have the time to be a full-time nightclub manager."

"You won't need to. Frank, who you haven't met yet, will take care of that. You would be more of a…resident manager. Take care of what you want to and leave the rest to Frank." Ted stood up. "Check this out." Ted walked over to the farthest bookshelf and pushed a decorative square in the upper corner. Stephen heard a click, then the bookcase swung forward.

"Secret door, my friend," Ted said, waving his hands like a magician.

"No way!" Stephen jumped out of his seat and moved closer for a better look. Looking through the open doorway, Stephen saw a narrow corridor with a staircase going up and down. "This is so cool. Where's it go?"

"Downstairs behind the kitchen and accessible to the rear door. Upstairs to the third floor and living accommodations." Ted pushed the bookshelf back in place. "But, let me show you the third level where you will be staying." Ted walked back out to the main room.

"The stairs going up to the third floor will be roped off; I didn't want to close it off entirely." Ted started walking up the staircase. Stephen gazed down to the first floor where he could see workers moving about and hear the buzz of power tools.

"Ted, I know this may be a silly question, but what about all the noise of a nightclub?"

Ted walked out into an open room. "The walls are noise insulated. Behind that locked door," he said, motioning to a thick Gothic-style door, "you're in the living room of your accommodations. You can't hear a thing beyond that door and no one will hear your freakish night terror screams out here."

Stephen shrugged. Ted knew and had experienced the effects of Stephen's nightmares on more than one occasion.

Ted walked toward two large French doors and swung them open to reveal a nice veranda outside. "I'm not sure what to do with this space yet. Maybe private parties or you can use it. I had this added, and in my opinion, it was worth every penny." A few chairs and a small table sat against the wall. Ted and Stephen stepped outside and leaned against the iron railings.

"I can see this was New Orleans inspired," Stephen said, admiring the view of Artman Street and beyond. They could see lots of construction along the street, but looking to the south, the view of the river really made you feel as if you were in the deep South.

"It is a New Orleans thing. We love to sit outside and enjoy the world with friends. Man, I may just stay here myself." Ted chuckled. "But, let me show you what I have been building up to."

Ted walked back to the ornate door that led to the living quarters. Stephen had only glimpsed the door when they had come up to the third floor, but as he got nearer, he saw how big, old and formidable it was.

The door looked as if it belonged in a castle. Intricate designs were carved upon its surface and iron bands spread across it, giving the door an impregnable appearance.

Stephen stopped in front of the door and touched some of the carvings. "Ted, what is this?"

"A door."

"No kidding. But is this real? Authentic? Are these real Templar markings?" Stephen was thoroughly intrigued, staring at all the designs.

Ted produced a key and moved to unlock the door. "They might be. I picked this up for a great price when I was in Turkey." Ted opened the door. "I couldn't pass it up and I thought it would look cool with the aesthetic I have going here. The merchant said it had 'magical protective powers' or something. Pain to ship it though."

The accommodations were a quaint space containing a living area, a kitchen, a sitting area and a spacious bedroom with a bathroom and closet.

"What do you think?" Ted asked as he walked through the area. "See that door past the kitchen? That leads out to the stairs and the secret door in the library."

"Ted, this is all amazing. I don't know what to say…" Stephen's mind spun with possibilities. "I have duties at the university."

"Yep, duties that will not be hampered by staying here."

"And I wish to continue my research into the paranormal," Stephen said.

"You can do that while staying here. I'll be a silent partner." Ted mimed zipping his mouth shut.

Stephen turned around and faced Ted. "Ted, I know this place is haunted…"

"I know, I know," Ted interrupted. "But I think the ghosts that are here will have others to bother besides you."

Gears were turning in Stephen's head. "You're going to pay me *and* give me an awesome place to live? What's the catch?"

"No catch. I need someone to manage the operations: book-keeping, ordering and some light accounting. Frank will run the staff and other aspects. I want you to continue your research, and in some instances, I want to be a part of it. Look, I don't have a lot that really interests me. My funds come from an overbearing family who only wants to see me make a profit. There is no profit in paranormal research. No offense."

"True."

Ted continued, "I have sold my family on the idea that there is profit in creating a trendy college town nightclub. I want to pursue my own passions, travel and explore. When I found out you were coming back to Strathmore to be a professor, the stars could not have been aligned more perfectly. This is a perfect setup, and you know it."

Stephen was impressed to say the least. Ted had spared no expense to turn DeMaine's into a fashionable hot spot. It had been a long time since Stephen and his friends had broken into DeMaine's and had experienced those strange events. It may have been scary then, but now everything was beautiful, new and exciting.

Stephen smiled wide. "I can't argue with that. It's a deal." He shook Ted's hand. "But I will only do it temporarily at first in case the ghosts here give me too many problems."

Ted smiled as Stephen began to walk about looking at his new digs. "They won't my friend. They won't."

7
---

*F**ridays at Strathmore are the best*, Evelynn thought as she left
Drew Hall. She'd just finished her only class of the day. There was
always a sort of excitement that ran beneath the surface on campus on
Fridays. It was a feeling full of freedom and possibilities.

Evelynn had only one thing left for today: ballet practice. She
thought ahead to her weekend plans. The first club meeting would
be Sunday evening, and she had to catch up on her reading for class.
She made it back to her apartment and saw Christine; it was 1:00 p.m.

"Hey Christine, how are you?" Evelynn tossed her book bag
onto the counter.

"Fine, thank you. Have you had time to think about whether
we should get cable this year? I don't really need it, and it's gotten so
expensive," Christine said from her bedroom.

No, I haven't really had time to give it a thought. Evelynn decided
to put an end to this reoccurring dilemma in Christine's life.

"No, I don't need it. I can find most of what I want to watch
on the internet or at the Student Union." Evelynn saw the mail and
began to sort through it. She liked mail. It felt like a secret admirer
sending her a special present. Her admirers, however, seemed more
interested in having her make payments or sign up for the latest Brad-
ford Exchange collection. A brown envelope from the Strathmore
Historical Society caught her eye and she grabbed it, throwing the
rest of the mail back onto the counter in a mess. She looked at the

mess, looked toward Christine's bedroom, shrugged her shoulders and flopped onto the couch.

Evelynn tore open the envelope and pulled out a single sheet of paper.

Dear Ms. Dumavastra,

It has come to our attention that Professor Stephen Davenport will be the academic advisor for the Strathmore University Paranormal Investigation club. Given your persistent inquiries regarding the Crimshaw Manor, the board has granted your request to visit and research the property. Mr. Jack Hannigan is the caretaker of the property and will provide you access upon certain conditions.

1. Your academic advisor must be with you during all visits.

2. There should be no damage to the property.

3. All research and findings will be shared with the Strathmore Historical Society. Mr. Hannigan can be reached at...

Evelynn was surprised, very surprised. She had been nagging the Strathmore Historical Society for about six months to get access to Crimshaw Manor. Now out of the blue they had granted her permission to research the property; she smirked at that word—research. Evelynn figured the Historical Society would only allow her access to investigate Crimshaw Manor if they believed it was to further their mission of discovering the history of Strathmore. Her investigation would probably uncover some historical clues, but most of the history had already been found and documented. It was the strange occurrences, the stories and the legends that Evelynn was interested in.

She grabbed her cell phone and punched in Mr. Hannigan's number.

"Jack here," said a chipper voice.

"Hello. Mr. Hannigan? My name is Evelynn Dumavastra. I am with the university and am interested in researching Crimshaw Manor. I was informed to contact you in order to do that... Research, that is."

A pause on the other end made Evelynn believe she had lost cell service.

"What's your name again, Miss?"

"Dumavastra. Evelynn Dumavastra with Strathmore University," Evelynn said, intentionally emphasizing her words.

"Yes, I remember now. Miss Strydecker told me you would be calling. I am to grant you access only with 'university adult supervision,'" he said mimicking what Evelynn believed was Miss Strydecker's snobbish voice.

"Yes, that is my understanding as well. Professor Davenport from the university will be with us at all times. When can we come out and explore the property?"

"In about three weeks. I am heading out to Colorado for a hunting trip, but I should be back around the twenty-fourth."

Evelynn was crushed. She was hoping to start the club's year off with a bang by getting to do an actual paranormal investigation at one of the area's local haunted houses.

"Is there anyone else that can grant us access?" she pleaded. "I am eager to begin researching and have waited a long time."

Jack paused before answering. She could imagine him mulling over who he could pawn her off on. But he said, "No, I'm the only one with keys. I'm sorry. It's just bad timing."

Evelynn was a quick thinker and tried another approach. "Mr. Hannigan, when did you say you were leaving?"

"Tomorrow. I'm catching a flight at 8:00 a.m."

"Can I meet you today?" Evelynn said. "Please."

"I don't know, Miss."

"Please, Jack," Evelynn said in the sweetest way she could.

"Well, if you can get here by 6:00 p.m., I guess so. But if not you will have to wait till I get back."

"We will be there!" After getting the details figured out, she hung up the phone. *Wow, things are finally moving.* She had been trying to get the club opportunities to do more than talk about paranormal investigations or watch *Ghost Adventures* on television, studying Zak and Aaron as they went into haunted locations. A quick recon mission and then the first order of business at the meeting on Sunday would be what to do at Crimshaw Manor. Evelynn grinned as she started to text Stephen to let him know what he would be doing this afternoon.

8

"I'm not mad." Stephen gripped the steering wheel a little harder.

"Well, something has put you in a foul mood," Evelynn said as she looked out the window.

Robb sat in the back seat, alone and looking like he wished he had somewhere else to be. Stephen glanced in the mirror to see Robb looking down at his phone. *Maybe I am in a foul mood.* Feeling silly, he calmed himself.

"I'm sorry. Guess I have been a little bit pissy." Stephen glanced at Evelynn "It's just…when you called I thought…never mind. How did you get permission to get into Crimshaw Manor? You did get permission, didn't you?"

Evelynn looked at the clock on the Jeep's dashboard. "I did and if you could go a little faster, that would be great. We can't be late."

"Don't worry, Evie," Stephen said. "We'll get there by six."

Robb smirked in the back seat at Stephen's use of a nickname for Evelynn. Stephen glared at him in the mirror, and Robb's grin disappeared. Evelynn smiled. They would get there in time; they had to.

◆ ◆ ◆ ◆ ◆

Evelynn had grabbed her research folder on Crimshaw Manor, stuffed it in her backpack and headed off to dance practice. As she briskly walked across campus, she had called Robb. As the club's vice president, she wanted his input and told him to meet her at the 7-Eleven at four. Robb said he was in, and Stephen had texted back saying he was free. She then placed her phone in her backpack and entered the dance studio.

At 4:10 p.m. Evelynn had showed up at the 7-Eleven feeling sore, tired and gross. She hadn't even had time to change out of her leotard and sweatpants. Evelynn had to practically run to get to the 7-Eleven on time, and she was still late.

"I'm sorry I'm late," Evelynn had started, but Stephen cut her off.

"It's okay. Robb filled me in." Stephen took her bag and opened the rear door to place it inside next to a big duffel bag.

"Okay, great," Evelynn said as she got into the Jeep. After ten minutes of awkward conversation and another ten minutes of silence, Evelynn had had enough when she had finally asked Stephen why he was mad. She now suspected she knew the reason.

Stephen broke through her thoughts, saying, "I know a little bit about Crimshaw Manor, but what's the truth behind it all?"

"Well, I'm glad you asked, Dr. Davenport." Evelynn grinned, thankful that Stephen was trying to break the ice. "Robb, hand me the folder in my backpack please." She stuck her hand toward the back seat.

"The My Little Pony one?" Robb said, digging into Evelynn's backpack.

"No, idiot. The one that says Crimshaw Manor. Thank you," Evelynn said, grabbing the folder.

Evelynn had been doing research on Crimshaw Manor the entire time she had been going to Strathmore University. It was sort of a local legend, and she was attracted to the stories.

"I've been working on this for some time," Evelynn said, pulling papers out of the folder and arranging them in some sort of order. Evelynn saw Stephen smile as she started to give her "briefing." She was in her element. The research, the organizing and the explaining of it all.

For the next thirty minutes Evelynn explained the story of Crimshaw Manor. Prior to the American Revolution, a large portion of

Virginia was owned by Lord Edmund Strathmore, the founder of the town and who the university was named after.

His estate was immense and his wealth even more so. After the French and Indian War ended, Lord Edmund Strathmore seemed to have disappeared. It was a mystery in and of itself. He had been a major figure in Virginia during the war and had increased his power and prestige during the conflict. After his disappearance the estate continued to flourish, eventually becoming the town itself. In fact, the university president's house and part of the administration building were once part of the Strathmore Mansion.

As the town grew, the Strathmore presence within the town seemed to lessen. After the American Revolution, records seemed to indicate that large portions of the estate were ceded over to the town itself.

In the year 1818, however, a manor was completed in the far northwestern portion of the Strathmore estate. The manor was built out of fine stonework and became the home of Jeremy Portis. After Lord Strathmore disappeared, Mr. Portis assumed control of the Strathmore Estate and all of its affairs. It was generally believed that Lord Strathmore had either gone back to England after the war or that he had died leaving behind no living heirs. Under Mr. Portis's control, the estate's wealth, power and influence increased, but there was no public record indicating how the increase was achieved. The public record only said that Strathmore Estate was in full operation, and the caretaker was Jeremy Portis.

In 1840 Strathmore University opened its doors. A large portion of its start-up costs were donated by the estate itself. Shortly after the opening of Strathmore University Jeremy Portis died, and a new caretaker moved into the manor: Benjamin Crimshaw.

Not much was known about Benjamin Crimshaw. There was no documentation about where he was from, but census records showed him living at the manor for several years. After the Civil War ended in 1865, records documented the marriage of Benjamin Crimshaw, age forty-eight, to a young woman named Elizabeth Cantor, age twenty. Elizabeth was from a very affluent family in Strathmore, and while the age difference was noticeable, the match made sense for their families. A year later the couple had a baby boy named Jonathan.

Due to Elizabeth's active participation as a benefactor of the university, the manor started being referred to as Crimshaw Manor. The name stuck and so it has been called ever since.

"Cantor Dorm is named after her," said Evelynn.

Elizabeth was the public relations manager of the Strathmore Estate. No one heard much from Benjamin, but Elizabeth brought the Strathmore Estate back into grace and prestige through donations and fundraising events for the university. The future looked bright for the Crimshaws despite rumors of Benjamin's oddities and their stressful marriage. Elizabeth became the face of Crimshaw Manor and the Strathmore Estate. Benjamin was seen less and less; he never seemed to socialize with anyone at any of the town's functions. Rumors flew. It was suspected that their age difference was one possibility of contention, but many believed Elizabeth's popularity may have been a sore issue between the two of them.

The winter of 1868, however, changed everything in Strathmore and, in particular, Crimshaw Manor.

"We're almost there," Stephen said, turning onto a dirt road that displayed a sign reading *Crimshaw Manor, a historic landmark. This way.* Evelynn looked up from her notes and relaxed when she saw the clock said 5:45 p.m.

"Funny how they never paved the road," she said.

"It's because they wanted to keep it as authentic as possible," Robb said, startling Stephen. Evelynn turned around and looked at him in surprise.

"What?" Robb said. "I know stuff. Crimshaw Manor is a historic site owned and operated by the Strathmore foundation. It is kept in as near-period condition as possible in order to preserve the history and legacy of the Strathmore Estate."

"How do you know that?" Evelynn asked.

Robb's grin disappeared. "That's what I was told when I got arrested for trespassing on the grounds last year."

"Really?" Evelynn exclaimed.

"And here we are," Stephen said, slowing the Jeep down in front of a huge black gate. The foreboding Crimshaw Manor loomed behind it.

9

The setting sun made the place appear darker. Jack Hannigan was standing outside of the gate looking at his watch when Stephen turned off the engine.

"Stay here," Evelynn said, handing Robb the folder and exiting the Jeep. Stephen looked at Robb, smiled and exited as well.

"I was just about to give up on you, Miss," Mr. Hannigan said. "I don't like being here after dark."

"I appreciate it, Mr. Hannigan," Evelynn said, extending her hand to shake his. "This is Mr. Stephen Davenport, Professor of… uh… He's a professor at the university."

Stephen glanced at Evelynn as he shook Mr. Hannigan's hand. "Pleasure to meet you, sir," he replied.

"I'm not sure what Miss Strydecker had in mind, but it's late and I don't have time to waste," Mr. Hannigan said, pulling a piece of paper from his jacket. He continued, "I am to have you sign this release form, Mr. Davenport. It says you will take full responsibility for any damages or injuries obtained while visiting Crimshaw Manor." Stephen slowly took the paper.

"A release?" he asked, a little surprised.

"Yep," Jack replied. "I was instructed"—he made quotation marks with his fingers—"to have you sign this prior to allowing you access."

As Stephen read the paper in the fading sunlight, he couldn't help but feel that someone was watching this spectacle. Glancing upwards, he thought he saw a shadow in one of the windows as if someone were upstairs. *Probably just a trick of the light.*

"Okay," Stephen said, as he signed the paper. "We don't plan to cause any damages."

"Good. Now that the legal business is out of the way, I will give you a quick tour of the grounds seeing as it will be dark soon," Jack said, then removed a large black iron key and fit it into the gate. Turning the key with a loud metallic clank, he swung the gates back. They made a screeching, almost screaming noise as they opened.

"Eerie, isn't it?" he said.

Jack walked Stephen and Evelynn up to the porch of the house. The last bit of sunshine was touching the tops of the larger trees. Already the surrounding forest was dark, and the grounds were flooded with shadows.

Crimshaw Manor was a large house but not as big as a mansion. It was made of stone and brick with a large, covered porch along the front. From the outside Stephen guessed the home to be two stories with a possible cellar or basement. The ground floor windows were shuttered, while the upper windows were not.

Stephen looked back at the gate and saw Robb getting out of the Jeep. The home sat in a clearing and was surrounded by a low stone wall, but the rest of the property was open grass area. A barnlike structure could be seen on the western side of the building, and he saw a garden with a low-fenced animal pen on the eastern side. The clearing wasn't particularly large, and the foreboding forest encircling it gave Stephen the impression of an angry mob wishing to reclaim this tiny bit of cleared land. Stephen glanced back toward the Jeep but didn't see Robb any longer. He started scanning the area when Jack started speaking.

"This large, black key opens the front gate. We keep it locked when no one is up here to prevent folks from driving onto the property. This silver key opens the doors of the manor, specifically the front and back doors. All the interior doors should be unlocked. If for some reason they are not or you accidentally lock one of them, this last key, the skeleton key, should be able to open them." Jack handed the keys to Evelynn.

"Aren't you going to show us around?" Evelynn asked. Jack looked at the fading sunlight then at his watch.

"Nope. Don't have the time. Vacation just started, and I'm off the clock." He started walking toward his pickup but continued speaking over his shoulder.

"Most of the upper rooms are empty. The main level has furniture and other antiques. Don't go into the basement; there's nothing there and the steps are unsafe." Jack climbed into his truck, started up the engine and left without another word.

Stephen looked over at Evelynn who was still standing on the porch holding the ring of keys, her mouth slightly open in amazement.

"Did he just give us the keys to Crimshaw Manor?" she said slowly.

"Yes." Stephen said, "The keys to the kingdom so to say." He raised his voice a little. "You can come out now!"

"I'm here," said a voice behind Stephen, causing him to jolt a little.

"Shit! How did you get over there?" Stephen asked Robb.

"Superior ninja skills," he said with a silly grin on his face.

"Did he really just give us the keys to Crimshaw Manor?" Evelynn said again.

"Yes, Evie, he did. Are you okay?"

"Hell yeah, I'm okay! I didn't think he was going to just give us the keys and leave us. I thought he was going to walk us through, hold our hands, tell us not to touch anything…you know. The tourist tour crap and then that would be it." Evelynn was grinning like Robb now. "Do you know what this means?"

"If we break anything, I lose my job," Stephen replied.

"It means we can really explore, really investigate. Professor Davenport, Robert," Evelynn said in a dramatic fashion as she placed the silver key into the front door lock and turned. "Let us explore Crimshaw Manor."

10

The key made a solid metallic clicking sound as Evelynn unlocked the door. Evelynn pushed the heavy oak door open, and everyone stood still not sure of what to do. The sun was dropping below the tree line, and all was dark within.

Evelynn thought for a moment and then said, "I'm guessing we don't have a flashlight, do we?"

"You can use your cell phone," offered Robb. Evelynn took her phone out, swiped it and saw her battery was at 35 percent. *That should be enough for a quick look,* she thought as she turned it on and entered the house.

Evelynn looked down the hallway and saw a backdoor that probably led to the yard out back. The foyer was a nice size and had a staircase going up the left side to the second level. To the right was a large dining room. There was a sitting room with a few period-looking pieces of furniture on her left. Stephen and Robb followed Evelynn inside, closing the door behind them.

"Wow. So, this is what Crimshaw Manor looks like on the inside." Robb moved his cell phone light around.

"You never told me that you had been here before. Care to elaborate?" Evelynn asked.

◆ ◆ ◆ ◆ ◆

Stephen moved into the sitting room with his own cell phone light illuminating the area. The room was simple, yet homey. A few chairs, a couch, some end tables. Stephen's steps caused the worn wooden floorboards to creak as he moved to the fireplace and the items on the mantle. He could hear Robb and Evelynn in the other room.

"It was during summer school this past year. John and I had nothing to do one weekend and decided to explore this place after seeing an old article about it."

"John? Asian John or Johnny Mendoza?" Evelynn asked.

"Asian John," Robb replied. "He's my roommate this year, and I'm pretty sure he wants to join the club. Anyhow… We drove up here but that big gate was locked. We didn't want to be turned away, so we jumped the fence. Not really hard to do; even you could do it, E." Robb continued, "It was late in the afternoon, but because it was summer, it was still sunny and warm outside. We didn't see anyone around, so we didn't think anyone was here. Well, John and I had heard the stories about the floating light, the screaming wail and the ghost lady, so we wanted to get inside and look around. AJ is remarkably good at picking locks, and he was able to open the front door. As we started to open it, the same guy who gave you the keys came around the corner and caught us. He must have been in the barn doing something. We got in trouble, had to apologize and got a lecture about vandalizing historical places."

"Did you get arrested?"

"Technically no, thank goodness. My folks would not have been happy about that."

Stephen was looking at a small photo on the mantel next to a candlestick holder and a small plaque that stated the items were original to the house.

"Kitchen is back here." Evelynn's voice came from somewhere on the first floor.

The photo was in an old-fashioned frame and depicted a young woman standing next to an older man in front of the manor. The woman was attractive, smiling and wore a dress that would have been popular sometime after the Civil War. The man was stern looking, big, forbearing and looked as if he did not wish to have his photo taken.

"What are you so interested in?" Evelynn said, startling Stephen a bit.

"I think these were the Crimshaws," Stephen stated, motioning to the photo. "You never did finish your story about the Crimshaws and what happened."

Evelynn looked at the photo. "It's rather tragic and terribly sad," she said as she sat down on one of the chairs. Stephen cringed.

"Should you be sitting on that? It's old, isn't it?"

Evelynn waved her hand in the air dismissively. "It's fine. This furniture was built to last. Anyway, it was the winter of 1868, and the entire area was hit by one of the worst blizzards ever recorded."

Stephen sat down on the other chair gingerly. Evelynn continued, "The blizzard was ridiculous, even by today's standards. It snowed for days, and some reports even said lightning was seen amid the howling winds and clouds. In the late 1800s they didn't have snow removal or anything like that. People died in bad storms and usually in the worst ways. People would be cut off from town, and if you were ill prepared it could cost you your life. In the case of the Crimshaws, they were not prepared."

Stephen noticed how quiet it was and wondered where Robb was. He wanted to see the rest of the house before the sun was completely gone. The shuttered windows on the first floor made it really dark, but the windows on the second floor would still allow the dwindling light in.

"Evie," Stephen interrupted. "I want to hear the rest of the story, but let's see the whole house before it gets too dark."

"Yes," Evelynn said, standing up. "Excellent idea. Where's Robb?"

Stephen shrugged his shoulders and yelled, "Robb! Where are you?" No response.

It wasn't like the house was so large that Robb couldn't have heard him. Stephen moved to the foyer and noticed the rear door was wide open. He moved down the hallway, past the stairs, the kitchen and another empty room that was off to the left. He reached the door with Evelynn right behind him.

Stephen stepped out through the rear door onto a stone step. The fields were empty, but as he looked toward the barn, he saw the doors move.

"Get back inside, Evie," Stephen said as a figure emerged from the barn. The figure stopped, looked back inside and then started to walk toward the house, quickly picking up speed.

"Get in! Get in!" Stephen backed up fast. He turned to look back at the figure one more time and realized it was Robb.

"What? What's happening?" Evelynn yelled behind him. Robb jogged up to the steps and looked up at Stephen.

"What are you doing?" Stephen asked Robb, who looked perplexed.

"I saw somebody. Or at least I thought I did," he said as he walked up the steps and entered the house. Robb closed the door behind him and looked back toward the barn.

"I was afraid I would be locked out," Robb said.

Evelynn asked, "What did you see?"

"Well, I was in the kitchen when something outside caught my eye. It was movement, quick and maybe only a shadow of sorts, but it looked like a guy running across the field and behind the barn. It was so fast and I only saw it out of the corner of my eye. I went to the backdoor and looked out the window. I swear I saw something go behind the barn."

"Like what?" Stephen asked. "A deer? A person?"

Robb shrugged. "I don't know. That's why I ran out the backdoor to see if I could catch a better look at what it was."

"Did you see anything?" Evelynn asked.

"No. Just a bunch of equipment in the barn. Man, it's a huge barn."

Evelynn started to say something when the distinct sound of footsteps could be heard on the wooden floorboards upstairs. Stephen raised his hand. "Did you hear that?" he whispered.

Robb and Evelynn both nodded. "Those were footsteps. Friggin' footsteps!" Evelynn said.

The footsteps stopped. They knew it was not the normal creaking or settling of the house, but the sound of someone walking. Stephen looked toward the front door, which was still closed. Unless someone had already been in the house, nobody could have gotten in without them knowing. Then again Robb had left via the backdoor without them realizing it.

Evelynn moved toward the steps.

"What are you doing?" Stephen said in a loud whisper.

"What we are here for." She started up the steps with Stephen and Robb following cautiously behind her.

11

"Wait...wait. Wait!" Stephen whispered loudly. The three were walking up the steps to the second floor. Evelynn was the closest to the top; Robb was behind Stephen.

"Evie, turn on your voice recorder app. I'll keep my light on," Stephen suggested. As they made it to the top of the staircase, the hallway revealed three closed doors on the opposite side and two closed doors near the stairs. Windows at both ends of the hallway let in the last rays of the setting sun.

Evelynn turned on her voice recorder and held her phone out in front of her. "Is there anyone here?" she asked. Only silence answered her.

"Let's check out these doors to make sure no one else is here," Stephen stated. He moved to the first closed door on the right, grasped the old metal doorknob and turned it slowly. They heard a loud creaking sound when Stephen turned the knob and opened the door.

After walking inside, Stephen noticed a fireplace on the far wall and a simple bed and table. No one was within.

Evelynn was still standing near the staircase and asked again, "If you can hear us, please make a noise." Again, only silence was her answer.

Robb decided to open the door directly across from the bedroom Stephen had entered. Another window showed the barn and fields behind the house. Long, dark shadows from the forest were quickly turning the yard into gloom. The room was empty of any type of furniture, but a closet door attracted Robb's attention.

He walked across the wooden floor slowly, each step making a low squeaking sound. *Creak. Creak. Creak.* Robb opened the closet but found it empty. He retraced his path quickly. *Creak. Creak. Creak.* He left the door open as he entered the hallway. Evelynn gazed at Robb with an incredulous look.

"What?" he asked.

"Can you make any more noise?" she replied.

Stephen suggested that they should explore the rest of the house quickly, and if time allowed they could conduct some Electronic Voice Phenomenon sessions, otherwise known as EVP. It is believed that voices and other sounds not capable of being heard by the human ear can be captured on electronic media, most commonly a digital recorder.

The next room was about halfway down the hall, near the top of the stairs. The three of them stood near the door. Stephen looked toward the foyer with an aching feeling in his stomach.

Knock.

Stephen turned back to Robb and Evelynn, figuring one of them had made the noise. Robb shook his head to indicate it wasn't him. Evelynn held her hand up, as if to hush him.

"Where did that come from?" she said in a low tone.

"I don't know," Robb said.

Stephen motioned toward the area they hadn't explored yet. "It had to have come from one of those rooms. I was looking downstairs, and it definitely came from behind me."

Evelynn opened the door in front of her and looked in. It was another empty room identical to the one Robb had checked out. Two doors were left on the floor, one on either side of the window at the end of the hallway. The sun had gone down for the most part, and the tree line was dark beyond the field.

Robb went to the door on the right, opened it and mouthed, "*Bathroom.*" Stephen went to the last door and motioned for Evelynn to stand back. He turned the knob slowly and then opened the door.

The room appeared empty. A fireplace was on the outer wall; a large bed and two chairs completed the scene. No one was within.

"I can let that last knock go as a random house noise; perhaps settling due to the temperature change." Evelynn continued, "But the footsteps were footsteps, not house noises."

Robb nodded in agreement. Stephen looked at his watch. It was about 7:00 p.m., and it was getting dark inside the house. Robb and Evelynn were mostly shadows themselves.

"Okay, let's regroup outside," Stephen said. "It's getting really dark in here, and my phone is about to die."

"There's still the basement to look through," Robb stated.

"Stephen, let's check out the basement and then come up with a plan," Evelynn said.

Stephen was getting a bit nervous about being in the house without proper equipment, but he knew that Evelynn would not even entertain the idea of leaving with the basement still unexplored.

"Okay, let's do the basement really quick and then regroup at the Jeep."

The trio walked out of the room and down the stairs to the foyer. Robb led the way, his phone light illuminating the space. The basement door was a solid wooden door located under the staircase. The first floor was extremely dark now, and Robb's light made deep shadows bounce around the room openings and around the corners.

Stephen got to the door, placed his hand around the cool metal knob and swung the door open. Immediately the hair on Stephen's neck rose as a cloud of cold air exploded out of the dark stairwell and struck him. It literally sucked the air out of him for a moment.

"What the hell?" Robb said, holding his light toward the door opening.

"Do you see this?" Evelynn exclaimed as she fumbled with her phone to start video recording. Stephen saw it. Heck, he sure felt it. Then he realized what it was.

"It's mist, Evie," he said, sort of puzzled. The mist settled in the hallway and floated above the floorboards as it slowly dissipated.

Robb was staring at the spot where the mist had disappeared. "Are you sure? I've never seen mist like that before," Robb said.

I haven't either, thought Stephen. He opened the basement fully and stuck his arm out, shining his cell phone light down the stairs. The darkness was deep. A tangible chill could be felt coming up from the stairs.

"Stay close behind me," Stephen said as he cautiously began to go down the steps. The wooden steps were old, and they creaked with every step he took. He tried to walk slowly, so as not to make noise, but quickly realized that was an impossible feat.

What a creepy basement, Stephen thought as he set foot upon the hard dirt floor. It was a dug-out dirt basement typical for its age. Some boxes were stacked by the steps as if the person who placed them there did not wish to go any further. Robb and Evelynn came down, and between the three light sources they were able to illuminate the area pretty well. The basement was about the width of the house. A strange structure stood at the rear, circular in shape and about four feet high.

Stephen sensed something. He couldn't put his finger on it, but something was odd. Evelynn noticed the object as well and moved deeper into the basement toward the object. *It was quiet*, Stephen thought. *Too quiet*. Not that the first floor was loud. It just seemed as if being in the basement dampened everything.

Evelynn walked up to the structure's edge, while Stephen and Robb followed.

"I think it's a well," she said.

Robb stopped and took a step back.

"What?" Stephen said to Robb, a little edgy by his sudden movement.

"Nothing good can come from a creepy well in a creepy basement in a creepy haunted house. You ever see *The Ring*?" Robb said.

Stephen smirked and turned toward Evelynn and the well. Evelynn was looking down into it.

"Wow! It's pretty deep. I think there is water down there."

Stephen stepped up next to Evelynn and cautiously looked over the edge. It *was* deep. A lot of work had gone into laying the stones. A steady push of cold air could be felt coming up from it. Stephen stepped back and noticed mist coming up from the well. He moved his cell phone light up to illuminate the faint flow of water vapor.

"Looks ghostly, doesn't it?" Stephen said. The well and the temperature changes of the house could be one possible explanation for the reports of ghost activity.

"It does," Evelynn replied.

"No…no… No!" Robb said suddenly.

Stephen and Evelynn turned toward Robb saw him shake his phone and then his light went out.

"That is weird," Robb said. "I had like 40 percent battery left before we came down here. Now there's nothing."

"It was drained," Evelynn said in all seriousness.

Stephen looked at his cell phone; it had 3 percent left and was already starting to dim his light. He was about to say they should go upstairs and back to the Jeep, when they heard footsteps on the floor above them. All three stopped and looked up.

"Oh shit," Robb said, coming closer to Evelynn, Stephen and the well. "That's loud."

The steps were indeed loud and different from before. While the earlier footsteps had sounded like a slow methodical walk, these were a fast *click, click, click*. It sounded like heels walking from the kitchen into the hallway. There was a *creak* followed by the slamming of the basement door.

12

"This is ridiculous!" Stephen commented, passing Robb to get to the steps. He stopped and listened. He didn't hear what he expected. He expected to hear the clicking footsteps walking toward the front door. What he heard was nothing. Either the person who closed the door was standing in front of the door or...

Stephen's cell phone turned off. Evelynn came over to the steps, and together they went up the stairs. Robb kept bumping into Stephen and Evelynn, obviously not wanting to be in the darkness of the basement anymore.

"Can you hurry up?" Robb said, running into Evelynn's back for a second time.

Stephen grasped the doorknob and turned it. For a brief second, he thought how bad it would be if it was locked. It wasn't and slowly Stephen opened the door. The entire house was now dark. Stephen didn't see anyone or hear anyone, and he quickly glanced to the front and back doors to confirm they were closed.

"Okay," Stephen said. "I'm going to conclude that there is definitely activity here."

"I knew that before we came." Evelynn said, "I've been recording since we went downstairs, and I'm hoping to have captured some EVPs."

"Evelynn, how much power do you have?"

Evelynn looked at her phone. "I have 20 percent. You?"

"I'm dead," stated Stephen.

"So am I," Robb said.

"All right, let's do this," Stephen continued. "Let's get to the Jeep, start charging cell phones and decide what we are going to do."

The trio walked to the front door and stepped outside. Strangely, it was actually lighter outside the house and a bit warmer. The open areas were still easily visible, but the edge of the woods was dark with shadows.

"Leave the front door unlocked. Evie, you still have the key?" Stephen asked.

"Yep, right here," she said, holding it up in front of her.

"Okay, good. Hold on to it."

Robb took a step away from Evelynn and Stephen.

"What are you doing now?" Stephen said, turning toward him.

Robb was looking toward the woods and commented, "I feel like something is watching us. We're too clumped together—easy targets."

Stephen shook his head and looked back toward Evelynn. "I'm going to circle around the house really quick. Stay here with Robb."

Robb turned back around. "Yell if you see anything," he said.

Evelynn was looking at her phone and stated, "Okay. I'm going to review the audio while you're strolling about."

Stephen stepped off the porch and began to walk around the house, occasionally looking up toward the windows on the second floor. As he turned the corner the dark shape of the barn came into view. *It's just fine sitting by itself over there*, he thought. Stephen was not interested in searching that structure anytime soon; perhaps during the daytime they would check it out.

While Stephen walked, he thought about everything. It was as if his thoughts were on a roulette wheel spinning around to different topics. Topic one was Evelynn and his unexpected feelings for her. Topic two was this investigation. Finally, there was the night-club manager job that Ted had offered him. He kept circling from

Evelynn to the manor to the nightclub, then it was back to Evelynn. The house. Evie. The nightclub. Over and over on repeat. *Oh hell*, Stephen thought. *I'm in trouble.*

He turned the corner of the house, all the while deep in thought. A noticeable chill came across the field making him wonder what could be hiding in the tree line. Stephen stepped up onto the back-door steps and checked the door. It was locked which was good. He wanted to be able to have some control over the access to the house. Stephen put his face up to the window and looked in. All he could see was a slight difference in darkness from the meager light of the upstairs windows. The shutters on the first floor made the ground level tomb-like in appearance.

This whole evening investigation had happened so quickly. And they were not the least bit prepared for it. He hadn't even heard all of Evelynn's research yet. Even without all the actual history, he knew some of the stories about Crimshaw Manor. Anyone who lived in Strathmore had heard it was haunted.

Living in Strathmore, he had grown up on the spooky stories often told of the manor. Strange lights when there was no electricity, shadows moving in the windows and even an occasional scream that would send shivers down the listener's spine. The explanations were always tricks of the light and teenagers playing around, but something just seemed strange about this house in the woods.

He thought about that and wondered why he had never explored Crimshaw Manor himself. He had explored Max Meadows near Wytheville, Virginia, visited the Iron Works haunting in Buffalo, New York and a few others in between. He figured it was one of those local things he would have gotten around to at some point, but he just hadn't.

During an investigation it was not unusual to hear noises, but he had never heard footsteps as pronounced as he had tonight. The recollection of the heeled footsteps and the closing of the basement door brought goose bumps up on his arms. He turned the corner and started up the last side.

He pushed Evelynn out of his thoughts and tried to remember the stories he'd heard of Crimshaw Manor. He couldn't remember it too well and knew that Evelynn would have the whole story and her own theories. He thought one of the stories he had heard had to do with Elizabeth Crimshaw walking through the…oh wait. Walking through the house! Were those Elizabeth's footsteps they had heard? Stephen turned the corner and saw Evelynn and Robb standing near each other.

He could tell immediately that something was happening or just had. Evelynn was standing slightly off to Robb's side with her arms folded across her chest. Robb was smiling like the Cheshire Cat.

"What's going on?" Stephen asked, coming up to them.

"Nothing other than Robb is an ass," Evelynn said, turning away from Stephen. Stephen looked at Robb, eyebrows raised.

"What?" Robb said, "All I said was that it was getting a little nippily out here. That's all."

Evelynn turned around and flung her arms down. It was apparent that she was feeling the cool air in only her leotard and sweatpants. Stephen took his jacket off and handed it to Evelynn. "Why didn't you say you were cold?" he asked.

"I wasn't cold with all the excitement going on inside." She put the jacket on and looked at Robb who was backing out of her reach.

Stephen decided to change the subject. "I've been around the house. All seems quiet now. I've been thinking"—and now he was thinking of Evelynn's reaction to the cold—"that we need to formulate a plan. I was thinking about pulling the plug for tonight…"

Evelynn interrupted him. "Stephen, no. We are actually getting activity here, and I may know why."

Stephen stopped her. "As I was saying I was *thinking* of pulling the plug, but since we have had some activity it would be foolish not to stay a little longer and see what else develops."

Evelynn bounced a little, obviously happy with that decision.

"We need to come up with a plan, so let me get the Jeep moved inside the gate before we warm up, charge phones and discuss our investigation," Stephen said.

13

S tephen pulled the Jeep inside the gate. At first, he was going to close the gate behind him but decided against it. Stephen had a fast charger and plugged in Robb's phone before turning on the heat. Evelynn had grabbed her folder, pen and pad and was writing down some notes while Stephen settled into the driver's seat. Robb pulled out some beef jerky, which stunk up the entire car, and offered to share it with them. Stephen, realizing he was hungry, thanked him and helped himself to some of the meat snack.

"What is the full story about Crimshaw Manor? You never did finish it," Stephen asked.

Evelynn looked up from her notes. "I forgot. Where did I leave off?"

"Something about a snowstorm and the Crimshaws not being prepared for it…" Stephen reminded her.

"Yes, they were not prepared for it in the least. It was the winter of 1868, and the worst blizzard ever seen in this area. It snowed and snowed, cutting the estate off from the town. Like I said, back then they didn't have snowplows. People just hunkered down and waited for the thaw." Evelynn continued, "It was about three weeks before anyone from town thought about the Crimshaws. No one had heard from them; no one had seen them. Some of the townsfolk figured they should check on them and made their way up here in the very deep snow.

"According to statements given later, when they arrived they noticed everything was very still. No tracks, neither human nor farm animal, were present. Only various wild animal tracks crisscrossed the property." Evelynn stopped and took a sip of water from her water bottle, then continued. "The townsfolk figured that the Crimshaws had left, gone to a relative's home or something. But when they discovered the carcasses of the horses, cattle and other livestock, they knew something was wrong.

"The livestock had died in their stalls and pens from exposure and starvation. Their dried, frozen bodies exhibited scavenger activity, but it was not like the Crimshaws to leave their animals uncared for. They entered the manor to check for signs of departure or if a note of explanation was present. What they found was not what they expected." Evelynn paused again, either for dramatic effect or to gather her thoughts. She continued, "The townsfolk found Elizabeth immediately. She had taken her own life in the foyer by hanging herself from the banister on the second floor. There was no sign of Benjamin or the baby boy, Jonathan. A search of the home revealed no clues. All of the Crimshaws belongings were still within. It is still a mystery to this day what happened to Benjamin Crimshaw and the young boy."

"They never showed up? Anywhere?" Stephen asked.

"No," Evelynn replied, shaking her head. "It was springtime when the house was officially closed up. It stayed empty for a very long time."

"Tell him about the ghosts and the deaths," Robb interrupted.

"The what?" Stephen said.

"Well, there are some strange occurrences related to the house." Evelynn stated, "A lot of the older records do document two unexplained deaths in the early 1900s. Since the house was empty, a caretaker from the town would come up once a month or so to check on things—make sure all was secure. Sometime in early 1901, the caretaker reported finding the front door had been forced open. Parts of the intruder were found inside…"

"Parts? Did you say parts?" Stephen questioned.

"Yes. A man's torso, missing its head, and only one arm were found. The records are not the best as you can imagine, but it was never determined who the parts were from or whether it was an animal attack or not. The second death happened in 1918. Same sort of scenario. A caretaker came up to check on the home, found the front door forced open and a foot still in a boot in the kitchen. Needless to say, the house gained a reputation and people started making up stories."

"Okay." Stephen said, "That was a hundred years ago. Anything current? Anything paranormal?"

Robb spoke up. "There are reports of people hearing a woman screaming and seeing a shadow walking past or standing in the windows."

"So, since 1867 nobody has lived in the home?" said Stephen.

Evelynn answered, "No, not really. It stood empty pretty much as is. There was a time period between 1923 to 1925 that a caretaker stayed. Then from 1930 to 1937 another caretaker and his family moved in. Nothing documented. In 1952 the home was established as a historic landmark, and the Strathmore Foundation officially purchased it. An unidentified family lived there for a year, but they left in 1979 complaining that there had been intruders inside the house. The last occupants of the house worked the estate as a period farm site and were there from 1986 to 1993.

"The last family stated in some correspondence that they would be awakened from sleep by odd sounds in the house: footsteps, whispers and the occasional scream. The teenage daughter left as soon as she turned eighteen, saying that the manor was haunted. She had personally seen the shadowy figure of a woman walking through the house."

Robb said, "There have been a lot of claims of seeing shadow figures and hearing screams. That was why I came up here in the summer. This place has been a paranormal mystery for over a hundred years, and it's right here in our area. Is my phone charged?"

Stephen picked it up and disconnected it. "It's at 60 percent. Should be good for now." He handed it to Robb who opened the door and got out.

"If it's okay with you, Professor, I will sit out here and observe. I just don't like being closed up in the car," Robb said.

"That's fine, just don't go too far off without texting or calling. I don't want anything happening to you. As soon as our phones get charged a little, we will go back in."

"No problem. I'll just get my duffel bag and set up over by those trees," Robb said grabbing his large black bag from the back and closing the door.

After Robb left, Stephen looked over at Evelynn. The moon had risen and was nearly full, casting a great deal of moonlight all around. Evelynn seemed lost in thought, looking out the window toward the house.

"What do you think, Evie?" Stephen said, plugging in his phone.

"About what?"

"Uh…about the house, the stories, the hauntings…"

"Oh," she said, sounding a little disappointed in his answer. Stephen was perplexed once again with the enigma known as Evelynn Dumavastra. She continued, "Well, being the first investigators to ever explore the interior of Crimshaw Manor and having already observed solid activity, I am thinking that the home is haunted."

Stephen looked at Evelynn ready to agree, but upon seeing her sitting in the passenger seat with his leather jacket on, he decided not to. She was exhausted and tired; it had been a long day, and the events from within the house had definitely drained them.

"Evie." He motioned for her to come over next to him. "What's bothering you? Are you still cold?"

Evelynn slid across the seat, but instead of sitting next to Stephen, she placed her hands on either side of his face and kissed him. Kissed him deeply, passionately. Electricity went through Stephen from the top of his head to the ends of his toes. Evelynn then sat upon his lap and kissed him again. "I still have deep feelings for you, Stephen," she whispered.

Stephen was confused. He thought their prior relationship had fizzled out; that she had not wanted to continue it. Apparently, he was wrong. "And I care about you, Evie. I never stopped loving you," he said as she again moved her lips over his, her tongue moving slowly, exploring. Stephen's mind was not ready for this, but instead of thinking he reacted.

As their long built-up passion was expressed, Stephen pushed down with his feet and inadvertently had Evelynn grind herself into him more. Stephen felt a strange tingling on his right leg. He tried pushing his right leg down hard, raising up on that side and lowering his left side. *Leverage*, he thought. Meanwhile, Evelynn continued the deep kisses until his leverage idea resulted in her head hitting the driver's window.

"What the hell are you doing?" Evelynn said, stopping to rub her head.

"Need to…adjust…something," Stephen commented, as he once again pushed down with his feet. He lifted Evelynn's body slightly with one hand and "fixed" his problem with the other. He lowered her back into his lap. Again, a tingling feeling strummed his leg.

Evelynn groaned and engaged Stephen's mouth again.

Another tingling feeling vibrated his leg. *What is that? Am I having seizure of some kind?* No, it was his cell phone vibrating; apparently it had fallen onto the seat during their encounter. He grabbed the phone and looked at the screen. There were several messages from Robb.

What are you doing?

Do you want something? Why do you keep tapping the brake lights?

The last one wiped the grin from Stephen's face as he read it.

There's somebody else out here!

14

"What are you doing? Are you looking at your phone?" Evelynn said, a little perturbed.

"Robb says there's someone else here. Let me check on him; I'll be right back."

"Fine. Don't be gone long, Professor." Evelynn moved back to the passenger seat.

"Don't plan to. Be back soon."

Stephen grabbed his phone, saw it was charged to 40 percent and gave Evelynn a quick kiss. He exited the Jeep and gazed about. The moon had risen over the treetops and had lightened up the open spaces. As Stephen let his eyes adjust to the darkness, he looked over toward Crimshaw Manor. He saw a figure near the corner of the north side of the manor and wondered why Robb was over there.

Stephen started walking toward the house and turned the corner. He didn't see anyone. Stephen glanced toward the barn again. Dark and scary. He didn't think Robb would have gone into it without checking in with him first. As if on cue Stephen's phone vibrated, informing him of a text message. It was Robb.

Where did you go?

Stephen texted back. *Where did you go? I saw you along the house.*

No. I'm in the clump of trees to the rear of the Jeep.

Okay, I'm on my way. Stephen placed his phone in his pocket, looked at the barn and thought about what Robb had said about seeing someone go into the barn earlier. They may have to clear the barn tonight just to make sure nobody was in there trespassing on the property. He would not be going in there alone, however.

Stephen walked the length of the north side of the house again and glanced up toward the second floor's dark windows. He thought he saw some sort of light but chalked it up to the moon reflecting off the glass. When Stephen turned the corner, he looked out toward the open field. Something caught his eye, a movement of some sort. He stopped and looked. A motionless shadow waited in the field. Stephen peered at it until it moved and began to eat grass. A deer. Stephen chuckled inwardly; the house had him seeing phantoms at every turn.

Stephen turned the corner and walked the length of the eastern side of the house, feeling like a security guard on his rounds. The thought of horror movies always showing the security guard getting picked off chilled him. When he turned the corner, he could see part of the Jeep. The exhaust was still running, which made him feel a little bit better. *Wow*, he thought. *It really is isolated out here.* What it must have been like back during the Crimshaws' days. Now to find Robb.

He saw the clump of trees behind the Jeep but didn't want to walk straight toward them in case Robb was still watching whatever he'd seen. Aware that he was still very visible in the moonlight, Stephen headed toward the tree line. He stepped into the trees, figuring he would be just another shadow among shadows. He followed the edge of the forest until he got within close proximity of Robb's location. Stephen crossed the small open space, walking toward the tree cluster. Since the moon was so bright, he didn't use his flashlight app. He wanted to conserve its battery and not to give away their positions.

◆ ◆ ◆ ◆ ◆

Evelynn plugged her phone into the charger and snuggled into Stephen's jacket. She could smell his scent on the collar and thought about what had just happened. She had been reluctant to get involved with any guy. It usually didn't work out. Guys either wanted something she wasn't going to give, or they just thought Evelynn was strange. Stephen, however, was different. He got her. He accepted her with all her strange behaviors and moods. It was just bad timing that their relationship hadn't worked out the first time. With Stephen graduating it hadn't seemed like a good idea to continue their relationship. It was a mistake. She remembered thinking he would move on, away from Strathmore, while she stayed and finished her degree. The fact that he was back and wasn't going anywhere changed everything. Evelynn was tired and drained from the events of the past few hours. She drifted away into sleep and entered the dreamworld.

Evelynn entered the dreamworld frequently, but her dreams were more vivid and meaningful when she was completely relaxed. In this state Evelynn would experience bizarre dreams that might not make any sense but at other times were very accurate. It was a matter of interpreting what they meant and what they represented. Sometimes the veil between the physical world and the spirit world was thin, and it was then that Evelynn would encounter spirits. Sometimes pleasant, sometimes horrific.

Evelynn's body relaxed and drifted away. It was a conscious decision to let go of her physical body. Letting go was difficult, because it involved letting go of control, of care, of decisiveness. It felt as if she floated away from herself and her cares. Like a leaf on a river, her spirit floated and drifted to wherever the current took her. Not surprisingly, as her spirit seemed to slow in the nonphysical stream, she found herself in the foyer of Crimshaw Manor. She felt cold, so very cold. Even though several kerosene candles lit the home, she began to shiver.

Evelynn's senses in the dreamworld were unpredictable. Sometimes all of her senses worked together; other times her senses phased in and out. Evelynn found herself seeing more than hearing at the moment. It was as if cotton had filled her ears. She concentrated and the noise that had been muffled became louder and louder. It was a hysterical, desperate sound. A woman's wails were coming from upstairs.

She looked up to the banister, and suddenly she was looking down into the foyer from the second floor. Her vision began to haze over, but she could still hear the sorrowful wailing coming from the room to the right. It was the first bedroom Stephen had checked out earlier in the evening. Evelynn hadn't really thought about moving, but again she was instantly standing in front of the door. A faint banging could be heard from within. *Tap, tap. Tap, tap.* The occasional "no" spoken between sobs pained her heart.

The anguish of the person within the room was overbearing, and Evelynn dropped to her knees. She knew the person crying and sobbing was within reach on the other side; their shadow was visible underneath the door. As Evelynn kneeled, she heard the woman from within croak out, "My poor, sweet, little Jonathan." Evelynn began to weep with this woman, and her vision began to darken. Loud, clumping footsteps could be heard coming up the stairs behind her. Apprehension and fear filled Evelynn as the figure strode into view on the second floor.

The figure had to be Benjamin Crimshaw. He wore black wool trousers, boots and a cotton shirt that had stains all over it. His hair was wild, and his eyes seemed yellow and angry as they turned their attention toward Evelynn.

♦ ♦ ♦ ♦ ♦

As Stephen entered the shadows, he hesitated for a moment to let his eyes adjust. He saw a downed tree with Robb crouched behind it absolutely still. Stephen looked hard and was sure it was Robb, but something didn't seem right… He was *too* still. Not wanting to call out to him, Stephen closed the distance quietly, focused upon the crouching figure behind the log. He did not notice the dark shadow above watching him.

The figure Stephen was looking at was wrong. It had a head and a torso, but it appeared to be aiming something at the rear of the Jeep.

He approached as quietly as possible until he got within six feet of the figure. The shadow from above soundlessly lowered itself to the ground behind the unsuspecting Stephen.

♦ ♦ ♦ ♦ ♦

Evelynn's dream-self recoiled in horror as the figure of Benjamin Crimshaw marched toward her. She scrambled backward like an awkward crab, imagining the woman inside the room doing likewise. Evelynn had backed to the end of the hallway, the window above her. She could feel the bitter coldness from the outside grabbing and penetrating her. The wind howled as if an angry animal was beyond the panes of glass wishing to enter.

The stench of Benjamin was excruciating, and Evelynn could feel the bile in her throat begin to rise. Benjamin stood in front of the door and produced a large black key from his pocket. He inserted it, turned it till a loud click sounded. Then with his massive hand he gripped the knob and opened the door.

♦ ♦ ♦ ♦ ♦

In the dreamworld Evelynn's vision was beginning to fade, and she felt as if she were floating upwards like a feather swaying to-and-fro. She heard a voice she believed was Benjamin's saying, "You need to eat. It had to be done."

A female voice replied, "No, you wicked man... No! Your sins will be known forever... May you burn in hell!"

♦ ♦ ♦ ♦ ♦

Stephen edged closer toward the figure. It wasn't a person at all but a crude representation of one with what appeared to be a loaded crossbow laid upon the tree aimed at the Jeep.

"Professor," said the shadow behind Stephen.

"Oh shit!" exclaimed Stephen, jumping and hitting the makeshift dummy, causing its head to fall off.

"Sorry, Professor. It's me Robb..." Robb crouched down, looking about.

Stephen blinked his eyes and stared at the dark shadow. He had heard Robb's voice but could only make out a dark figure about Robb's height crouching near him.

"What the hell?" Stephen asked.

Robb was dressed in a full black ninja outfit and was motioning for Stephen to duck down next to him. "I'm not sure where it went."

Stephen wasn't sure what to say. He looked at Robb and asked him, "Why are you wearing that?"

"To be unseen, one with the shadows. But, Professor—"

"And what is this, Robb?" Stephen grabbed the crossbow.

"It's a crossbow. But I need to…"

Stephen was standing in front of Robb looking at the crossbow and still not understanding.

"Professor. Look, I'm sorry I frightened you."

"You didn't frighten me," Stephen lied.

"Well…startled you then. But there *is* someone else out here. I think it's the same person I saw run across the field toward the barn earlier."

Stephen held the crossbow in his hand. He couldn't believe he hadn't known Robb had brought it. The bow was cocked with a bolt ready to go. "I can't believe you brought a dangerous weapon with you. What were you going to do? Shoot someone?"

Robb dropped his head like a scolded dog. "It's not dangerous as long as you don't touch the—" Robb's finger touched the trigger mechanism and with a sudden *swoosh* the crossbow fired its bolt in the direction of the Jeep.

◆ ◆ ◆ ◆ ◆

Evelynn's feather feeling came to an end, and she now stood in the foyer facing the main door. Something was bumping against her upper back, but for some reason she couldn't turn around to see what it was.

Bump, bump. Bump, bump.

The front door opened, and a blast of cold air blew snow into the foyer. Benjamin stood in the doorway; a hulking, dirty, crazed-looking man. He looked in Evelynn's direction and screamed, "No!" Then ran toward her. The terror mixed with anger in his eyes frightened her to the point of throwing her back to the physical world.

Evelynn's heart was beating hard. At first, she was confused as to where she was. She slowly took in the lights of the dashboard and the radio. Glancing to her right, she saw a dark figure pressed against the window peering in at her. The only barrier between them was a thin glass window. A sudden loud explosion came from behind her, and Evelynn screamed.

◆ ◆ ◆ ◆ ◆

Everything happened at once. For Stephen and Robb time seemed to slow down. Stephen saw Robb's finger touch the trigger. He tried yelling out a warning, but he was too late. The crossbow fired the bolt straight toward the Jeep. Their eyes followed the path of the bolt as it flew straight and true, striking the spare tire on the rear of the Jeep. An explosive sound filled the area as the bolt punctured the tire. Evelynn screamed, and for a brief, horrifying moment the most terrible thought entered Stephen's mind. Thankfully, he could see the shaft sticking out of the tire, so he knew Evelynn was okay. What was perplexing, however, was that there was someone leaning up against the window looking into the Jeep.

"That's him!" exclaimed Robb.

The figure backed away from the Jeep at the sound of Evelynn's scream and the tire popping. It crouched and turned its head toward the clump of trees where Stephen and Robb were standing. Even though it was nighttime, the nearly full moon shone down upon the figure. It was a man, devoid of clothing; long, wild hair covered most of his head and shoulders. It actually appeared to snarl at them before turning, crouching down on all four limbs and loping across the field at an unnatural speed, disappearing within the shadows of the woods.

"What the hell was that?" Robb said in a shock.

Stephen didn't have an answer. He began to run toward the Jeep, toward Evelynn.

15

As Stephen ran toward the Jeep an unexpected stench assaulted him. It dissipated in the open air, but whatever it was reeked of urine, sweat, decay and death. Stephen grabbed the handle and yanked so hard he almost ripped the handle from the locked door. Evelynn had jumped into the driver's seat, and for a few seconds Stephen thought she was going to put the Jeep into gear and punch it.

"Evie!" yelled Stephen. "It's me. Are you okay?"

The door lock clicked, and Stephen opened the door. Evelynn was sitting in the seat looking blankly out the front windshield.

"Stephen," she said calmly. "What was that?"

"Eve. I don't know. You okay?"

"Yes, Stephen. Yes, I am." Evelynn turned her head toward him. "Is that...*thing* gone?"

Robb had now come up next to Stephen. He had taken off his ninja hood. "Did you see that thing? Ugh. What's that smell?" Noticing Evelynn, Robb raised his hand and waved. "Hey, E."

"I'm not sure what it was. I think it was a man," Stephen said, not sounding too sure.

"What? Like a crazy, meth-headed redneck?" Robb continued, "No way. Did you see it take off? It was like an orangutan or chimp. Oh shit! It was a skunk ape!"

"A bigfoot, Robb?"

"Sort of, but it's the Florida version with orange hair, and it always has a terrible stench."

Stephen thought about that and dismissed it. The most probable explanation was Robb's first comment: a crazy homeless local, probably high.

"I'm not sure if we should stay here any longer with that crazy guy running around," Stephen said. Evelynn was finally calm after the shock of what had happened. She turned off the Jeep, got out and came around to where Stephen and Robb were. She handed the keys to Stephen and said, "It's only 8:30 p.m. That freak is long gone. Probably was as scared of us as we were of him. Let's stay a little longer while we still can. No one has ever had this opportunity before."

Stephen looked at Evelynn and then at Robb. "Fine. But we are either in the Jeep or in the house with the doors locked." They agreed. Robb retrieved his crossbow and bag, threw them in the backseat of the Jeep and locked it. Then they entered the house and locked the front door behind them.

"You know, we are really not prepared at all to stay out here," Stephen commented. He turned on his flashlight app, and the three of them entered the parlor on the left. Robb went to make sure the rear door was locked and when he returned Stephen spoke up. "Okay. Let's get a plan together. I'm not liking what just happened. If we see him again, we leave. No arguments." He continued, "Since we have been here, we have heard knocks, footsteps and had a door apparently close on its own."

"Don't forget the skunk ape," Robb said.

Stephen looked at Robb. "Yes, and the skunk ape," he conceded.

Evelynn was seated on the couch, quiet and introspective.

"Eve. What's wrong?" Stephen asked.

"Nothing's wrong. I'm just thinking. After you left the car to check on Robb, I sort of fell asleep… I dreamed," she said.

Stephen knew what she meant when she said that. He didn't know much about it, only what she had told him. He didn't know what to make of it other than that she had some sort of precognitive dreaming ability. Whatever she had dreamed seemed to have made an impression on her.

"What did you dream?" he asked.

"I dreamed about *her* and this house." She continued, "Something bad happened here. Something really bad happened to the young boy, Jonathan, and I think Benjamin had something to do with it."

Evelynn recounted her dream as best she could, and when she was done Robb spoke up. "I guess that means Evelynn's going to have to spend the night here."

"Shut up!" Evelynn said.

"Not going to happen," Stephen replied.

"Okay then." Robb said, "Just trying to break up the serious vibes. I'll just sit over here…and not say a word." He motioned as if he was locking his lips up and throwing away the key.

"Didn't you say Elizabeth Crimshaw was found hanging from the banister?" Stephen asked Evelynn.

"Yep. I think she is buried in town at the old Strathmore cemetery. Most people thought it was suicide. Maybe it wasn't."

"She probably haunts this old house… I bet it was her footsteps that we heard," Robb said, breaking his silence.

"There are stories of seeing shadows and hearing a woman's scream. Maybe it is her ghost after all," Evelynn said.

"Well, let's see what we can do to communicate with her if that is the case." Stephen continued, "Let's do some EVP work. Robb, how about the basement?"

"No, thank you. I can't get the image out of my mind of some freaky dead girl coming out of that well," he said.

Stephen thought about that and now he couldn't get that picture out of his mind either. "Okay, how about Evelynn goes upstairs to the room she saw in her dream. It sounded like it was Elizabeth's room. Robb, you go with her. I'll stay on the first floor."

"You're not going to the basement?" Robb asked with a grin.

"Uh…no," Stephen replied.

16

E velynn and Robb walked up the steps. Evelynn cringed as each step up the old staircase creaked and groaned.

"Step on the sides," Robb said.

"What?"

"Step on the sides. That's where the stringers are that support the steps. Less likely to make noise that way."

Evelynn did as instructed and smiled, amused by Robb's useless knowledge. They made it up to the second floor and looked in both directions down the hallway. All the doors were closed except the one across from Elizabeth's room.

"Robb. Didn't you close that door?"

"Yeah, I thought so."

The door was opened about four inches. Robb walked up to the door, opened it fully and said, "Anyone here?" No answer. He closed the door and then moved over to Evelynn who was standing in front of the room they thought belonged to Elizabeth. She felt odd after having the dream of being up here not very long ago. She turned her head to the right and looked to see if Benjamin was coming up the steps. He wasn't, of course. She grasped the doorknob and turned it.

Evelynn opened the door slowly. The hinges squealed in protest. Entering the room with only their flashlight apps, Evelynn couldn't help but feel differently than she did earlier with the sunlight coming in through the window. Now she felt like an intruder invading Elizabeth's private space.

Evelynn was pretty certain now that this had once been Elizabeth Crimshaw's bedroom. History depicted her as a strong young woman who had saved and revitalized the town and Strathmore University. But Evelynn's brief dream of the past painted a different story. She had only felt despair and abuse coming from the poor woman in this locked room.

"Did you hear me, E?" Robb asked, bringing her out of her deep thought.

"No. What did you say?"

"I said, 'what do you think is haunting this place?'"

"Well," Evelynn said. "I think it is Elizabeth who is still here. It's just to what extent."

"Like a ghost?"

"Something like that. People use 'ghost' as a generic term. You took Parapsychology 101, right?"

Robb nodded and moved over to stand by the mantel of the fireplace.

"There is something here. It's not a poltergeist, but it could be a haunt, spirit, specter or remnant."

"Remnant?"

"Yes, a remnant is a 'ghost' that stays here in this world doing the same thing it did in life. Sort of a residual haunting in that the spirit repeats the thing that was either so important or so tragic that it imprints itself in time. It's different from a residual, which is simply a loop of energy that replays itself repeatedly. A remnant can interact outside of its reason for remaining fettered to the physical world."

Robb looked at Evelynn. "Okay, so it's a ghost."

"Yes, Robb. It's a ghost." Evelynn looked around the room and thought about Elizabeth Crimshaw. If Evelynn interpreted her dream correctly something terrible had happened to the boy, Jonathan. Elizabeth was not part of whatever had happened and had been locked in this room by Benjamin. *What had he done?*

Robb moved over to the window and was looking outside into the moonlit yard and fields. "I really don't know what that was at the Jeep, Eve. I watched it for a while. I was in the trees when I saw it on the far side of the house. It was looking at the Jeep where you and the professor were." Robb turned to face Evelynn. "It began to sniff the air like a dog. What kind of—"

Knock.

"Did you hear that?" Evelynn whispered. She turned on her voice recorder.

"Who is here with us?" She waited.

"What happened to you? Are you Elizabeth?" she asked. Robb heard something and started waving his hands. Evelynn wasn't sure what the noise was and wondered if it was Stephen on the first floor. It did sound like talking. Evelynn looked at Robb and asked, "Are you hearing—" A short, distinct scream cut her off mid-sentence.

Robb's eyes grew wide. "Oh shit! Did you hear that?"

"Yes." Evelynn said, "I should have it recorded." Evelynn turned off her recording app and noticed a message from Stephen saying that he was going down to the basement.

◆ ◆ ◆ ◆ ◆

Stephen walked the entire first floor again, wanting to really get the feel of the house. He walked back out to the foyer and heard Robb say, "Anyone here?" Stephen heard footsteps as Robb and Evelynn entered Elizabeth's room. He decided to walk into the dining room which was partially underneath them.

The floors creaked as they moved above, their steps loud as they walked across the floor. Their muffled voices could be made out if Stephen closed his eyes and concentrated.

Stephen panned his phone around the dining room. Not much was in here other than a large table and six chairs. He took his phone, turned off the light and turned on the voice recorder. It was dark! He knew the moonlight was bright, but the shuttered windows were like brick walls keeping any light from coming in.

Knock. Was that Robb and Evelynn?

"Is anyone here?" He waited.

"Why are you still here?" he asked.

Knock. Stephen made a mental note to purchase some two-way radios in order to communicate better with Robb and Evelynn. He couldn't pinpoint the direction of the noise since he could still hear the other two above him, but the knock had sounded louder as if in the dining room.

"What do you want?" Stephen asked. He started to move toward the kitchen, asking questions and waiting for a response.

"Can you see me?

"What is your name?"

Stephen could hear Evelynn and Robb carrying on a full-blown conversation. This wasn't going to work being on the floor directly below them. He thought about it and then texted Evelynn. *I'm going to the basement.* Stephen stood at the top of the steps feeling the damp, cool air flow around him and looked down into utter darkness. It was by itself a very creepy basement, but the old well just put it over the top. With no light source other than his flashlight app, Stephen descended the steps into complete darkness.

It took a little getting used to, but Stephen could feel the air as it passed by him. At least he kept telling himself that's all it was. As Stephen stepped upon the dirt packed floor the hair on his arms started to stand up. He was careful as he walked past the debris and entered the larger portion of the basement.

His light source did little more than light up a few feet in front of him. He moved slowly and out of the corner of his eyes he thought he saw movement. Remembering the mist from the well, he didn't give it as much attention as he might have before. He walked closer and could make out the well's outline. Robb was right; it was a creepy well in a creepy basement. Stephen decided to turn on his voice recorder and begin an EVP session with what little light he had.

"Hello. Is there anyone here?"

Cool air swirled past Stephen's arms.

"Can you make a noise, any noise, to let me know you are here?"

"*Here…*" said a voice.

A chill ran along the back of Stephen's neck. "Wow. Did I just hear you?" he said.

No response. Stephen was about to ask another question when he heard the noise of something shuffling in the darkness. It was a very slow and deliberate noise that would start and then stop. He didn't see anything moving in his small area of light, but he didn't want to move yet since something was happening. Closing his eyes, he willed his hearing to focus; he strained his ears to listen. There in the darkness he thought he could make out the sound of someone weeping. A low sob came from somewhere in the darkness.

"Whoa… Is there someone here? Why are you crying?" Stephen asked while backing up slowly toward the steps. He decided he didn't like being in the basement by himself and with that thought he started walking toward the steps that led to the first floor.

◆ ◆ ◆ ◆ ◆

"I'm not sure, but I feel like something is here with us," Robb said.

Evelynn silently agreed with him. Since they had heard the scream, Evelynn felt as if someone had entered the room with them. She was standing near the window looking toward Robb when she saw it. Saw *something*. Evelynn wasn't sure what to say. She wasn't sure what she had seen.

"Robb. I think I saw something in the hallway."

"Really? Like what?" Robb moved to the doorway.

"I'm not sure. A shadow?"

Robb stopped at the threshold and stuck his head out into the hallway. Moonlight streamed in through the windows at each end of the hallway, making it easy to see.

"I don't see anything, E. It's as empty as—" In the darkness the slow squeal of hinges could be heard. "Eve! I think I just heard a door open down the hallway." Evelynn moved up to stand behind him.

"Okay. Let's go check it out."

Robb left the room and pointed his cell phone light down the hallway. They walked past the doors. All were closed till they got to the end. The door of the room on the left was slightly ajar.

◆ ◆ ◆ ◆ ◆

The hair on Stephen's arms was standing on end. His neck felt cold as he placed his foot on the first step. He heard a low, moanful sob coming from the darkness in the direction of the well. He raised his light, but its illumination did not go that far. Holding the phone up even higher as if it would provide more light, Stephen heard the shuffling noise he had heard before.

Stephen felt fear rise up within him. He couldn't say exactly *what* he was afraid of other than being in a dark basement with a well and definite paranormal activity.

"Is anyone here?"

The shuffling was coming toward him slowly in the darkness as if it took great effort to move. Stephen took another step up still holding his phone out. Stephen began to feel light-headed.

He peered into the darkness toward the source of the noise. He wasn't sure what he was doing, but he waited, staring into the dark looking for anything, anything at all. No more noise came from the darkness, but Stephen felt as if something was standing, looking, staring at him from the darkness.

Stephen lowered his hand with his cell phone and shifted his weight slightly as if to turn. As he turned he saw something move at the edge of his illumination. He quickly raised his cell phone higher, and there at the edge of the circle of light was a form standing still.

He could not fully make it out, but it appeared to be a woman with long hair wearing a long dress or nightgown. Stephen was shocked. A feeling of intense sadness entered his chest, a racking ache of the soul. He could not move; she stayed where she was. He tried to make out any features, note specifics, but he could not take his eyes off the area where her face was. Looking intently, he saw movement within the shadows of her face. Her mouth moved, and then a scream of unearthly pain and anger echoed in the dark basement. So chilling, unnerving and unnatural was the sound that Stephen turned, ran the few remaining steps upwards to the safety of the first floor and slammed the door behind him.

◆ ◆ ◆ ◆ ◆

The slamming of a door startled Robb and Evelynn. Robb jumped into a fighting stance, while Evelynn just jumped backward. Looking at the door they saw it was still slightly open and realized that the noise had come from downstairs.

"Evelynn! Robb!" Stephen yelled, running up the steps two at a time. Evelynn moved to the top of the steps.

"What? What is it?" Stephen's eyes were wide. Evelynn couldn't tell if he was scared or excited.

"I saw her. I saw her, and I heard her," Stephen said quickly.

Click.

"Oh no," Robb said, walking back toward the bedroom they had just left.

"I was in the basement when I heard a noise that sounded like sobbing, and I saw a woman standing not ten feet away from me," Stephen said.

"Uh, guys," Robb said quietly.

"Did she say anything?" Evelynn asked, "What did she do?"

"Evie, it freaked me out. She knew I was there; she could see me or at least sense me."

"Uh, guys. The door just closed." Robb was pointing at the bedroom.

"What?" Evelynn said, turning around to look. "Oh my gosh, it did! It was just open; we saw it and were going to go in."

Stephen came up the hallway and moved in front of the door next to Robb. Evelynn hung back a bit in the hallway. Stephen looked at Robb, nodded and opened the door. They entered not knowing what to expect, but the room appeared empty. Stephen moved toward the far window pointing his light in all directions.

"Crap, now what?" Robb said, looking at his phone which was dark. "I don't have any power. It was just charged."

"Maybe your battery stinks," Stephen said.

Evelynn was still in the doorway looking in when she heard the faint *click* of a door opening. She turned toward the direction of the sound and saw a shadow the shape of a person go into Elizabeth's room.

She wasn't sure if she'd seen anything. Robb and Stephen were debating about Android and Apple phones, so she walked down the hallway to the door that she seemed to constantly be standing in front of. This time the door was not closed.

While Robb and Stephen continued their discussion, Evelynn slowly pushed the door open fully and went into Elizabeth's room. As she walked toward the center of the room her flashlight app dimmed. She had 5 percent power left. *That's not right*, she thought. *It had been powered up almost to 100 percent prior to coming into the house.* A breeze of cool air brushed past Evelynn, and she knew she was not alone.

17

"Having an iPhone is not a symbol of economic superiority, Robb. It's just a phone that I like," Stephen said.

"But you believe it is a better phone."

"It is."

"Why? What makes big brother Apple so much better than Android?"

"Well, for one thing the battery lasts longer." Stephen held out his phone to prove it, but the power read 3 percent. "That's odd," Stephen said, puzzled. "It should not be that low."

"Ha! So, it's not only my phone losing power. E, how's your battery?" Robb said turning around. "E?" Robb moved out into the hallway looking left and right.

Stephen looked at his phone perplexed. Something was draining the power. A common belief among those that studied the paranormal was that spirits needed energy in order to manifest or interact with the physical world. This energy could be acquired through the manipulation of power sources such as electronics and people.

"Robb, I think I know what is draining the phones. Robb?" Stephen heard a *click* and *creak* outside the room, so he looked toward where Robb was near the doorway, but he was no longer there.

"Robb?"

♦ ♦ ♦ ♦ ♦

Robb slowly walked down the hallway, past the landing when he heard *click* and *creak*. Robb turned back around and froze in place. Every closed door was opening ever so slightly. Robb was shocked and a bit frightened. He began to back up, past the banister and toward Elizabeth's room.

◆ ◆ ◆ ◆ ◆

Evelynn stuck her hands out and felt a column of coldness near her. "Is someone here with me?" The cold column seemed to blow away and down. A sound like a sob came from the area near the fireplace. Evelynn began to get a tingling feeling in her feet similar to the needle sensation when a body part falls asleep. A charge of electricity moved through her body causing her to shiver. Evelynn looked toward the fireplace and started to see something forming out of the shadows.

It was similar to developing a photograph. A dark shadowy shape appeared, and the longer she stared at it, the more defined it became. Unlike television, when a ghost is viewed in real life, it is not a glowing person at all. The figure crouching on the floor had definition, but it was difficult to make out very many details. Evelynn saw a woman in a long dress or nightgown with long, disheveled hair, crouched over what looked to be a small notebook, writing and weeping.

Evelynn stood still, breathing as little as possible so as not to break the moment. She pushed away her feelings of shock and fear and tried to note as much detail as possible. She thought she heard Robb in the hallway.

"E. E, something's happening out here," Robb said.

"*Shh.* Don't move, Robb. Are you seeing this?" Evelynn said, not taking her eyes off the apparition.

"Seeing what? All I'm seeing is every friggin' door in the hallway opening up on its own."

Evelynn continued to watch the spirit that she believed was Elizabeth. As she did, Elizabeth's form became clearer to her. She seemed to take no notice of Robb or Evelynn speaking to each other; but

Evelynn still didn't want to move. Elizabeth was obviously in distress, frightened and extremely sorrowful. Her shoulders quivered with each sob. Evelynn could feel her pain, her anguish; she suddenly felt herself becoming cold and tired.

Elizabeth was writing frantically when suddenly her head snapped up at the sound of loud footsteps coming up the stairs. As her image began to fade, she closed the notebook and faded into the darkness.

"NO! LEAVE HER ALONE!" The words boomed through the hallway. Robb turned toward the sound coming from the top of the stairs.

"Oh, shit," Robb said.

Standing at the top of the steps in the feeble light of the cell phones and the meager moonlight was a large man with long wild hair and even wilder yellow eyes. A stench of urine, sweat, decay and death flooded the hallway. Robb took another step backward into the doorway of Elizabeth's room and said, "It's the skunk ape."

◆ ◆ ◆ ◆ ◆

Stephen was just leaving the room he had been investigating when he heard someone yell. *That's not Robb*, he thought. His suspicions were confirmed when he looked down the hallway and saw the dark form of the thing that had been looking into the Jeep earlier. It started to walk toward Robb and Evelynn.

"Hey! Hey, you! Stop!" Stephen yelled.

The "creature," because that was the only term Stephen could think of to describe it, turned and glared at him. The yellow eyes focused on him with intense hatred, and with astonishing speed it closed upon him in two bounds.

Stephen instinctively threw up his arms and braced himself as the creature slammed into him. The force almost pushed him off his feet, but Stephen was able to grab one of the muscular arms as it tried to grab his throat. The creature's other arm pinned his left arm against his body.

The shock of being grabbed and slammed backward almost made Stephen panic. He held on tightly to the creature's arm, knowing that releasing it would mean a steel grip upon his throat that would certainly choke him. Stephen was tall but this thing was taller. At least six feet, five inches tall, the nasty-smelling humanoid thing had leathery dirty skin and hair that was matted and tangled with bits of twigs and leaves clinging to it. Stephen felt what he imagined were its claws biting into his side. The pain helped him focus his attention enough to look it in the eyes. What Stephen saw made his blood chill.

The creature's face was covered in hair that was as unkempt as the rest of his naked body. Its yellow eyes were as intense and focused as a predator looking at its prey. When the creature opened its mouth, a putrid odor assaulted Stephen's senses and revealed canine-like teeth that Stephen felt no human being should ever have to see. Breaking its left arm free of Stephen's grip, it grabbed his throat and began to squeeze.

Stephen's back slammed up against the window at the end of the hallway. Pinpoints of light flashed in front of his face. He could hear his blood pounding in his ears, and somewhere beyond he heard Evelynn scream.

Stephen was in trouble and he knew it. He couldn't breathe, and if he didn't break this stranglehold on his throat soon, he was going to pass out. He began to beat furiously at the head and arm of the creature, trying his best to break its grip. It was having no effect, and soon he would not have the strength to do much of anything else.

Thump. The creature and Stephen momentarily stopped and turned to look at the cause of the noise. Protruding from the wall was an odd-shaped half-moon object. Suddenly, Stephen felt a sharp stabbing blow to his right thigh at the same time the creature yowled in pain and released his grip on Stephen. He slumped to the floor, looking at the strange starshaped object sticking out of his leg.

Stephen saw the creature hold its shoulder and turn around just in time to see Robb in midair, feet extended, coming toward him.

Robb's speed and the impact of his feet into the creature's chest completely caught it by surprise. Robb landed on the hallway floor and tumbled to the side, while the force of the impact windmilled the creature backward, over Stephen and into the hallway window with a crash. The momentum of its body took it through the window into the darkness.

Robb and Evelynn ran up to Stephen who was trying to get up but couldn't due to the pain in his leg.

"Stephen! Stephen! Are you okay?" Evelynn frantically asked, reaching him first.

Stephen was confused by what had just happened and why his leg was not working properly. Reaching down he discovered that impaled into his thigh was a metal star.

"What the…" He moaned.

Evelynn was wrapping Stephen's leg with a cloth doily she had grabbed from Elizabeth's room as Robb went to look at the shattered window.

"Sorry, Professor. I didn't mean to hit you, just the skunk ape."

Robb popped his head out of the broken window. Looking down some twenty feet or so he saw some of the broken frame and nothing else.

"Of course," he said.

With Stephen balanced between Robb and Evelynn, they hobbled down the steps and into the foyer. The ninja star was still in Stephen's leg, but the bleeding had stopped. Robb directed Stephen to a chair and went to the front door. Trying and failing to open it, he remembered Evelynn had the key.

Evelynn saw Robb's failed attempts and remembered they had locked the doors. Producing the key, she opened the front door and carefully looked out to see if the creature was still about. All appeared to be quiet, so with some effort they walked to the Jeep.

"I can drive," Robb said as he and Evelynn placed Stephen into the front passenger seat.

"No, no, no." Stephen continued, "Eve can drive."

Robb didn't say a word and got into the back seat. Evelynn started the vehicle and began to drive away from Crimshaw Manor. It was only 10:30 p.m., but it would be a while before they reached Sacred Heart Memorial Hospital.

Everyone was quiet as if speaking would ruin some sort of game. Finally, Stephen said between gritted teeth, "Robb, I'm not mad at you. Just wished your aim would have been more on target."

Evelynn tried to hold in a laugh, but it came out in an ugly mess and looking at Robb's face made her laugh even harder. Stephen even began to chuckle as well, releasing the mood, the fear and the excitement that they had just experienced.

Robb looked at the two of them laughing. "Uh, okay. I'll work on that."

18

A college town hospital on a Friday night has a constant stream of patients coming in with injuries ranging from the serious to the stupid. Sacred Heart Memorial had seen it all, so when Stephen came into the emergency room with a ninja star in his thigh, the nurse looked at him, handed him a clipboard and placed him in a room without so much as a raised eyebrow.

Stephen was given a shot for the pain, and as he started to go to happy land he told Evelynn to take Robb back to the dorms and to get some sleep. Evelynn was going to say more to Stephen, but he drifted off and was soon out of it. Evelynn was tired but too wired to go to sleep yet. She wanted to discuss and understand what had happened tonight. Finding Robb, she drove him back to campus and dropped him off in front of his dorm.

"Well, I guess that's that?" he said grabbing his bag of things.

"That's what?" Evelynn asked.

"Well, let's see. A skunk ape attacked our academic advisor, I threw a ninja star into his leg and then drop-kicked a friggin' creature out of a two-story window. Oh, yeah, I forgot about shooting a bolt into his Jeep. The way I figure…that's it. We're not going to get to go back. I might even get expelled."

"You're not going to get expelled, Robb." Evelynn said, "And I don't think that's the end of it. We did exactly what we set out to do."

"Put the professor in the hospital?" Robb remarked.

"No. Well…yeah, you did that, but seriously, Robb, we all experienced paranormal activity. We saw things; I saw *her*."

"I didn't see anything, E, except a crazy stinky skunk ape."

"You didn't see Elizabeth in the room right before your skunk ape thing came up the stairs?"

"No. When I came down the hallway, I saw every door on the second floor open up one by one like someone was checking the rooms."

"Checking the rooms?" Evelynn asked.

"Yeah. The professor and I were in the one room when I realized my cell phone battery was about to go out…yet again. When I asked you about your battery you weren't in the room any longer, so I walked down the hallway to where you were. As I did…" Robb took a moment as if reliving the experience. "One by one the doors opened as if someone or something wanted to look inside."

"Robb. We are going back tomorrow, today, whatever day it is. Leave Stephen—the professor—to me. What time is it anyway?"

"11:30 p.m. Why?"

"Can you write up what you saw and experienced tonight while it's still fresh in your mind?"

"Yeah. But since we finished early, I was thinking of going out."

"Really?" Evelynn was taken aback. "After all that's happened, you're going out?"

"E, it's Friday night in Strathmore. I need to relax the way that I relax. I'll write up your 'after action report,' and we can discuss it Saturday. How about 3:00 p.m. at the Starbucks on Elm Street?"

Evelynn gave in. "Fine. Get some rest, Robb. We are going back tomorrow night, and this time, we will be better prepared."

Robb agreed, hoisted his bag over his shoulder and walked into the dorm. Evelynn was going to drive back to her apartment and rest but thinking of Stephen at the hospital all alone unsettled her enough that she drove back to the hospital. After lying about being his sister from out of town, she was escorted to his room where he was asleep in bed.

Evelynn's body was beyond exhausted, but her mind was on overload. They had experienced more paranormal experiences tonight than she had ever before. After writing down her notes, she flipped the channels on the TV and then decided to review the recordings for any EVPs. If anything would calm her down, it would be listening to stupid recordings of her asking questions.

It didn't take long for Evelynn to fall asleep in the chair next to Stephen's bed. Around seven o'clock a nurse came in and proclaimed that Stephen was being discharged. Evelynn opened her eyes to see Stephen sitting up in bed finishing his breakfast.

"Good morning, Evie. I didn't want to wake you. You needed the sleep," Stephen remarked.

"Wow. I didn't realize how tired I really was." Evelynn winced at the stiffness in her back and neck.

"It was a long day and an even longer night."

Evelynn got up and moved to his side. "How's your leg?"

"Fine for the most part. Seven stitches, and it still hurts." Stephen continued, "Also, I didn't get a single question as to why a ninja star was embedded in my leg." He held up a lidded cup with the star.

"Seven stitches. Can I see?" Evelynn asked with a grin.

Stephen moved back the sheet, exposing his leg with a dressing on it.

"It's covered up for now. Maybe later."

Evelynn placed her hand upon his thigh. "That's a pretty short gown, Mr. Davenport." She slowly moved her hand up his thigh, a devilish look in her eyes.

"Yep."

"You wearing anything underneath it?" Evelynn asked.

"Nope."

Evelynn moved her hand up under the gown, causing Stephen to jump a little.

"Evie...not here..." Stephen whispered.

"Why not? What's the worst that can happen?"

"You can get caught and expelled from the hospital. I don't take kindly to being lied to about you being his sister," said the nurse who had just entered the room. "You come with me." She indicated to Evelynn. "And you, Mr. Davenport, are discharged. Someone will be in to wheel you out."

◆ ◆ ◆ ◆ ◆

A half hour later Stephen was wheeled to the hospital doors with a cane in one hand and a fistful of papers in the other. Evelynn pulled the Jeep up to the curb and drove away from the hospital once Stephen was inside. Evelynn was quiet, and Stephen looked at her with a smile on his face.

"So, what happened with you and nurse hard-ass?"

"I got banned from the hospital," Evelynn replied, embarrassed.

Stephen burst into laughter. "Banned? I don't think they can do that."

"She said I was not welcomed back unless I was in need of real medical attention."

"I warned you," Stephen said, chuckling as Evelynn hit him in the arm.

As they drove out of the parking lot, Stephen told Evelynn to drop him off at the old funeral home DeMaine's. Evelynn thought he was joking, but when they pulled up to it, she was surprised by all the new construction.

"I heard this place is haunted," she remarked.

"It is."

"So, you are living in a haunted funeral home? Really? A professor of Paranormal Studies living in a haunted funeral home. Wow. You couldn't make this up." Evelynn laughed.

"First off, it's not a funeral home…anymore, and second, I have only slept here off and on for the last week."

"Seen anything?"

"Not yet." Stephen said, "But I can feel it. I visited this place a long time ago and had a bad experience. Remind me to tell you about it sometime."

Stephen explained his new business arrangement and escorted her through the front doors. As they entered the first-floor bar area, Evelynn was amazed. The club was nice. It seemed like there were a few things left to do, but the bar, the paneling, the tables and the lighting were top notch. They slowly made their way up all the stairs to the third floor and came to the huge door to Stephen's apartment.

"Oh my gosh, what is this?" Evelynn said, looking at the large decorative door.

"It is an ancient door that Ted picked up overseas. It is a little over the top, but it really keeps the noise out." Stephen opened the door and the two walked into the apartment.

"Wow, I am impressed," Evelynn remarked, looking about.

"It is pretty cool. The grand opening is in another month. That's when my stress level will really rise." Stephen sat down in a recliner in his living room. "Eve. We need to talk about what happened last night."

Evelynn was in the kitchen opening cabinets and the refrigerator. She wasn't sure if he was talking about *them* or the house. "You don't have much do you?" she said, examining the apartment. "Yes, I agree. I have been going over what happened and wrote some notes. I am meeting up with Robb at 3:00 p.m. so we can be better prepared—"

"We are not going back, Eve," Stephen said flatly.

Evelynn turned to face him. "Yes, we are."

"Eve. That thing may have seriously hurt one of us last night. I can't risk any of you getting hurt."

"That's understandable, but we are going back. We need to go back."

Stephen began to say something, but Evelynn raised her hand to stop him and continued, "We experienced something last night that paranormal researchers dream of. This is exactly what we need to be doing. I know that…that thing attacked us, but we can be better prepared if, and that's a big if, it comes back." Evelynn paused. "We experienced so much last night. I saw her, Stephen. I saw Elizabeth in her room. After going over everything from last night, I don't know if we will get another chance to explore this haunting."

"Why do you say that? What's the rush?"

Evelynn sat down on the couch, still a bit tired from the previous night. "First of all, I don't think the caretaker was supposed to have given us the key to Crimshaw Manor. I am sure that by Monday we will be reeled in by Miss Strydecker. Secondly, I think that all the activity we experienced, minus the attack on you and Robb's misthrow, happened for a reason. A lot of reports speak of hearing noises, having an object moved, or seeing shadows but never all at once. I think something has occurred or is occurring that either weakens the veil between the physical and spiritual world or strengthens the spirit of Elizabeth. Something happened at that house to keep her there. I think we need to find out what that is."

Stephen was thinking. Evelynn could almost see his thoughts upon his face. He knew she had made some good points.

"Okay, Evie. We will go tonight and wrap it up. Any sign of danger and we leave."

Evelynn only nodded enthusiastically, knowing she would not have to debate her cause further. Stephen continued, "Okay, it's 9:00 a.m. now. I can't really drive at the moment. What time are we meeting with Robb?"

"Three o'clock."

"All right. I need to make some calls and go over to my mom's house before we meet up."

"I am in desperate need of a shower," Evelynn said.

Stephen gazed at her. "You can use mine if you like. It is working."

"Maybe next time. I really need to stop by my apartment, get some 'proper' clothing, food…"

"Okay. Why don't you take my Jeep? I'm in need of cleaning up too. I'll take an Uber over to where you're meeting Robb, and we can discuss the investigation to date."

Evelynn agreed and gave him a quick kiss. "You still need to finish what you started last night in the Jeep, Mr. Davenport."

Stephen looked at her. "I'm a little banged up right now, Ms. Dumavastra, but I think that can be arranged in the not-so-distant future."

◆ ◆ ◆ ◆ ◆

Stephen and Evelynn were coming down the last steps to the first floor when Ted walked in holding something in his hand.

"Ted." Stephen said, "How are you? I would like you to meet a student of mine…Evelynn Dumavastra."

Evelynn shook Ted's hand. "Nice to meet you, Mister…?"

"Rexpen, but please call me Ted. It is likewise a pleasure to meet you, Ms. Dumavastra," Ted said and then addressed Stephen. "What happened to you? Does it have anything to do with this?" Ted held up Robb's crossbow bolt and handed it to Stephen. "Found it sticking out of your spare tire on the back of your Jeep. Thought it was a gag, but your spare is very flat."

Stephen chuckled. "Great. I forgot about that. Yes, but it's a long story. What brings you by today?"

"I just needed to finish up some details and wanted your input," Ted said.

"Looks like your other duties are calling." Evelynn continued, "See you at 3:00 p.m.? Nice to have met you, Mr. Rexpen," she said.

Ted looked at her, bowed his head slightly and said, "Ted please, and it was my pleasure." As Evelynn walked out Ted continued to look at her.

"Very nice. Have I met her before?" Ted said.

Stephen was opening the office door. "I don't think so. Why?"

Ted followed Stephen into the office. "Very attractive. Are you two involved?"

Stephen looked at Ted, a little surprised by the question. "Yes. We are involved, but obviously since she is a student and I am a professor, it is something I want to keep on the down low."

"Yes, I see."

Ted and Stephen talked business awhile and decided to keep the name DeMaine's for the nightclub. It was nice to keep the history and lore of old Strathmore, and since there was plenty of both within these walls, why change it? They decided on a date for the opening and a few other minor things. When they were done, they both sat across from each other in the office.

"So, how is your teaching gig going?" Ted asked.

"Good. I am teaching Parapsychology 101 and Research Methods in Parapsychology. I am really enjoying it."

"That's good. And the club? How is that going?"

"Funny you should ask. The first meeting is actually this Sunday evening, but we have begun an investigation already here locally."

"Really?" Ted said, sitting up straighter.

Stephen went about telling Ted the *Reader's Digest* version of events that had taken place at Crimshaw Manor. Ted laughed about crossbow incident as well as the ninja star accident.

"This Robb person sounds like a dangerous guy," Ted said jokingly.

"I have to say in all seriousness that if it were not for Robb, I am not sure what would have happened with that…thing choking me."

"Are you going back?"

"I think we have to. There is evidence that still needs to be reviewed onsite and, while we have some EVPs to analyze, we don't have anything concrete. We just weren't prepared, and chances are that since we broke a window, we will not get another chance to investigate come Monday."

Ted contemplated that, stood and then paced about. "If you have a key, then I can get someone out there to replace the window. What if I could get some equipment for you? Would that help?"

"Heck yeah, it would!" Stephen said, "I was going to go by Walmart and pick up some common things like digital recorders and flashlights, but if you can get your hands on any other real equipment, I would appreciate it. I have never really experienced this level of activity before."

"Okay, you got it. Let me work on this, and I will be in touch." Ted turned and exited DeMaine's.

Stephen used his cane to walk over to the bar where he then sat upon a stool. He was deep in thought again about all the reoccurring subjects that fought for his attention. *If life is going to be this hectic, I might not survive my first year back,* he mused. Then again, he was living his dream; what could possibly go wrong?

19

Stephen was ready to leave for his mother's place but had forgotten his keys and a duffel bag in his apartment upstairs. He had been going back and forth over the past couple of weeks, slowly moving stuff out of his mother's home and into his new living arrangements. Surprisingly, Stephen's mom was happy that he was moving out on his own but reminded him not to be a stranger.

Stephen looked at all the steps and silently groaned. This injury was, no pun intended, a royal pain. He began the slow journey up, taking note of all the nice furnishings that had been installed. He heard a bang somewhere on the second floor and figured it was a worker. However, in this building he couldn't deny that anything was possible.

When Stephen made it to the third floor, he was slightly out of breath. *This is ridiculous*, he thought. He had not gotten used to the cane yet and trying not to use his right leg was becoming problematic and painful.

Once at the third level he started heading for his big black door. As he hobbled over, he noticed a figure standing near the veranda doors. At first Stephen figured it was a worker and he wondered why the worker was just standing and looking at him. He waved, but the figure did not. Stephen turned to insert the key into the lock. Glancing back, he saw no one standing there. *So, it begins.*

Stephen unlocked and opened "The Big Black Door," grabbed his keys, wallet, backpack, duffel bag and a fully charged phone. Thankfully, the door swung easily upon its hinges despite its size. He smiled to himself because that door would from now on need to be known as "The Big Black Door." He would have to inform the staff to feign ignorance about what was beyond "The Big Black Door," because he did not want people to know that he resided beyond it. There was also the fact that it added a bit of mystery to the place. Perhaps he would use the back entrance more frequently.

Getting down to the first floor was much easier; he chose a sort of controlled fall method using the railing for support. While leaving the hospital he was advised to stay off his leg and to elevate it. He hadn't and the throbbing pain made him acknowledge his failure to follow the doctor's orders.

Walking toward the front doors, Stephen heard a door open behind him. Frank walked into the bar from the back rooms with a box of liquor.

"Hello, Mr. Davenport,"

"Hello, Frank. Is anybody working on the third floor right now?"

Frank placed the box down. "No. Shouldn't be. Everything is done on the third floor. Have you moved in yet, sir? I would like to go over some of the features of your living quarters."

"I should be fully settled in a few days. Thank you, Frank." Stephen chuckled to himself about being referred to as Mr. Davenport and sir. Ted hired people for specific reasons and demanded a disciplined business approach. He would try to help Frank loosen up some once he got settled in. Stephen left DeMaine's and entered the awaiting Uber he had requested.

◆ ◆ ◆ ◆ ◆

Evelynn made it back to her apartment and found Christine watching the television in the living room. They exchanged pleasantries and caught up on some things, but when Christine made a comment about her wearing the same clothes from Friday and not making it home last night, she had to excuse herself. Evelynn liked Christine but wasn't in the mood to feel bad or to have moral judgements placed upon her. She was very happy with everything that had happened in the last twenty-four hours.

Once in the bathroom Evelynn cranked the hot water to high. As the room filled with steam, Evelynn peeled off her clothing and added it to a growing pile. *I really do need to do laundry.* The hot water performed magic upon her body. Between the dance practice, the events at the manor and sleeping in a chair at the hospital, she had become a walking muscle cramp. Her body began to relax, and in doing so she started to feel more alert and cleaner. She thought about all that had happened and was eager to discuss it with Robb and Stephen. The one thing she still had to do was listen to the EVP sessions she had recorded at the house. It was a tiresome task. She tried to review them at the hospital, but it was so boring she'd fallen asleep before having heard any of it.

Evelynn exited the shower, toweled off her lean body and threw on some comfortable clothes. She wanted to review the EVPs prior to the meeting at 3:00 p.m. Sitting on her bed, earbuds in, she started to listen to the recordings. After a while Evelynn couldn't believe what she was hearing. Grabbing a notepad, she began to review and write notes.

◆ ◆ ◆ ◆ ◆

Stephen was not accustomed to riding in the backseat of a vehicle. It was rather nice not having to concentrate on the task of driving, and it gave him time to think. It would take about twenty minutes to make it to his mom's house. This allowed him to ponder the activities of the past twenty-four hours.

His first thought naturally went to Evelynn. What had happened in the Jeep and then at the hospital was incredible and unexpected. He liked Evelynn. *Really* liked her. Their past relationship hadn't worked out because of the timing of the semester and his graduation. He suspected things had been going on in Evelynn's life at the time as well and that her past relationship experiences might have been holding her back. He allowed Evelynn to be herself and accepted her for who she was. Some guys, especially college-aged guys, had a hard time doing that. He never understood why that was; perhaps a lack of maturity or self-confidence.

Things were great with Evelynn, and he didn't want to mess that up. His being a professor and her a student could be an issue if someone wanted it to be; however, it wasn't like she was in any of his classes. They would need to be careful though. Some people were petty when others were happy. Putting his personal life on the back burner, Stephen began to think about the investigation and all that had happened. The spirit of Elizabeth Crimshaw had freaked him out a bit, but the physical attack by the creature was the more serious issue. Stephen needed to get a few things from his mother's house and Walmart before going back to Crimshaw Manor.

◆ ◆ ◆ ◆ ◆

Evelynn pulled her earbuds out and looked at her notes. She had listened to the recordings several times and was pretty sure of what she had heard. She noted the times and would have Robb and Stephen listen to them before telling them what she believed the recordings said.

Much of the recordings were just of what was happening while the three of them were investigating. The first interesting EVP was of the footsteps in the hallway. It was unmistakably the sound of someone walking. The second interesting portion occurred while down in the basement with Robb and Stephen. She wasn't sure but during the group's conversations about the well and the cell phone battery drain she believed she heard a voice say *"looking."* She had reviewed this several times to verify that it wasn't any of them saying this, and it wasn't. The last two EVPs occurred upstairs at Elizabeth's room. Evelynn's recorder had captured a scream that sounded like a woman's. It was faint but noticeable. The final EVP was when Evelynn had seen Elizabeth crouching down and weeping in her room. During the several questions that she had asked, a voice could be heard saying *"read."*

Looking at the time and realizing how fast it had gone, she changed her clothes, made sure to grab a jacket and stuffed a few things into her backpack. She had a lot to discuss prior to heading back to the house.

◆ ◆ ◆ ◆ ◆

Stephen received a text from Ted about the same time he arrived at his mother's house. He saw that her car was gone which gave him a sense of relief and then guilt. He wanted to get in and get out. Even though he loved his mom…he just didn't have time to explain his injury. It would lead to her wanting to know how things were going in his life, which would lead to a meal being made and hours later he would still be here. *Wow, I'm really a bad son. All my mom wants to do is spend time with me.* He would stop by and spend time with her after this investigation. Maybe even take her out to Red Lobster. She would like that and then he would answer all her questions.

Stephen paid the Uber guy and looked at Ted's text. *Working on the glass guy. Have gear for you. Will drop off in office.* Stephen texted back. *Cool. Great. Thank you.* Pulling out his old key, he entered the house. This was home, and it always would be. Not wanting to delay in his task he pushed away memories and went to his old room. Stuffing a few things into his bag, he placed it near the door and went down into the basement where a lot of Davenport generational history was stored.

His dad had been sort of a pack rat. Some people would say a hoarder, but he had been organized and everything was stored on the shelves in the basement alike to a museum storage facility. His dad had always said that family history was important and knowing the past was something you should be proud of. Stephen knew what he was looking for and figured it was still here. He found the bin that contained stuff from his grandfather's time. In it was a box containing items from his grandfather's brother, Stephen's Gruncle Mike, who had flown fighter planes in Asia with the Marine Corps during World War II. He opened the box. On top there were letters, a journal, medals and photos. After pushing those items aside, he saw what he was looking for. Wrapped up in an old rag was Gruncle Mike's Smith & Wesson .45 caliber revolver.

Stephen wasn't sure if his dad had remembered this was down here or not. He knew his mom didn't. Stephen had found it one day long ago and had made a mental note of it but knew it was not a toy to be played with. He pulled it out and examined it. The pistol had been issued to Lt. Mike Davenport, USMC while serving in the Pacific in World War II. It was a blued .45 caliber revolver with a swing-out cylinder and a lanyard ring in the butt that was standard issue for aviators. Gruncle Mike had replaced the wooden grips with ivory ones. When asked why he had done this he would reply, "Just like 'Old Blood and Guts' General Patton." There was no ammo for it, at least that he could find, so he simply took the .45 and placed it in his backpack. Going back upstairs he ordered another Uber, grabbed a bite to eat, wrote a note to his mom and then headed to Walmart.

20

Evelynn arrived a little before 3:00 p.m. at Starbucks. She didn't see Robb, so she found a table near the front and scrolled on her phone. At 3:15 p.m. Evelynn noticed a bright blue Ford F-150 pickup pull up to the curb out front. The driver, a cute young blonde, was obviously dropping off her passenger with lots of smiling and giggling before finally kissing them. Some of the older citizens of Strathmore eyed this spectacle before the passenger exited the pickup. It was Robb.

Robb waved at the blonde who then pulled away from the fire lane without looking, cutting off another vehicle. Robb entered Starbucks, saw Evelynn and gave her two quick shots from his finger pistols. Evelynn laughed. *What a goof.*

"So. Did you have a good night?" Evelynn asked Robb as he sat down.

He acted like he didn't know what she was talking about but then quickly looked out the window and back to her. "Oh, that... Yes, I had a wonderful time."

"Did you do what I told you to do?"

"I don't recall you telling me to do anything."

"Your notes, your analysis..."

"Oh, yeah. Here you go." Robb reached into his pocket and pulled out a folded piece of yellow legal paper.

"Do I really want to touch this?" she asked him.

"Really? Please grow up, E." Robb mocked her.

Evelynn smiled. "What's her name?"

Robb actually blushed a little. "Samantha? Savannah, maybe?"

Evelynn hit him on the arm. "You don't even know her name!" Evelynn said a little too loudly. Robb rubbed his arm where she had struck him.

"Hey, it's not like that. She told me, but she sort of has a Southern accent...like deep South, and rather than being rude and asking her to repeat her name, I figured it would come up again naturally."

"And until then?"

"Well, I'll just give her a nickname or shorten her name."

"Is that why you call me 'E'?" Evelynn asked.

"Nah. Evelynn is just too long...three syllables."

"Oh my gosh, Robb."

Stephen arrived shortly thereafter and was happy to see Evelynn and Robb in deep discussion with notepads, folders and their cell phones on the table. They had obviously started talking about the investigation.

"Sorry I'm late. What did I miss?" he asked.

"How's the leg, Professor?" Robb sheepishly asked. "I can't tell you how sorry I am for hitting you with that star."

"Robb," Stephen began, "if it wasn't for you, I may have been seriously hurt or worse. I'm just glad you didn't hit me another several inches over." They all chuckled at that. "So, what's going on?"

Elizabeth had a legal pad out and started to break down the events of the prior night.

"If we go chronologically with the examination of each person's experiences then I think a lot of insight may be gained," Evelynn said.

"That sounds like a perfect idea. Please begin," Stephen commented.

Evelynn began recounting the events as they had occurred. She spoke about the history of the Crimshaw family again, bringing up the fact that Benjamin Crimshaw and the young boy, Jonathan, were never found; only Elizabeth was found, and that was because she had been hanging from the banister.

"I think we would all agree," Evelynn said, "that whatever the event was that caused Elizabeth to kill herself or had her murdered—"

"Murdered?" Robb said, surprised.

"It's possible. We don't know." Evelynn continued, "Either way it is the reason Elizabeth Crimshaw is haunting the manor."

Evelynn continued with the timeline starting from when they arrived at Crimshaw Manor and were "mistakenly" given full access to the house. They spoke of the footsteps that they had heard and wondered if it may have been a residual sound.

Stephen spoke up. "Possibly. But I don't want you to eliminate any hypothesis. Residual hauntings may take the form of sounds or images. Just like a recording of something in audio or visual format or even both. I would not discount it as simply residual, because it may be just as possible from spiritual manifestation."

"Would that still be the case with the knocks, bangs and such?" Robb asked.

"Yes. Think about it. The footsteps were factual. There is no mistaking them and no other explanation could be attributed to such a sound in the hallways. The knocks and bangs could be related to other factors. They are stand-alone sounds that *could*, and that is the key word here, be made by something else that is explainable." Stephen continued, "As paranormal researchers our job is to investigate and present all facts, sort of like an intelligence officer. The facts will draw a conclusion one way or another. Does that make sense?"

Robb nodded his head in agreement. Evelynn went back to her notes. "During our initial examination of the home, Robb said he thought he saw something run across the backyard toward the barn. Are we assuming this is the creature—"

"Skunk ape," Robb said.

Evelynn ignored the comment. "The creature that was at the Jeep and then attacked us upstairs?"

"Uh…yeah." Robb said, "Without a doubt. I didn't imagine something going to the barn."

"Robb. Didn't you say you went into the barn?" Stephen asked.

"I did. Didn't really explore the barn though. I was just looking for anybody that might have been in there."

"What was in there?"

"Don't know for sure; it's a big barn. but I saw a tractor, lawn mower, some fencing and tools. Common stuff for a barn."

Evelynn asked, "Did it look like anyone or anything was living in there?"

"From what I saw…no. But again, I didn't explore the whole thing."

"The next big event that occurred was at the Jeep," Evelynn said a little awkwardly. Stephen smiled to himself.

"When the skunk ape went after you?" Robb asked.

"Robb, I don't think it was a 'skunk ape.' I'm not a cryptozoologist, but aren't those things said to be in Florida? Have you ever heard of a skunk ape going into houses or speaking English?" Stephen asked.

"No," Robb said, a little dejected.

Stephen continued, "I'm not sure what it was…but I'm not ruling out anything."

"So, what you're saying, Professor, is that it *could* be a skunk ape."

Stephen laughed and shook his head.

"Enough about your friggin' skunk ape, Robb," Evelynn exclaimed. "I'm trying to talk about the dream I had."

Robb chuckled. "Okay… What about your dream? I have dreams. Some are very, very interesting."

"No, not like your perverted fantasy dreams." Evelynn continued, "I had a dream of what I believe may have happened at the house." Evelynn stopped and looked at Robb, waiting for a comment.

"Go on," he said.

"Well, I have to say"—Evelynn lowered her voice—"I don't claim to say that these dreams, these images are anything. However, in the past when I have had them they have been pretty accurate, and I know about actual events that I should not have had any knowledge of…"

"You're a witch," Robb whispered. *Whack!* Evelynn's fist slammed into Robb's arm again.

"Dang!" He said, "I'm just joking. Man, you are bruising me a lot lately."

Stephen lowered his head into his hands. "What are the specifics of your dream?" he asked.

"It's difficult to answer that. I wrote up some notes at the hospital, because I tend to forget the details when I wake up. I remember being in Crimshaw Manor outside Elizabeth's room. She was weeping, crying, totally in despair. She had been locked in there by Benjamin. I remember her saying something about Jonathan." Evelynn closed her eyes in order to aid her memory. "Benjamin came up the steps and unlocked the door. I couldn't see inside her room but could imagine Elizabeth on the floor looking at Benjamin in disgust. He then said something like 'it had to be done' and he wanted her to eat… I remember her screaming at him that his sins would be remembered."

"What sins?" Stephen asked.

Evelynn opened her eyes. "I don't know, but I think Benjamin did something to their son, Jonathan."

Evelynn pulled out her laptop and headphones. "Hey, I almost forgot, but I wanted you guys to listen to some EVPs and tell me what you think."

She opened the laptop, found what she was looking for and said, "This one was recorded down in the basement when all of us were there." She handed Stephen the earbuds and played it.

Stephen's eyes lit up. "Wow!" he said. She then played it for Robb who likewise looked excited when he heard the voice.

"What do you think it is saying?" Evelynn asked them.

"It's a female voice," Stephen said.

"Is it saying 'looking'?" Robb asked. Stephen nodded his head in agreement.

"Yes." Evelynn said, "That's what I believe too." She then played the second EVP, and both heard the voice say "read."

"That's amazing, Evie. Great job," said Stephen.

Thinking out loud, Robb said, "Looking. Read. Looking. Read. Looking to read? Read what?"

Evelynn said, "Looking to read…what was written? Like a note, letter—or a journal!" Evelynn was excited. "Oh my gosh. When I saw Elizabeth in her bedroom she was writing in a journal!"

"Your sins will be remembered," Stephen said quietly.

"So, we're looking for a journal?" Robb asked.

"Possibly," Stephen said. "Eve, what kind of archives does the university have for the Crimshaws?"

"Quite a bit seeing as they were huge benefactors of the university and influential in the area. I can check that out, but I'm sure I would have remembered finding a journal by Elizabeth Crimshaw if I had located it while researching the house," Evelynn said.

"Good. Anything more to discuss regarding last night?" Stephen asked.

Evelynn looked at her legal pad and then gingerly opened up Robb's folded note as if not wishing to touch it. She scanned it and then commented, "Robb, when we were upstairs you said you saw the hallway doors open?"

"Yes, I told you that before. While you were in Elizabeth's room and the professor was in the other room, I started walking down the hallway to find you. When I got to the door you had opened, I heard the clicking of doorknobs and the squeal of hinges as each door was opened."

Evelynn pondered that and said, "You did mention that. You said you felt as if someone or something was checking each room…"

"Or looking into each room." Stephen said, "Elizabeth is not a residual spirit." Evelynn was nodding her head in agreement.

"No." She said, "She can interact with the physical world. That would explain your sighting in the basement and her acknowledgement of your presence."

"By screaming at me?" Stephen asked.

"By letting you know how much pain she is in. We have to help her," Evelynn replied.

Stephen thought about that for a moment and then stated, "Eve. We're researchers. We investigate and document the paranormal."

"We do, Stephen, but in this case, we can help her spirit be at peace. Imagine for a moment that something so tragic, so utterly terrible happened in your life that it fettered you to this world, not allowing you to pass over; and by not passing over you were doomed to live in isolation, unable to interact with this world. You are literally living as a ghost. For whatever reason Elizabeth has been able to communicate with us. She wants our help. I'm going to help her, Stephen."

Stephen was silent for a moment. He had to know that when Evelynn had made up her mind it was futile to argue with her, but more importantly she was right.

"Okay, Eve. We will do what we can to give Elizabeth closure. I'm not sure what that may be, but we will try."

The group ordered more coffee and had a snack. They continued to talk shop and discuss their plans. They wanted to be out at the property earlier to set up and explore in the daylight hours.

"I think we should explore the barn to make sure the creature isn't living in there," Stephen said.

"Yeah, that would be smarter to do in the daytime." Robb continued, "We need a K-9. E, what about Geist?"

Evelynn laughed.

"Geist?" Stephen asked, raising an eyebrow.

"Yes. He is my dog, a Jack Russell. His full name is Poltergeist," said Evelynn.

Stephen laughed. "You named your pet dog 'Poltergeist'?"

"Yes. Yes, I did. I call him 'Geist' for short, and no, Robb, I'm not bringing my dog on this investigation," she said.

Stephen stopped laughing and said in all seriousness, "It would be interesting. Animals are very attuned to spirits."

"I'm not bringing my dog."

"Okay, okay. That's fine. I did get some items at Walmart and some other equipment is going to be available for our use from a friend of mine," Stephen said.

"Cool. What kind of stuff?" Robb asked.

"The stuff I got from Walmart is pretty generic, but we were so ill-prepared last time that I want tonight to be a more organized investigation. I bought some flashlights, notepads, two-way radios and lots of batteries."

"That's going to be really helpful." Evelynn continued, "The cell phones were really not the most ideal items to use."

"No, they weren't," Stephen said. "They were good in a pinch, but having equipment specifically designed to do specific functions is best. I'm not sure what Ted was able to acquire, but knowing him it will be technical and elaborate. Did you say you had a friend who was good with computers? A tech guy?"

"Yeah. Asian John," Evelynn said.

Robb spoke up. "Asian John is my roommate and he is in the club; at least, he signed up for it."

"Is he good with electronics, computers and audio/visual equipment?" Stephen asked.

"Yes, he is." Robb said, "I'll text him to see if he is available."

Robb pulled out his phone and started texting. Evelynn was looking at something on her laptop when Stephen caught her attention. She looked inquisitively at him as he raised his eyebrows up and down several times. She snorted out a laugh before covering her mouth.

"Okay. He's in." Robb said, "Just one thing?"

"What?" asked Stephen.

"He is a little sensitive about his Asian background. He hates stereotypes. Just remember that."

"Not a problem." Stephen looked at his watch, it was just about 4:00 p.m. "Wow! We are already losing daylight. Robb, can you and John be out in front of your dorm around 5:00 p.m.?"

"Sure," Robb replied.

"Okay." Stephen said, "We will drop you off, go pick up the equipment and then swing back by the dorm to pick you guys up. Sound good?"

They agreed and eagerly exited the Starbucks to begin their second night of investigation.

21

With Evelynn still driving Stephen's Jeep, they dropped off Robb at his dorm and drove toward DeMaine's.

"How's your leg?" she asked Stephen.

"It hurts; it throbs a lot."

"You should stay off it like the doctor said."

Stephen turned and looked at her. "We both know that's not going to happen. At least not till after this investigation. Besides, what do you know—you're banned." He smiled.

"Shut up." Evelynn laughed. "I figured I would mention it anyway. Oh, do we have time to drive by the library? I would like to take another look at the Crimshaw collection for Elizabeth's journal."

"We have time, but maybe you should go and do that while I go back to DeMaine's and go over the equipment."

Evelynn thought that was a strange response. "What? You don't want to be seen with me?"

Stephen cringed. "Evie, I think that us being seen together at the campus library will only start rumors."

"Screw them. So what if you're a professor."

"But you're a student."

"Not your student." Evelynn was getting upset.

An awkward silence settled between them which lasted for the next few minutes. When they reached DeMaine's, Stephen got out of the Jeep and came around to the driver's side.

"Eve. I didn't mean to upset you…"

"I know," Evelynn said, a little calmer. "You're right. I just don't like having to do something or not being able to do something because of what others think."

"I know that. You're very independent, and I like that about you."

Evelynn smiled. "You like that…about me?"

"I do." Stephen kissed her. "Can you pick me up around 4:30 p.m.?"

"I will. See you then."

◆ ◆ ◆ ◆ ◆

Stephen entered DeMaine's as Frank was getting ready to leave. He told Stephen that a few more things needed to be done on the first floor and in the kitchen area, but everything was on schedule. Stephen told him to have a good rest of the weekend and locked the front door behind him. He then went to the office to see what Ted had managed to find on such short notice.

He entered the office, leaving the door open. No one was in the nightclub and being alone at DeMaine's kind of spooked him a little. Leaving the door open allowed him to hear more of the building and to see if anyone or anything was nearby.

Sitting on the table were two black, briefcase-sized plastic cases, a larger black plastic case and a duffel bag. He opened up the first case. It had foam padding protecting a 35mm camera, flash, lenses, film and a camcorder. The second case contained a digital recorder, a monitor, an Ovilus and a mobile Wi-Fi hot spot. The larger box held two REM pods and a spirit box while the duffel bag had extension cords, batteries, battery chargers and a light stand. Ted had resources, that was for sure.

The Ovilus was an interesting piece of equipment. It was square-shaped and had a display and speaker. It could produce words from an extensive vocabulary list within the device, the idea being that spirits could use energy to form words. The REM pods looked like short coffee cans with lights and an antenna on top. When placed in an area, the lights would flash and an alarm would sound to indicate that something had come in contact with it. The final item, the spirit box, was a device that scanned various radio frequencies at a very high rate of speed. The white noise generated was believed to be a means for spirits to communicate with the living.

Stephen carefully examined the equipment. He was familiar with most of it, having discussed such equipment in his class from time to time. The REM pods and the Ovilus were nice and appeared to be brand new by the plastic wrapping around them. Stephen looked at the Ovilus and was about to turn it on when he heard some noises coming from upstairs. It sounded like machinery of some sort, but nothing he had heard before.

Wondering if a workman had left something on, he began the climb up the stairs. The noise sounded like several machines were working away directly above him. Stephen's ascent was slow; his leg throbbed. As he passed the first landing, he believed he heard talking amidst the clamoring of machinery. *What the hell?*

The second floor was dark, and the noise and voices seemed to be coming from the bar area. Nothing was there. Nothing other than tables, chairs and the bar. As if a switch had been flicked off, all noise suddenly ceased. Stephen stood still, looking into the dark gloom of the second floor. Shadows among the shadows seemed to move from the corner of his eye. Each time he moved his eyes to follow the shadows, nothing was visible. But something was there, when he was not looking directly at them.

Any regular person would have been frightened by the audio and visual experience. Stephen, however, was used to seeing things when others did not. He had foolishly thought that the spirits of DeMaine's would have simply left over the years or maybe passed on. It seemed that he was wrong. Stephen turned around and descended the stairs, thinking that lights and security cameras would be a great addition to the nightclub. While slowly walking down the stairs, Stephen did not notice the figure that had been near the corner of the bar, nor did he observe it as it began to drift toward the bathrooms and disappeared among those shadows.

◆ ◆ ◆ ◆ ◆

Evelynn texted Stephen and informed him that she'd had no luck in locating Elizabeth's journal, and that she was on her way over to pick him up. Stephen packed up everything and exited DeMaine's. He sat on a bench under the overhang out front, thinking as he waited for Evelynn.

The fact that Elizabeth's spirit was a haunt was an important point. It meant that she could interact, that she was aware of the team's presence. *Why has no one else ever experienced what we did?* It could have been that people were frightened and left before having an actual sighting. It could be that no one had been in the home when Elizabeth materialized. But, why now? What was it that made Elizabeth's spirit capable of interacting the way it did? It took energy for a spirit to materialize and manipulate. Draining cell phone batteries should not have provided enough energy to do that; at least, Stephen didn't think so.

Evelynn arrived and picked up Stephen. They headed over to the dorm and saw Robb and John standing near the parking lot. John Lee was about five foot eight and thin. He had dark, neat hair, and he dressed fashionably well.

"You must be John," Stephen said as they exited the Jeep.

"Yes, sir. Pleasure to meet you," John said, extending his hand. Stephen shook it. A firm confident handshake.

"John, it's my understanding that you are in the Strathmore University Paranormal Investigations club?"

"Yes, sir. I joined this semester."

"Excellent. I haven't met all the students yet. Have you had any experiences with the paranormal?" Stephen asked.

John glanced at Robb, who was loading up his bag of many things. "I didn't know that was a prerequisite," John said.

"It's not." Stephen continued, "It's just that this is not a joke or a television show. We are doing real research, which may be unsettling."

"I understand that, sir. I believe Robb said you had equipment that you may need help with. May I ask what kind of equipment?"

"You may," Stephen said with a smile. "We have some camcorders, a monitor, a few REM pods."

"If you don't mind, Professor, I brought some additional video cameras and monitors. It was no problem."

Stephen was impressed. "No, I don't mind at all. In fact, I would appreciate anything to help us document what is happening at Crimshaw Manor."

John loaded his equipment, closed the rear hatch and then turned to face Stephen.

"Robb said something about a skunk ape?"

Stephen groaned as he got into the Jeep and pulled out of the lot.

22

E velynn tended to drive a bit faster than Stephen was used to, which, in turn, kept him glancing at the speedometer. *It would be easier to just not look*, he thought. John talked about his background as they raced through the countryside. He was a computer science and mathematics double major. He had a talent for it and would have good career possibilities, which made his family happy, but he was intrigued by the unknown, the weird and the unexplained. He had always liked to read and used to sneak books about the strange subjects he enjoyed in between his science and math books. He had a traditional Korean family, but he was not very traditional, which irked his mother and father. But as long as he excelled in academics, they didn't pester him about his foolish hobbies.

The team gave a rundown of what had happened the night before.

"Are you serious?" he asked skeptically.

When Evelynn described their encounters with Elizabeth, John became very quiet.

"So, you all have seen a ghost?" he said, looking at each of them.

Evelynn and Stephen nodded, but Robb was playing a game on his phone. "Not me. I only saw the doors open on their own," Robb said.

John grinned and replied, "This is going to be off the hook!"

The sun was still high up in the afternoon sky when Evelynn pulled up to the Crimshaw gate. Evelynn sat in the seat for a moment as if waiting for something, but then she exited the Jeep, opened up the gate and got back in.

"I could have done that," Robb said.

"Yeah, you could have…but you didn't," she replied.

Robb mouthed the words *"but you didn't,"* getting a chuckle from John. The house looked the same as they had left it. The only indication that they had been there the night before was the noticeable broken window on the second floor. Evelynn parked the Jeep in approximately the same place as the night before. As they began to unload the Jeep Stephen asked Robb jokingly, "You didn't bring that crossbow, did you?"

Robb reddened a bit and replied, "No, Professor, I didn't." Stephen thought about the fact that he had placed Gruncle Mike's .45 revolver in his own backpack. He knew he was being hypocritical, but hopefully they would not need it.

Evelynn produced the black key and opened the door. Even with the downstairs shutters closed, beams of sunlight came into the house from the upper floor windows, giving more of a sense of ease than the previous night. The downstairs rooms, however, still harbored dark shadows.

"I think we will set up a command center here in the dining room," Stephen said, setting down some of the equipment boxes. He looked around and realized that there were no outlets visible. "I'm not sure what we are going to do about power for the equipment," he said.

Evelynn looked up from what she was doing and said, "There should be outlets somewhere. People lived in this house when electricity was around."

John was near the wall and bent down. "Here's an outlet." He pressed on a wooden tile that covered it up. "I guess they wanted to hide it."

"Yes. Probably for historical aesthetics," Robb said.

They plugged in a power strip, but nothing happened. "Hmm. What's the deal?" Stephen asked.

"Might be that the power is actually turned off since nobody lives here; nobody living that is," Robb commented.

"I'm guessing the fuse box is turned off. Might be as simple as turning it on." Stephen continued, "I'm guessing the most obvious place for the fuse box would be..."

"The basement," Robb said, groaning.

Stephen nodded and looked at Robb. Robb shook his head side to side slowly. John, watching this silent communication between Stephen and Robb, asked, "What's the big deal about the basement?"

◆ ◆ ◆ ◆ ◆

John walked cautiously down the steps into the dark basement. Stephen and Robb stood at the top of the stairs.

"I don't know what the big deal is. It's just an old empty... What the..." John said as he stepped onto the hard dirt floor and scanned the space. "Is that a well?" he said loudly.

"Yep. Don't fall in," Robb yelled down.

"Let me know when he flips the box," John heard Stephen say. He then heard footsteps as Stephen walked back to the dining room.

John had no intention of going near the well. Obviously, the professor and Robb didn't like the basement. He knew that Robb had a dislike for small spaces, which was funny since he was smaller in stature, but the basement was rather large. It just didn't have any windows. He saw the fuse box and went over to inspect it.

"Found it," he said. The handle on the side was down in the off position. He pushed it up with a loud metallic clank. "How's that?"

"Yes! We have power," yelled Stephen from the dining room.

John began to turn toward the stairs when a noise came from the darkness of the well. He swung his light around as a chill came up his back. His flashlight revealed nothing that he could see, and he walked quickly to the stairs and up out of the basement.

♦ ♦ ♦ ♦ ♦

They gathered around the dining room table, which was now the command post where all the equipment was laid out. Stephen had opened the black plastic equipment cases and laid out the Sony HD digital camcorder, the full spectrum 35mm camera, two digital recorders, two handheld radios, three flashlights, a lot of batteries, two REM pods, the Ovilus, the spirit box and the mobile hot spot. The monitor was already on the table, and John had set out the equipment he had brought.

John explained that he was able to bring the equipment because he was part of the tech club, and that it was not to be handled by anyone but him. He looked at Robb when he said this. John placed on the table two direct feed cameras, tripods, portable lights, cords, cords and more cords, a power box, desktop computer with monitor, two audio mics and batteries for the various items.

"Wow," Stephen said. "I'm impressed with your equipment."

Robb snickered.

"Thank you, Professor. When Robb told me about what you were investigating, I figured having stuff that could really document and cover the entire house would come in handy," John said.

Evelynn picked up the 35mm camera. "Is this a full spectrum camera?" she asked with interest.

"It is," Stephen replied.

A full spectrum camera could film in the entire light spectrum from ultraviolet to infrared. This meant it had the potential to capture images not visible to the human eye and not processed out by most modern digital cameras. Evelynn seemed excited to see the camera in action.

Stephen sat down and gazed about. The team, his team, was working together like a well-oiled machine. Everyone naturally filled a role without being asked. Stephen was happy and exhausted as he thought about the investigation.

"Eve, are you and John good here with setting up the equipment?" Stephen asked.

Evelynn looked up from examining the equipment on the table. "Sure. Why?" she asked.

"I'm going to take Robb with me and check out the barn before it gets dark." Stephen stood.

"Okay. I think we will run cords and set up the cameras, lights and mics," Evelynn said.

"Sounds like a plan, but make sure you go together as a team. I don't want any solo projects. Understood?"

"Aye, aye, Captain," Evelynn said, saluting Stephen.

He smiled and motioned to Robb. "You ready to explore a barn?"

"Sure." Robb said, "Why not? What could be in a barn next to a haunted house after all?"

◆ ◆ ◆ ◆ ◆

Stephen and Robb walked out the backdoor, down a few steps and out into the backyard when Robb stopped.

"What's up?" Stephen asked.

"You know we never did really talk about the skunk…creature thing. When I did my flying dropkick it went out that window and fell two stories to the ground."

Stephen looked toward the broken window. "I know."

Robb continued, "It fell, what? Twenty feet? Then disappeared into the night?"

Stephen returned his gaze to Robb. "I know."

"So…"—Robb seemed to drag out the word—"any comments about that? Concerns?"

"I do have concerns, Robb. I saw that thing up close. Looked it in the eyes, smelled its putrid breath…"

"Okay, that's cool. Didn't mean to bring up bad memories." Robb turned to walk toward the barn. Stephen started limping after him.

"No, I'm sorry. I am concerned about what that was. I just haven't been able to rationally explain it and that bothers me. So, Robb," Stephen said changing the subject, "What's the deal with the ninja stuff?"

Robb shrugged his shoulders. "No deal. I'm a ninja; I've been training for the past three years."

"Really? So, you're a true ninja?"

Robb turned and smiled. "I am not confirming or denying anything, Professor."

It was five o'clock and the afternoon sun was still over the top of the trees, but it would not be for much longer. It would start to get dark in about an hour, and like yesterday, they were running out of daylight.

The barn was huge. The large sliding barn doors were closed but opened easily with Robb and Stephen pushing on them. Once inside, the barn opened into a large area. A modern tractor was present along with a riding lawn mower. Weed eaters, gas cans, and other tools sat along one wall while a set of stairs led up to a loft on the other side. A door could be seen along the back wall flanked by what looked like old stables or pens.

Stephen looked at the steps and sighed. He was tired of climbing stairs with his gimpy leg. He turned toward Robb and said, "You want to check out the loft area?"

"Sure." Robb bounded up the wooden steps. Stephen watched him till he disappeared behind some hay bales.

"See anything?" No answer. "Robb, is there anything up there?" There was still no answer. Stephen moved toward the steps, already regretting violating his rule about staying together. "Robb!"

"Yes, Professor," said Robb, his voice sounding far away.

"You okay?"

"Yeah, just checking on all the bales. Making sure there's no hidey-holes."

"Hidey-holes?" Stephen said to himself.

♦ ♦ ♦ ♦ ♦

Evelynn and John were so engrossed in their own tasks that when Evelynn looked up from the full spectrum camera, she was surprised that Stephen and Robb had already left. She looked at her watch which showed it was a little after 5:00 p.m.

"John," she said.

"Yes," John replied while still looking at the computer screen.

"What are your thoughts about the paranormal? I kind of got the feeling you were just joining the club because of Robb."

John stopped what he was doing and looked at Evelynn. "I don't just follow Robb around like a puppy. I actually am interested in the paranormal."

Evelynn hadn't meant to offend him and stated as much, then asked, "What part? What of the paranormal interests you?"

John thought about it and said, "Well, the ghost thing does intrigue me, but honestly I think a lot of 'knocks' and EVPs are nothing more than random sounds."

"Interesting. So, you're a skeptic?"

"No. I just think that a lot of those shows on TV 'see something' but never seem to capture it on video."

"Like the bigfoot shows?"

John stopped and stared at her in disbelief. "No. Bigfoots are real. There is plenty of evidence that these creatures exist."

"Okay," Evelynn said slowly. "I seem to have hit a nerve."

"No, you didn't. I'm just amazed that people think bigfoot creatures are a myth. Did you know that some folks believe the government is aware of them but keeps it a secret? That's why the Appalachian Trail was created. It allows them access to large parts of the Eastern United States."

"I did not know that," Evelynn said with a smile.

"It's true. Now tell me about this skunk ape that attacked you guys."

♦ ♦ ♦ ♦ ♦

Robb and Stephen had looked through most of the barn. While it was large, a lot of it was open space. The sun was starting to cast shadows across the fields, and even though the front barn doors were open it was still somewhat dark in the portion of the barn under the loft. Eventually Stephen found a light switch and turned it on, thankful that electricity was present in the barn.

"Wow, that helps a lot," Robb said.

They finished looking in the rear portion of the barn. The six stalls were empty except for the occasional extra building material such as shingles, fence poles and a roll of aluminum. A worktable sat near the center of the area. Stephen went to the rear door and opened it up, allowing the setting sun's beams into the barn.

"Robb, are you sure that creature came to the back of this barn when we first got here yesterday?" Stephen asked.

"I am now. I was 80 percent sure that I saw something race across the rear of the house and behind this barn. With the door here it could have easily come in here."

"But you said you came in here."

"I did, but I didn't really explore this place. I looked around down here, didn't go up into the loft and as I was walking back here, I kicked over a shovel leaning against the wall… Oh shit!" Robb moved toward the stall nearest the tractor. "It's gone!"

"What's gone?"

"It was kind of dark in here yesterday; I didn't have the lights on or even have the doors fully open. I was walking around the side of the tractor"— Robb replayed his previous motions—"and sort of tripped over a shovel leaning against the wall here." He motioned to his right. "I picked it up and set it in the stall."

"I don't see it."

"Exactly! Unless someone came here today the skunk ape must have moved it."

Stephen walked into the stall. It was one of the two larger animal pens. The floor had dirt and hay and the old remains of a feeding trough but not much else. If the creature was using the barn as a place to bed down, this wouldn't be it. It would make more sense to make a "hidey-hole" out of hay in the loft.

Stephen moved around the pen, looking for any sign of something living in there. As he moved toward the rear of the pen, his foot struck something in the hay.

"What's that?" Robb was watching Stephen.

"Don't know." Stephen kicked away the hay, revealing wooden planks.

"It's wood," Stephen said, still removing the hay. "It's a trapdoor."

"No friggin' way!" Robb said, coming into the pen. "This is like *Scooby Doo, Where Are You!*" Stephen looked at Robb and inwardly laughed at his excitement and because he was right, the trapdoor was precisely like something out of a mystery novel.

Stephen and Robb removed the old hay that covered the trapdoor. It was approximately three feet by three feet with an old iron ring at one end and large hinges at the other.

"Do you think it's in there?" Robb asked, looking at the trapdoor and back to Stephen.

"Only one way to find out." Stephen bent down to grasp the ring.

"Wait! Wait! Wait!" Robb exclaimed, exiting the stall. He returned quickly with a hoe in hand. Stephen looked at him and nodded his approval, then pulled on the iron ring. It swung open with minimal protest revealing a set of stairs going down into darkness. Stephen looked at Robb who was holding the hoe in a ready-to-strike position.

"You didn't bring a flashlight or walkie-talkie by chance, did you?" Stephen asked.

"No. Didn't think we would be exploring anything."

"Okay, hold on and let me text Evelynn real quick."

Stephen pulled out his phone and texted: *We found a trapdoor in the barn. Going to check it out.* Within a few seconds the chime on Stephen's phone indicated a text. It was from Evelynn. *Okay, be careful.*

"All right. Robb, I'll go first; you follow and don't hit me with that thing."

Robb nodded and Stephen flicked on his flashlight app and started down the steps. It wasn't a long descent, but Stephen had to stoop a bit so as not to hit his head against the ceiling. The room was small and appeared not to have been used in some time. Cobwebs were present everywhere, along with old crate boxes and jars stacked about.

"I think this was a cellar of sorts where folks would keep their canned food and other supplies," Stephen said.

"Uh…what's that?" Robb motioned toward the far wall. Stephen aimed his light in that direction and saw a square opening in the wall. It was about three feet tall by three feet wide; the bricks had been removed and tossed to the side some time ago. Stephen bent down and looked within. His flashlight only illuminated so far.

"It looks like another chamber or room," Stephen said.

"Is anything in there?" Robb asked, looking around. "You know what would be really bad right now?"

"What?" Stephen asked, standing up.

"If that trapdoor fell down and trapped us in here."

They both turned and looked toward the small square opening above them.

◆ ◆ ◆ ◆ ◆

Evelynn and John made a rough sketch of the house and discussed the setup of the cameras and mics. It was decided that since Evelynn and Stephen had both had experiences, his in the basement and hers in Elizabeth's room, those would be the prime spots for the direct feed cameras. John carried a tripod and camera down the basement steps, while Evelynn followed him carrying a flashlight and two very long cords.

"So, let me get this right." She said, "You are skeptical about ghosts, yet you are not skeptical about bigfoots...or are they called bigfeet?"

"I told you I'm not skeptical about ghosts; I just haven't seen a lot of evidence proving their existence," John said, setting the equipment down.

"But you have seen evidence regarding bigfoot?"

"Yeah. There are castings, hair fibers, and even bones. Not to mention an abundant amount of video."

Evelynn wasn't sure if John was serious or not. He was a hard read. "What about UFOs?"

"Not sure but leaning toward believing. The government has kept a lot of information classified."

"Like what?" she asked.

"You know stuff about the Greys, abductions, alien technology."

"I don't know much about all that. Wouldn't you think when we went to the moon, we would have found some evidence of aliens or at least made contact with them by now?"

John stopped after setting up the tripod and looked at Evelynn. "That didn't happen." Now it was Evelynn's turn to stop and look at John in disbelief.

"What? You don't believe that we landed on the moon?" she asked incredulously.

"I don't want to upset you," John said, sounding sincere.

"You're not. This is fascinating to me."

"Well, think about it, Evelynn. Do you really believe that in 1969 during the height of the Cold War that the United States landed on the moon? That we spent several hours up there and then came back to Earth never to return? I'm just saying that I think it was a hoax or propaganda. Ever see the movie *Capricorn One*?"

Evelynn was speechless. Apparently, John had several opinions on conspiracies and theories about large bipedal creatures.

"All righty, John. Very…interesting." She started laying out cords in the basement.

◆ ◆ ◆ ◆ ◆

Robb and his hoe came up out of the trapdoor first. The barn had become darker since the sun was setting. Stephen followed and dropped the door back in place with a loud *bang*.

"Okay, let's head back to the house. You're sure that there was no evidence of anything living in the loft?" Stephen asked.

"Yeah, I didn't see anything that lead me to believe a skunk ape or crazy man was living up there."

"Okay. And there was no indication of anything living down in the root cellar."

"Well…"

"Well what?" Stephen replied.

"We didn't go into the chamber through the wall."

"Do you want to crawl in there?" Robb shook his head no. Stephen continued, "I think it was the beginning of an expansion to the cellar. We didn't see anything down there that would make me think someone was living there."

"Yeah, I guess you're right."

Stephen walked out the backdoor. Robb started to follow but stopped prior to leaving the pen. He turned around and walked back over to the trapdoor, placing the hoe over top of it. He then left to catch up with Stephen.

Stephen and Robb entered the manor about the same time Evelynn and John came up the basement steps, taping cords down with duct tape.

"Howdy," Robb said, walking down the hall.

"Hello. Did you guys find anything in the barn?" Evelynn asked.

"No, not really." Stephen said, "But I think that creature has been in there. How are things going here?"

"Slow, but good. Come on over to the command center, and I will show you what John and I have come up with."

The command center looked like a real command center. Cords came up out of the basement like tentacles and led to a central power box under the dining room table. A light plugged into the outlet gave the dining room a much cozier feeling than the flashlights. The main monitor with the secondary monitor next to it and a laptop occupied the table.

"Wow, you have been busy." Stephen commented, "What is all this?"

"Well, we're not really all set up yet, but this main monitor here"—John placed his hand on the large one Ted had supplied—"is Monitor One. If we had more cameras, I could really make great use of this. It can easily accommodate six screens but seeing as we only have two cameras, I decided to only put one camera on it."

"Which camera? Where?" Stephen asked.

"In Elizabeth's room. Well, we still have to place it in there. I believe that is a major hot spot," Evelynn said.

John continued, "Monitor Two"—which displayed the basement and the area around the well—"is hooked into the direct feed in the basement. Both rooms have a mic set up to capture any audio."

Robb was looking at the setup and commented, "Why is there no picture on Monitor One?"

Evelynn and John glared at Robb. "Because laying cable and taping it down is a pain. We haven't even made it upstairs yet," Evelynn said. Robb shrugged his shoulders.

"Okay." Stephen said, "Looks good. We can help with the cords to Elizabeth's room. Do we have enough?"

"Oh, yeah." John said, "I brought enough; that's for sure." He pulled out one of the duffel bags crammed with spools of black cable.

The team grabbed the spools of cable, camera, mic and tripods and headed up to the second floor. Once at the top of the stairs, Robb sat down the tripod and mic he was carrying while the others continued into Elizabeth's room. A light breeze was coming through the broken window at the end of the hallway, and Robb wanted to see it again in the daylight.

He saw dried blood on the floorboards, and when Robb looked up toward the window, he saw his star embedded into the frame. "Hello, my little friend," Robb said to himself. He then gently and carefully grabbed hold of the sharp object and pulled it out. "Might need you again." He gingerly placed it into one of his pockets. He then carefully stuck his head out the window, making sure not to cut himself on the shards still in place and gazed about in the daylight.

It was a good drop to the ground. Robb could see some of the broken window pieces on the grass, and he believed there might be a faint impression where the skunk ape landed.

"Be careful." Evelynn's voice came from behind.

Robb turned around with a very serious look on his face. "E, that thing shouldn't have survived a fall like that. At the least it should not have been able to get up and disappear into the night that quickly."

"I know. I don't think it was human."

"I don't either." Robb said, "But, E... It spoke. I don't know if you heard it, but it spoke."

Evelynn was silent. She wasn't sure whose voice she had heard on the tape during the event but now knew it wasn't Robb or Stephen who had shouted in the hallway.

"I thought I heard it shout something before Stephen was attacked."

"It did." Robb lowered his voice. "It said 'Leave her alone.'"

23

E velynn became very quiet. Robb broke the silence. "I'm assuming that he was talking about your ghost Elizabeth."

Evelynn looked at Robb. "Are you sure he said that? Are you sure he said 'Leave her alone?'"

"Yeah. I was standing in the hallway and all the doors started opening... I told you all of this..."

"I know. Keep going."

"You said you could see Elizabeth's spirit. I looked into the room, saw you looking toward the fireplace—"

"And you didn't see anything?" Evelynn interrupted.

"No! Oh my gosh, Evelynn! You really do have an attention issue. I told you I did not see anything, then the skunk ape was at the top of the steps and yelled, at me I guess, to leave her alone. Maybe he's got a thing for you, but I got the impression he was talking about the ghost that you said was in the room with you."

Evelynn was thinking. Robb was right. The creature had to have been talking about leaving Elizabeth's spirit alone.

"Hey! Where are you guys?" Stephen said from down the hallway.

"Right here. On our way," Evelynn said. They walked back down the hallway and entered Elizabeth's room. John had set up the tripods for the camera and mic and was now attaching them to the apparatus. Stephen was starting to connect cords to each other and spooling them out.

"Stephen, Robb and I were talking, and I'm starting to run ideas through my head," Evelynn said.

"Oh no," Robb and Stephen said in unison, groaning.

"No, these ideas are more like a hypothesis. Do you remember when the creature was in the hallway?"

"Uh, yeah. Can't forget that," Stephen said.

"What made you come out into the hallway?"

Stephen could tell Evelynn was thinking something through, so he said in a calm voice, "I realized that the cell phone battery drain was probably linked to spirit activity using the energy in the batteries to manifest action or substance. I started exiting the room because everyone had left me, and I heard some commotion in the hallway. I came out into the hallway…"

"And it was on," Robb said.

Stephen looked at Robb, then back to Evelynn and with a smile said, "Yes, it was on."

"Robb said the creature spoke to him."

"What? Why didn't you tell us?" Stephen asked Robb.

"Holy shit, really? Really! You two pay more attention to ghosts than to what I say," Robb said, frustrated. John laughed.

Stephen felt bad. "I'm sorry, Robb. I do recall you saying something about it, but I must have been focused on something else. What did it say?"

Robb recounted his story again, emphasizing certain details to make sure Stephen and Evelynn were paying attention this time. John listened as well since he had finished attaching the equipment to the tripods. When Robb was done, Stephen appeared deep in thought.

Evelynn waited for Stephen to come to the same conclusion that she had. Finally, she said, "You do know what this means, don't you?"

Stephen looked at Evelynn. "That he is connected to her in some way."

"What? Wait a second." John said, "Are you saying that the skunk ape was a ghost?"

"No, not at all." Stephen said, "In fact, it is neither. I fought with that thing, and it was no spirit…"

"And skunk apes don't speak," John said.

"That we know of," Robb added.

"It is protective of her." Evelynn said, "It was aware of her spirit being here—being in that room…"

"And it knows we have communicated with her, and that we are back for a second night," Stephen said.

"Oh, crap," Robb and John said in low tones.

"So, is it her guardian?" Evelynn asked.

Now it was Stephen's turn to think. He tried to rationalize different theories but could not come up with any. This thing, this creature, was aware of a spirit's presence and wanted to protect her. This was now becoming much more serious.

"Are the doors locked?" Stephen asked.

"Yeah, both front and back," Robb said.

"That didn't seem to stop him last night," Evelynn said.

"Are you saying this creature is going to attack us tonight?" John said nervously.

"Don't know. Maybe. Maybe not. I'm thinking that a lot of what we may be thinking is just the stuff of movies. That creature, I believe, is more of a crazy mountain man than anything supernatural. The legends of Crimshaw Manor being haunted are well known around here; perhaps he has lost touch with reality and believes he must protect her. I don't know. But more than ever we need to be careful and aware." Stephen continued, "Let's finish setting up the equipment and come up with a game plan over dinner. I brought subs if anyone is interested."

They agreed and started taping down the cords, making sure that they were secure and would not become a tripping hazard on the steps. The broken window was an issue that could potentially contaminate any EVPs or allow bats, birds or anything else to come inside. With the wonders of duct tape and some materials they found, they were able to close off the broken window. The drawback was, however, no ambient moonlight was available from that end of the hallway.

They ate and discussed various thoughts about the investigation. Eventually the discussion came back to Elizabeth's journal. Since it was not in the collection at the library, it was most likely lost to time. Tonight's focus would be to try and make contact with Elizabeth and figure out why she had not crossed over. Easier said than done.

"Why not use a Ouija board?" John offered up.

"No," Evelynn said quickly.

"No way," Robb echoed. Stephen remained silent.

"Why not?" John said, "I see that on some of those shows you like."

"Too easy to summon something else." Robb said, "Ghosts are one thing, but demons are a whole different ballpark."

"You believe in demons?" John asked.

"Yep," Robb said, not expounding on it.

"And you?" John asked Evelynn.

Evelynn looked at John and said, "Of course, I do. Don't discount something so quickly. I am not very religious, at least formally, but I do believe in an afterlife. The point is evident by the very spirits we investigate and document. I don't think it is hard to continue that line of thought and believe that there are evil entities interacting between the physical world and the spiritual world."

"Stop please," Robb said, standing up. "I'm serious. I can do the ghost thing but talking about demons is going to just freak me out all night."

"Ha. You're so funny, Robb." John said, "I learn something new about you every day."

"Fine, Johnny Lee. I'm afraid of demons. You have never even seen a ghost or a skunk ape yet."

"Well, we're not investigating demons or demon possession here." Stephen commented, "This is a classic haunt. Elizabeth, who killed herself—"

"That's an assumption," Evelynn interrupted.

Stephen continued, "You are correct. Elizabeth, whose body was found hanging in the foyer and whose spirit was sighted by myself in the basement and by Evelynn in the upstairs bedroom, must be here due to some unfinished business."

"How so?" John asked.

"Spirits fail to pass over to the afterlife and remain here for a variety of reasons. Emotion is a powerful force, and within that category alone you have sorrow, anger, revenge, regret... The list goes on. Evelynn believes that we can figure out what is keeping Elizabeth here, and in doing so help her move on," Stephen said.

"But the skunk ape creature thing is not a ghost," John stated.

"No. It is not," Stephen replied.

"Okay." John said, "Glad to know."

Stephen stood up and tried to lighten the mood. "All right. Everything is operational, correct?"

"Correct," John said.

"All right then. Let's go dark and begin tonight's investigation," said Stephen.

"Go dark?" John asked.

"Well, as dark as possible. In this house that won't be too much of a problem," Stephen replied.

"Why? Why not have lights on so we can see?" John asked.

"It has to do with the electromagnetic field, called EMF for short, that is generated by man-made electrical devices." Evelynn said, "Spirits are more likely to be documented if the EMF is as low as possible."

"Common knowledge, bro," Robb said, smiling. "That business about being afraid of the dark has a whole new meaning now, doesn't it?"

Stephen said, "For now I want to have teams at all times. Evelynn, why don't you and I begin to do some work in the basement. Robb and John can man the command post. Sound good?" They all agreed and prepared for the investigation.

24

E velynn had taken the full spectrum camera with her as she walked
down the steps into the basement. Stephen had grabbed the
Ovilus and one of the radios, leaving the other one with Robb and
John. Stephen felt uneasy as soon as he laid a foot on the step to the
basement. He could feel the damp air coming up from the basement.
Logically, he knew it was from the well and that it wasn't unusual
whatsoever, however it was still a creepy sensation that made him feel
uncomfortable.

John had placed the camera and mic in the far corner near the
fuse box. The cords ran along the wall and up the steps. John and
Evelynn had done an excellent job with taping the cords down on the
steps, eliminating any chance of tripping on them. There was enough
room under the basement door for the cords to continue their journey to the command post, allowing Stephen to close the door and
eliminate any noise contamination from the rest of the house.

After closing the door Stephen turned on his flashlight and
finished walking down the steps. He could hear Evelynn already
snapping photos with the full spectrum.

"Stephen, can you turn off your light when you get down here? I
want to take some overalls without any lights on."

Stephen made it down and came over to where Evelynn was
standing near the camera. He turned off his flashlight and was
engulfed in total darkness.

"Oh, wow. Now that's dark, really dark," Stephen said.

Evelynn chuckled. "Well, yeah. No windows; no ambient light."

It was so dark that Stephen almost felt as if he was floating in space. As he became adjusted to the darkness, he realized his hearing seemed to have taken over as his dominant sense. He moved slightly forward, bumping into Evelynn from behind, his hand making contact with her buttocks.

"Oh," Evelynn said with surprise. "I hope that's your hand on my ass and not a spirit's."

Stephen gave a squeeze. "What are you talking about? I'm not touching you." Evelynn giggled, and then a voice in the darkness spoke.

"You guys do realize the camera allows us to see everything happening down there even in total darkness, right?" Robb said over the radio.

Stephen and Evelynn laughed again and then became serious. Evelynn took several photos and viewed them on the camera's view-finder. The photos were amazing in clarity and had a purplish hue. Nothing appeared out of the normal except in one photo of the well. In it a mist could be seen seeping up and out of it. At first glance one might think it was paranormal, but it was quickly determined to be water vapor and dismissed as such.

"You can turn on the flashlight if you like. I'm good with the overalls."

Stephen turned his flashlight on and instinctively scanned the area. It was a huge basement that he hadn't been able to fully see last night due to only having his flashlight app. There was not much of anything down here except a few boxes that were near the steps. Several brick columns supported the first floor, and with the well on the far side, deep shadows were created by the flashlight's beam.

"Eve, I'm going to try the Ovilus. Does the light interfere with the full spectrum?"

"No, it will be fine. I will just take random photos as it suits me. Might catch something."

Stephen nodded and turned on the Ovilus. It was a square device about six inches by four inches with two short antennas on top, a display screen on the front and a speaker on the back. In a nutshell, it was an electronic speech-synthesis device that would take readings of electromagnetic waves in the area and then convert them to a word which would be displayed on the screen and sounded through the speaker.

"Okay, it's on," Stephen said. "You want to do an EVP session?"

◆ ◆ ◆ ◆ ◆

Robb and John sat at the dining room table watching the monitors. The only light in the room was from the screens themselves, and after a few minutes they decided to lower the screen setting so as not to blind themselves.

"So, what's the deal with Evelynn?" John asked.

"What do you mean?"

"She's kind of hot. Is there something going on with her and the professor? She constantly refers to him as Stephen."

Robb seemed to think for a moment. "Yeah, I guess so now that you mention it."

"Isn't that frowned upon by the school?"

"Probably." Robb said, "Not my business. Evelynn's a big girl and doesn't do anything she doesn't want to. I think there is some history there or something. Why?"

"I'm curious. I'm just saying…she's pretty hot."

"Dude, what are you thinking?"

"I'm just saying"—John now regretted saying anything—"that, you know, she's like hot and…uh…just forget it."

Robb began to laugh at John's discomfort.

An hour or so went by without any activity. Evelynn and Stephen had not received any activity on the Ovilus, and the review of the EVP session yielded nothing. Robb and John watched the monitors, but with no activity their attention began to wane. John began scanning his laptop, while Robb scrolled on his cell phone. When a loud beep echoed through the house, everyone became alert.

"What was that?" Robb said to John.

"I don't know. I think it came from upstairs."

The radio squawked and Stephen's voice came through the device. "Was that the REM pod I heard?"

John looked at Robb, embarrassed that neither of them had been paying attention.

"Uh…yeah," Robb said into the radio, cringing. Four seconds went by in silence as Robb and John waited for a reply.

"You don't know, do you?" Stephen said.

They were busted, and they knew it. "Sorry, Professor. But—" Robb began to say when the beeping sound came again in two quick bursts. John actually was looking at the monitor and saw the lights on the REM pod light up in the upstairs hallway.

"Robb! Robb! The remmy pod is lighting up!" John said excitedly.

Robb keyed the radio. "Professor. The REM pod in the upstairs hallway is having some activity."

Evelynn and Stephen came upstairs to the command post.

"What's going on?" Stephen asked the duo.

"Nothing now." John replied, "The REM pod gave two short beeps and the lights came on."

"I'm guessing something is up there?" Evelynn said. "Who wants to go with me?"

John was out of his seat before Robb had a chance to respond. "I guess John does," Robb said, sitting back down.

"John, take the camcorder with you. We'll keep watch here at the command post," Stephen said.

Evelynn took the radio from Stephen, checked the batteries and asked John if he was ready. John was a bit nervous but wasn't going to pass up this opportunity to work with Evelynn.

The two departed the dining room and started up the steps. Both had flashlights and, like before with Stephen, Evelynn requested John to turn his off while she took some overalls with the full spectrum.

"John, let's take overalls of the entire second floor now, so I don't forget," Evelynn said.

"Sounds good to me." John said, "When should I start using the camcorder?"

"Wait till we start in the hallway."

Evelynn moved from room to room snapping approximately two to three photos per room. As she began moving away from the room across from Elizabeth's, Evelynn scanned the photos that she had just taken.

"That's odd," she said, stopping in the hallway and looking at the display screen.

John moved closer to Evelynn. "What?"

Evelynn held up the camera and John leaned in close.

"Look, I've been taking photos of all the rooms with the full spectrum camera. Just now I took three photos. Look at this one."

Evelynn showed John the display screen which showed the room in a purple hue. A strange small shape was partially blocked by the closet door.

"What's that?" John pointed to the shape.

"I don't know. Look at the first photo; nothing. The second photo has that small image by the closet. Then the third photo once again has nothing."

John was standing very close to Evelynn, and he inhaled her scent deeply. Evelynn put the camera down and stepped away.

"Did you just smell my hair?" She smiled.

John was embarrassed. "No! No, I didn't. I'm just surprised by that image you showed me."

"Mm-hmm." Evelynn grinned. She keyed the radio. "Stephen. We were just in the room across the hall from Elizabeth's. Caught something on the full spectrum. Just note that in the log."

"Will do," Stephen replied.

Evelynn turned to John. "Okay, this is Elizabeth's room and where I saw her spirit. I think this area is a good hot spot—" Evelynn was suddenly interrupted by the sound of the REM pod beeping twice in the hallway.

25

"Oh shit! Oh shit!" John exclaimed. "Is there a ghost over there?" He had jumped when the REM pod went off and was now dancing around unsure of what to do.

"John, calm down and listen." John stopped moving and looked at her. "It's okay. It may or may not be a spirit. I am assuming there is since this is the third time it has gone off. It may be just letting us know it is here."

"All right...I'm good. What should I be doing, Evelynn?" John appeared to be calmer.

Evelynn replied in a low, calm voice, "Turn on the camcorder and just start filming down the hallway." Evelynn then keyed the radio. "Did you guys see that?"

Stephen replied, "No. The direct feed camera doesn't cover that portion of the hallway, but we can hear you. I think there is definitely something up there in the hallway. Do you want to try the spirit box?" Evelynn stated that she would and pulled it out.

She moved toward the area of the REM pod and turned on the spirit box. At first the white noise startled both Evelynn and John, but after adjusting the volume and other settings, the white noise became tolerable.

"Is anyone here with us?" Evelynn asked. "We are here to help." She paused. "What do you want?" The white noise would fade in and out with static like a wave as it swept through radio frequencies.

Suddenly a voice, small and childlike, said, "*Mama.*" Evelynn and John froze in place.

"Dude, did you hear that?" John asked.

Evelynn had, and she motioned with her hand for John to be quiet. The spirit box continued to sweep the air waves, and occasionally the sound of what Evelynn believed to be crying would come through. It sent shivers down her spine. Evelynn continued for several more minutes asking questions, but no further responses came through. After a few more minutes of silence, she turned off the spirit box.

"Is it gone?" John whispered.

"Maybe. What did you hear, John?"

"Sounded like a kid crying and asking for his mommy."

"Yeah, that's what I thought I heard as well." Evelynn stood, still thinking and listening. As Evelynn stood there, the sound of a knock penetrated the silence.

John's eyes grew wide. "Did you hear that?" he asked.

Evelynn nodded her head and pulled out the Ovilus and the digital recorder. Sometimes if one method didn't work, another one would. She turned on the Ovilus and sat it down by the banister. Holding the digital recorder, she began to ask questions.

"Is there anyone here with us?"

"Are you Jonathan? It's okay, we won't hurt you."

"Can you touch the device in front of me and make it light up?"

Evelynn asked the questions slowly and paused between each one, straining her ears to hear the slightest noise. She began to walk toward the end of the hallway with the broken window, motioning for John to stay where he was at the other end. She looked at the window and the material they had taped to the window. It moved in and out with the air current, giving Evelynn the impression that it was breathing.

Evelynn asked several more questions, walking back to the top of the steps. She was about to review the recorder when a word came over the speaker of the Ovilus.

"*Evil.*"

"Whoa…what did that say?" John asked.

The Ovilus spoke again in its computer-generated voice. "*Despair.*"

Evelynn didn't know if it was the eeriness of hearing a voice say the words or something else, but the hair on her arms began to stand on end. Without touching the Ovilus she bent down to look at the screen when a third word came across the speaker.

"*Killed.*"

Evelynn wasn't sure, but she now felt that they were not alone and that Elizabeth was nearby. She asked in a low voice, "Is that you, Elizabeth?" There was no response, but the feeling was unmistakable that someone, *something* was near. She closed her eyes and waited.

◆ ◆ ◆ ◆ ◆

Robb and Stephen had been watching the monitor that was connected to the camera in Elizabeth's room. The mic was sensitive and allowed them to hear what was going on in the hallway. Stephen was itching to ask Evelynn to ask certain questions but keying the radio could potentially ruin the moment. Instead he and Robb watched and listened. They were so intent on looking at and listening to the monitor that neither of them heard the back doorknob as it slowly began to turn.

The doorknob turned slowly, so slowly, as if the person on the other side did not wish to be heard. Luckily Robb had locked the dead bolt prior to the investigation that night. The knob twisted one way. Stopped. It twisted back the other way and stopped. After a brief moment a sudden *bang!* sounded from the backdoor.

"Did you hear that?" Stephen asked.

"Hear what?"

"Like a bang or something."

"Did it come from upstairs?" Robb asked.

"I don't think so." Stephen got up and went out to the hallway. He looked up and saw Evelynn near the banister. Stephen glanced left toward the front of the house and then looked right to scan the rear of the house. A shadow outside the backdoor moved away from the window.

"Oh crap," Stephen muttered.

♦ ♦ ♦ ♦ ♦

Evelynn closed her eyes and relaxed. She was aware of John about twelve feet away. She was also aware of Stephen and Robb in the dining room on the first floor. She felt as if someone else was near her.

Evelynn asked in a low tone, "How can I help you?" Concentrating on her hearing, a slow feeling of detachment crept over her. It was an odd conscious feeling of letting go. She then heard a dull *bang* from downstairs and opened her eyes at the same time the Ovilus said, "*Here.*"

"Oh man, it said 'here!'" John said, still holding the camcorder up and filming the area. Evelynn turned toward John and for a split second thought a shadow moved past him. She wasn't sure if it was the lighting or because she had just opened her eyes, but she didn't say anything to John.

"Evie," Stephen said from the foyer. "I think something is outside."

"What? What did you see?" Evelynn asked.

"Not sure. A shadow? It was at the backdoor."

"Don't tell me you're going outside Stephen."

"No. I'm not about to do that. I think that we'll be fine as long as the doors remain locked."

"What?" John said, walking to where Evelynn was at the top of the stairs.

"It's back?" Robb asked, coming into the foyer. "That's not good. Not good at all."

"John," Stephen started. "Switch out with Robb. Eve, can you make contact with Elizabeth's spirit?"

Evelynn looked at Stephen with a look that said "what the hell do you think I've been trying to do?" at which point Stephen began to realize what he'd said. "I know you're working on it; maybe you might have a better response in her room. You're doing a fantastic job, Evelynn," Stephen awkwardly said.

Robb walked past Stephen on his way to take possession of the camcorder from John. As he did, he quietly said, "Smooth, Professor. Real smooth."

26

R obb checked the battery of the camcorder as he walked up to the second floor. He had a good two hours left of filming.

"Hey, E. Pretty cool stuff happening up here? We couldn't see it but could hear the REM pod and Ovilus."

"Yeah," Evelynn replied. "But it's just confusing me more as to what is really happening up here."

They left the REM pod where it was, picked up the Ovilus and went into Elizabeth's room. Evelynn had been writing some notes, while Robb sat down on the floor near the door. Evelynn walked over and sat on the edge of the bed.

"E. What did the Ovilus say? We couldn't hear as well as we would have liked."

Evelynn picked up her notepad. "The first word that came across the Ovilus was 'evil.'"

"That's not good."

"The second word was 'despair,' followed by 'killed' and the word 'here,'" Evelynn said, setting her notepad down beside her.

"So, evil, despair, killed and here. Wow. Fun place."

"It is interesting." Evelynn continued, "The Ovilus creates words from the energy that is present at that moment. These are not necessarily words spoken. It is not an EVP."

"Okay. Still the general impression is similar to the Delta Kappa Pi sorority house—evil and depressing."

Evelynn was going to comment but decided against it. She needed the EVP session to be reviewed and decided that in order to make the most of the time Stephen or John could do it. She informed Robb she would be right back and took the digital recorder with her as she left the room.

♦ ♦ ♦ ♦ ♦

Evelynn came into the dining room where Stephen and John were. After discussing it Stephen stated he would review the EVP session while Evelynn used the other digital recorder. Stephen watched Evelynn as she walked back up the steps to the second floor. She was thinking, he could tell, about the investigation and maybe something else. She was zoning in; he could sense it.

"John, make sure you watch both monitors. I'm going to review the EVP session."

"Will do, Stephen."

Stephen looked at John and raised an eyebrow.

"I mean…yes, Professor. I will do that."

Stephen hooked up the headphones to the digital recorder and began listening. Reviewing EVP sessions was not exciting. He would have assigned the task to John, but he had not been trained on how to do it. Stephen didn't want to take the time to train him now. Listening to an EVP session required focusing on the audio, scrutinizing every voice or noise, analyzing it, putting it in context of any questions asked or actions made. Anyone could listen to an audio and listen for an unusual voice saying something, but a lot of information was obtained from other noises. A good investigator would note the noises they heard or made as a reference for the analyst reviewing it. The ability to note take and ultimately put everything in context to what was going on during the recording took experience and skill. Stephen sat back and pushed play to begin the EVP session.

♦ ♦ ♦ ♦ ♦

Evelynn returned to a completely dark room. The house was generally all dark, but she figured Robb would have had his flashlight on. Robb had gotten up and moved to the window, looking out into the moonlit night. He turned toward Evelynn as she came in.

"You know it's weird to be standing here in the dark with it so silent looking out the window. This is the same view that Elizabeth Crimshaw would have had."

"Dang, Robb. You're going to become a paranormal investigator yet," she said.

"Maybe. When it's really quiet and I just sit here, I can't help but think about what it was like for her. Like what you told us about her being locked up in here in despair."

"Yep. That's what the Ovilus said... Why don't we try something? I'll need your help though. It's a method that I'm working on in which I close my eyes, relax and walk through a space in an attempt to not be distracted by the physical world and 'see' what the spiritual world allows. I'll just need you to make sure I don't fall down the steps or out the window," Evelynn said with a laugh.

"Okay, that's cool. Just tell me what to do."

Evelynn explained that the best results came when a person using this technique was relaxed and not afraid of running into anything or distracted by having to manipulate any items. The first thing they did was open all the doors on the second floor. Since most of the rooms were relatively empty, this was an ideal space for this technique. Going back to Elizabeth's room, Evelynn and Robb practiced walking the path that she would take several more times. They would leave Elizabeth's room, walk across the hallway into what they were now calling Jonathan's room and then down the right-hand side of the hallway, going into each room and finishing in Benjamin's.

◆ ◆ ◆ ◆ ◆

Stephen sat up quickly as he listened to the recording. "What the heck?"

John, who was still a little edgy, jumped a little. "What? What?"

Stephen jotted something down on a notepad and then said, "Sorry. I'm hearing some strange things on Eve's EVP. Let me finish and then we can review it together." For the next several minutes Stephen listened, reviewed and wrote. On more than one occasion, he exclaimed, "Wow!" Finally, he pulled off the headphones and moved over to John and his computer.

He plugged the digital recorder into the laptop and pulled up the program they used for digital recording analysis. It displayed a graph and other readings. The digital recordings Stephen was most interested in were marked down on his notepad.

Stephen explained to John the need to be thorough and to document everything. When analyzing any evidence, it was important to be able to put it into context with other evidence or knowledge. Many times, something by itself would have little meaning but combined with other bits of evidence, it could lead an investigator to a new path or help solve an unanswered question.

Stephen pulled up the first EVP he had marked. Evelynn could be heard walking about and asking questions. In between questions the sound of a child crying could be heard.

"That's eerie," John said. Stephen did not disagree. It sounded as if the child had been crying for a long time and was alone.

"This one really intrigues me. What do you hear?"

Stephen pushed the play button and the two of them listened to Evelynn asking more questions and pausing for answers. A voice said, "*He killed.*" John's eyes grew wide. "Wow," John remarked. Another clip sounded like more crying but from a woman instead of a child. Finally, Stephen pulled up the last EVP.

"This last one is remarkable. I'm not sure of what I hear after the first voice. Here. Just listen."

John was fascinated now. He watched the screen as the monitor displayed the audio in graphic form. Suddenly, they heard a female scream followed by a strange sound.

"Oh wow, Professor…" John said, "That's freaky. I don't remember hearing any of that while we were up there."

"I know, John. That is why we do multiple methods. What do you think that noise was after the scream?"

John appeared to think about it and asked to hear it again. Playing the EVP again they focused on the noise after the scream. It was an odd sound that happened right after Evelynn asked, "How can I help you?" There was a whooshing noise like something was passing by, followed by a sharp crack and a strange noise that could only be described as something straining.

"I'm not sure what that noise is, Professor." John leaned back in his chair. He then looked over at Monitor Two. "What happened to that?" Stephen looked at the monitor along with John. What they saw was a blank screen, totally dark in the basement.

27

"So this walking with your eyes closed thing is a paranormal technique?" Robb asked Evelynn.

"It is a theory. A sort of meditative state in which one opens themselves up to the habits or routine of a spirit. It's called *Spiritus Viatorem*, which is Latin for spirit traveler."

"Sounds like shadow walking," Robb replied in all seriousness.

"Shadow walking?"

"Yeah, it's a ninja technique where one does things blindfolded or in complete darkness. It is meant to teach you to rely on senses besides sight. Your theory sounds like you're letting something possess you."

Evelynn was quiet at that comment. There had been stories of those who lost their way while conducting this technique and of having a spirit take over, to some extent, the person's movements. The idea of something else controlling her was a feeling she did not like. Those were stories; however, Evelynn would keep them in mind if things started getting weird.

They walked the path they were going to take a few more times to become familiar with it, and then once in Elizabeth's room Evelynn began to prepare. She sat on the edge of the bed and started to remove her shoes and socks.

"Uh, what are you doing?" Robb asked, watching her.

"I'm making myself comfortable. I am more balanced and grounded with my feet having direct contact with the floor. Direct contact with the area the spirit would have walked in life can't hurt either."

"Are you going to be taking off any more clothes?" He grinned.

"No, you degenerate imp!" Evelynn exclaimed. "This is serious. Are you going to help me or not?"

"Yes, E. I will help you. What do you want me to do?"

"Can you record with the camcorder, watch where I am going, gently guide me if I am going to obviously run into a wall or something and be quiet the entire time?"

Robb cocked his head, looked up to the left, contemplated and then replied, "Yes, I can."

♦ ♦ ♦ ♦ ♦

"That shouldn't be doing that," John stated, looking at the monitor.

"What happened? Did it go out?"

"No, it's on. There's just no picture. It's almost like something is covering up the lens."

"Let's go check it out." Stephen keyed his radio. "Robb, Evelynn. Camera went out in the basement. We're going to check it out."

"Ten-four," Robb said.

Stephen grabbed a flashlight and the radio; John took only a flashlight. Once in front of the door, Stephen hesitated. John was looking at him, and when Stephen realized he was just standing there he turned to John, smiled and said, "Just spooked a little. Ready?" John nodded and Stephen opened the door.

Like before, cool air rushed into the hallway, making John gasp a little. Stephen aimed his light down the steps, thinking back to the night before when he saw Elizabeth's spirit watching him from the edge of the shadows. A shiver ran down his spine. Rather than going slowly down the steps, Stephen proceeded down quickly in order to get this over with. John was a bit more tentative in coming down.

At first Stephen shone his light beam erratically all over the basement. It didn't take long to see that nothing was there. John walked over to the camera in the corner near the fuse box. It was on. Everything checked out at first glance as normal. Just no picture.

"This doesn't make sense. Maybe the humidity messed it up," John said.

Stephen walked over to the well and cautiously investigated it. He could see water at the bottom, which was far down. Robb was right; this was a creepy well. Stephen moved away, not turning his back to it and went over to John.

John had the camera open and was making sure everything was clean when Stephen began to ask, "So, what seems to be—" The sound of footsteps above them made him stop mid-sentence. John had heard them as well and looked at Stephen.

"What was that?" John whispered.

"Footsteps," Stephen whispered back. He keyed the mic. "Are either of you on the first floor?"

Robb's voice came back loud in the silent basement. "Nope. Still in Elizabeth's room."

Stephen thought for a moment before responding to Robb. "Okay. Just be aware that we definitely heard some footsteps on the first floor. We are in the basement checking on the equipment."

There was a slight pause and then Robb's voice came over the radio. "REM pod just went off up here. I'm guessing activity is picking up."

Stephen inquired about the camera John was examining. When John said he needed to look at it a bit more, Stephen suggested they take the camera back to the command post. He really didn't like not being able to observe what was going on upstairs. John unplugged the camera and grabbed it along with the tripod and started moving toward the steps.

"What about the mic?" Stephen asked.

"It's on a separate line. We can leave it down here and at least hear what's going on or if the pod thing goes off."

◆ ◆ ◆ ◆ ◆

Robb and Evelynn both heard the REM pod go off after Stephen said he had heard footsteps downstairs. The conditions were about as perfect as they could be for trying the *Spiritus Viatorem* technique. Evelynn asked Robb if he was ready and then closed her eyes. She needed to relax and clear her mind. After several minutes Evelynn stood and, with eyes closed, walked out the door and into the hallway. She moved slowly. The temptation to open her eyes was great. She walked across the hallway into Jonathan's room, still thinking about running into something and had to remind herself to relax or this would not work. She had to trust Robb to not let her run into anything; that was a leap of faith she would have to take.

Evelynn stopped and decided to focus on her other senses. The floorboards under her bare feet were smooth and cool. Her ears were the next sense to become keenly acute. She could hear Stephen and John moving from the basement to the dining room. She could imagine them going into the dining room and sitting down. Letting her mind relax, she opened it up to the house to what had been here and what was here. She began to feel light-headed, and without realizing it she began to walk.

◆ ◆ ◆ ◆ ◆

John and Stephen had gone back to the dining room and had just sat down when Stephen looked at the monitor.

"What is she doing?" he said aloud, mostly to himself.

John looked at the monitor. "Is she sleepwalking?"

"No, I think it is a technique that she has been exploring."

John seemed satisfied and after looking at all the wiring and parts, flipped the power switch on the camera. An image of the dining room appeared on the monitor.

"Excellent. What did you do?" Stephen said, surprised to see the back of his head on the monitor.

"Uh, I flipped the power on," John said a little bewildered.

"Well, good job."

"No…that should not be the answer. It wasn't working…now it is. It doesn't make sense."

Stephen grinned. "Welcome to the world of the paranormal."

◆ ◆ ◆ ◆ ◆

Evelynn felt Robb's hand on her arm gently indicating she should not proceed in that direction; she altered course and continued. While entering Benjamin's room her left shoulder struck the doorframe and her left knee the bed frame. It distracted her more than hurt her, but once back in Elizabeth's room she was both surprised and rather proud of making the walk without opening her eyes.

Stephen and John made their way upstairs to see how things were going. Stephen explained the issues with the camera in the basement, and now that it was working, he wanted to place it in the hallway to watch Evelynn's *Spiritus Viatorem* work.

"Do you want to see me run into something?" Evelynn jokingly asked.

"No." Stephen said, "I think that you may be onto something. I'm thinking that Elizabeth may be able to connect to you. At the moment this is where the activity is, so let's focus on the upstairs."

They decided to set up the second camera at the end of the hall near the broken window. Making sure to tape down the cable securely, Stephen and John headed back down to the dining room, while Evelynn and Robb went back to Elizabeth's room to discuss the plan once more. The path was to go from Elizabeth's room across the hall to Jonathan's room, come back out to the hallway, proceed down to the spare room and finish up in Benjamin's room. They had decided that the bathroom was not a probable area of investigation. Evelynn performed the walk several more times in order to relax and walk without thought.

Becoming more confident and comfortable, Evelynn began to walk the path with the intent of letting go. Her bare feet made little noise as she exited Elizabeth's room and went into Jonathan's. Like before she felt light-headed, but this time she embraced it rather than shying away from it. It felt like going down a drain, round and round, yet without becoming dizzy.

Letting herself go, she knew she was moving, but it didn't matter to her. It was an unconscious thought as she floated within herself. A sudden movement within her closed vision state almost made her think about opening her eyes, but instead she watched it pass by and continued to let her conscious self relax.

Evelynn felt a light cool movement of air upon her face. Not thinking much about it, she wondered if someone had opened a window or a door or had just walked past her. She heard the sound of footsteps in the distance, a door slamming shut and crying or, more precisely, weeping behind her.

"*He mustn't know,*" said a faded voice somewhere to her right. Was she still in Jonathan's room? Evelynn moved, where she wasn't sure, but ahead of her was a less dark area. She went toward it, and as if coming out of a cave she began to see wispy gray images before her.

Evelynn concentrated on what was before her, and as she did the images became more distinct. She was looking down the hallway of the second floor. She could even see the window at the end of the hallway near Elizabeth's room. Warm, bright sun came through the window, making the dust in the air dance about like fairies. Giggling came from Jonathan's room, and suddenly she was there in the doorway looking in.

The images flowed in and out of clarity as if a tide would bring them in and then take them away. Evelynn saw the room as it had been, crib against the wall along with a small bed and dresser. A rocking horse sat motionless near the window and in the corner a rocking chair held the occupants of the room. Evelynn gazed upon the scene in easy contentment. Elizabeth, no longer the image of a young woman in fear, anguish and despair but one of youth and beauty, sat upon the rocking chair with a young blond-haired boy about two years old upon her lap. She had a book open and whatever it was that they were looking at made the young boy giggle and laugh with each turn of the page.

Evelynn smiled or at least she believed she was smiling. Elizabeth and Jonathan did not seem to notice the shadow that was Evelynn watching the two of them. *Am I a ghost?* Evelynn thought. Content to watch the happy mother and child, Evelynn would have stayed, but an unknown force tugged upon her like a rope around her waist. As if the tide was rushing back to sea, so too did the images, and Evelynn was in the hallway of grayness again.

◆ ◆ ◆ ◆ ◆

Stephen looked at the monitor and was fascinated by what he was watching. Evelynn had been able to perform the *Spiritus Viatorem* technique. At first her movements seemed awkward, hesitant and reserved, but after exiting Jonathan's room, she almost seemed to have glided with purpose down the hallway toward the broken window until she stopped, turned and went back to Jonathan's room. Something was there. Evelynn was reacting to something in the room.

◆ ◆ ◆ ◆ ◆

Another breeze brushed across Evelynn; it began cool and then became cold. The grayness faded, distorted and became like fog. She began to feel afraid. She heard weeping, banging and cursing from below. Suddenly, Evelynn was back in Elizabeth's room, gazing at the opposite of the scenario she had just experienced. Evelynn no longer saw the happy, strong mother. Instead, a shell of a person was lying upon the bed, weeping with her back to the door.

Evelynn felt this woman's pain. She could feel this woman's hopelessness. She felt a chest-wrenching sadness that made her soul ache to its core. Evelynn watched Elizabeth as a buzzing noise sounded behind her. It was distant at first but then became louder.

Evelynn watched as the vision faded, and the feeling of being back in the house came over her. She opened her eyes slowly, already knowing what to expect. She was in Elizabeth's room, looking upon the bed that Elizabeth had just been lying on.

28

Robb watched in awe and silence as Evelynn seemed to move like her eyes were wide open. Robb had both the camcorder and digital recorder out and was recording all that was happening while being mindful not to let Evelynn run into anything. By the second one it seemed to Robb that Evelynn didn't need any guidance; she moved as if by an unknown will.

Robb was physically closest to Evelynn during the process and could see things that he knew the professor and John could not. He thought they would be interested in capturing Evelynn's face on video because much of what she was experiencing in this "spirit" state was being expressed across it.

While in the hallway Robb could tell by Evelynn's expression that she was experiencing something unknown. Inquisitiveness was the mental image that came to his mind, but when she entered Jonathan's room Evelynn's body expression changed. She became relaxed, more at ease and at one point a smile came across her face. It reminded Robb of watching his young niece sleeping and having a good dream. These good vibes, however, came to an abrupt end when Evelynn walked across the hall and into Elizabeth's room.

Robb could feel the difference as they entered the room; he couldn't explain it, but there was a stark difference between the room across the hallway and this one. Evelynn's entire body stiffened, her face tightened and her jaw clenched. He could see some sort of pain reach her and affect her emotionally. That was when the REM pod pierced the silence, sending Robb almost into cardiac arrest.

"Oh shit!" Robb exclaimed, rushing out into the hallway expecting another attack. The REM pod was blinking erratically and buzzing as loud as it could. Words suddenly came from the Ovilus in quick succession.

"*Killed.*"

"*Evil.*"

"*Read.*"

Then all fell silent. Evelynn stepped out of the bedroom and into the hallway, looking as if she had just woken up.

"What did I hear? A voice saying something?" she asked.

Stephen's voice came over the radio. "It was the Ovilus. Come on down to the command post and bring it with you, please."

◆ ◆ ◆ ◆ ◆

Once in the dining room the four of them relaxed, ate some snacks and gathered around to discuss all that had happened. Stephen looked at the display screen of the Ovilus and informed them of the words that had been generated. Killed, evil, and read. While they had heard the other words from the Ovilus earlier, the word *read* hadn't been said before. Evelynn relayed her experiences while performing the *Spiritus Viatorem* technique.

"I saw Jonathan." Evelynn said, "A beautiful boy of maybe two. That was his room across from Elizabeth's. I'm certain now that Benjamin did something…something evil."

"That oval thing said 'killed,'" John said, interrupting her. "Maybe Benjamin killed Jonathan."

Everyone fell silent knowing that if anything would drive a mother to the level of sorrow that Elizabeth experienced, it would be the loss of a child.

"It also said 'read.'" Stephen said, "That seems a little out of place when compared to 'killed' and 'evil.'"

"If it is Elizabeth communicating with us, then it is obvious she wants us to read something," Evelynn remarked.

"Read what?" Robb said.

"Her journal." Evelynn replied, "It has to still be here."

Stephen stated that the EVP sessions Evelynn had done had been reviewed, and he wanted Robb's and Evelynn's opinion as to what was being said. He set it up, looked at John and pushed play. The words "*He killed our son*" were easily heard by all.

"Well, that pretty much clears up the word 'killed' from the Ovilus," Robb said.

The sound of crying was unnerving, but it was the final EVP noise that sent chills down Evelynn's spine. It was when Evelynn was at the top of the stairs near the banister and asked, "How can I help you?" A woman's scream could be heard on the recording. Robb suddenly stood up, obviously unnerved. The scream was followed by what could only be described as a whooshing noise, a crack and a strange straining noise. Evelynn's face became white.

"What? What is it, Eve? What is it that you hear?" Stephen asked, seeing her reaction to the EVP.

Evelynn stood up, wrapping her arms about her. *Did it just get colder in here*? she thought.

"I've heard that noise before," she said, her eyes a bit damp.

"Where?" Stephen asked.

"When I was in the dream state. In the foyer right after Elizabeth hung herself."

"Oh my gosh! It's the rope straining on the banister," John said excitedly.

"Oh, for the love of Peter Frampton!" Robb exclaimed. "I can't stand this. Did Elizabeth kill herself or not?"

"I believe she did." Evelynn said, "I think that whatever Benjamin did to Jonathan was too much for her. Too much pain, too much grief."

"Well, suicide is a likely cause for a haunting, but I still think that something is keeping her here," Stephen stated.

◆ ◆ ◆ ◆ ◆

All this information, combined with the anxiety, stress and fear, sunk into the group as they sat there contemplating. A lot of activity had happened over the course of the last twenty-four hours and everyone felt it. Evelynn was mentally tapped out, feeling like an iPad that had been given to a five-year-old. Robb was keyed up but knew that sometime soon he would crash. John was still on hyper alert due to not having been here the night before, and Stephen was thinking of a thousand things. He would have preferred to have done the investigation over a series of days but come Monday morning this would most likely be the end of their free reign at Crimshaw Manor.

"What's our plan, Stephen?" Evelynn asked, breaking the silence.

"Well," Stephen began, "I believe the key that would really, fully explain what happened here is in Elizabeth's journal. I don't believe it exists anymore, so finding out the truth is going to be difficult."

"We can use the spirit box again," Robb said.

Stephen nodded his head. "We can. I'm thinking that we should—"

John interrupted Stephen. "Something is in the basement." He removed his headphones and unplugged them, letting the audio come through the speakers. The noise was very faint but sounded like something scraping across the basement floor.

"What is that?" Evelynn asked.

No one had an answer which led to the conclusion that someone needed to go down there and find out what was making the noise. No one spoke up. Stephen wasn't going to ask a student to do something he wasn't willing to do. Even though his leg still hurt, he stood and grabbed a radio and a flashlight.

"Okay. I'll check it out. Now that the camera is working, we can put it back up in the basement. It seems to be the second most active area," Stephen said.

They retrieved the camera from the upstairs hallway, and Stephen, John and Evelynn went to the basement. Robb stayed behind to monitor the screens. The three went down the stairs and scanned the area with their flashlights to see if anything was in the basement; it was empty and still.

Stephen asked Evelynn to scan the floor to see if any marks or evidence was present while John replaced the camera. Nothing was found which was not unexpected. John finished setting up the camera and checked with Robb who said that it was transmitting fine. John then went back upstairs to stay at the command post with Robb. Evelynn decided to stay with Stephen and see if any more contact could be made with Elizabeth in the basement.

Stephen glanced down at his watch. It was about three o'clock in the morning. He was feeling exhausted but wanted to run with this investigation while the activity was strong. He pulled out the spirit box and set it upon the floor near the well. Evelynn stepped away as he did so.

"What's wrong?" Stephen asked.

"Nothing… Just not a fan of the spirit box."

"Really? Why not?" Stephen was intrigued.

"Don't know. I just don't like it. The sounds it makes just kind of grate my nerves."

Stephen had never heard that before and coming from Evelynn, it made him smile. "Do you want to go back to the command post?"

"No. It's okay. I'll just keep my distance."

Stephen nodded and turned on the spirit box. For the next thirty minutes nothing came through the device. It only made white noise and was beginning to grate on Stephen's nerves as well. Finally, he turned it off.

"Seems like this area is quiet," he said.

"Perhaps. Or maybe the spirits are just tired." Evelynn responded, "Maybe they don't like that noise either. Here." She motioned to the floor. "Let's just sit and be quiet. Let's hear this space with no devices."

Evelynn sat down upon the basement floor, her back against a wall. Stephen joined her.

◆ ◆ ◆ ◆ ◆

Robb and John had been sitting, watching a lot of nothing on the monitors. Robb was fidgeting. He kept stretching his legs out, cracking his knuckles, standing up suddenly and then sitting down.

"What's wrong with you, dude?" John asked, seeming tired of Robb's erratic movements.

"Nothing's wrong; just getting tired and stiff."

"Okay, so what… Do you want to take a nap? I can take care of this if you need a quick sleepy-poo."

"Nah, I'll be fine. Just need to get my blood moving." Robb stood, went over to the foyer and started stretching. He decided to make good use of this downtime and began to go through some katas. Katas were detailed choreographed movements done in a set order and pattern to aid in memorizing and perfecting moves, kicks, blocks and strikes. After several sets Robb took a break and had some water. *The foyer here is a nice size,* he thought. He imagined that at some time there may have been a bench or table here occupying some of the space. He looked up toward the stairs and remembered that this was where Elizabeth's body was found by the townsfolk, hanging from the wooden banister at the second floor.

Oh man, Robb thought as he started to go back to the dining room. Upon entering the room he found John where he had left him, sitting in front of the monitors. The only thing different, however, was that John was out cold sleeping in his chair.

Oh, so you give me crap for being tired and then you're the one that takes a sleepy-poo, Robb thought. With a grin upon his face Robb stealthily walked over to his bag of many things and opened it up.

◆ ◆ ◆ ◆ ◆

Sitting in the dark was challenging. The fear was ever present, and more than once Evelynn's hand reached over to make sure Stephen was still beside her. It was easier on her mind to simply close her eyes as opposed to looking into the darkness. Keeping her eyes open made her see things, darker shapes within the darkness. It was a strange, unnerving feeling being in complete darkness, and Evelynn understood these feelings that were dwelling below her emotional surface.

"Are you awake, Stephen?" They had been sitting in darkness for what seemed like hours but it had only been twenty minutes or so.

"Yep. Still here," Stephen replied.

Stephen was acutely aware of how hard the floor was. His butt and legs were getting stiff, and he was becoming sore from the experience. His hearing, however, had become much stronger. He had heard noises in the darkness during this time. He could hear very faint sounds of movement, but he dared not move or speak for fear of the noise suddenly stopping. Now that Evelynn had broken the silence it didn't really seem to matter.

"Did you hear anything?" she asked.

"Yeah, I thought I heard something over on the far side of the room, but I am not sure what it was."

"Really? I haven't heard anything except Robb and John doing something upstairs," Evelynn remarked.

"Well, I can't say it was anything. Could have been my imagination. You done with this technique?"

"Yeah." Evelynn flipped on her flashlight, momentarily startling Stephen. "This didn't really do anything other than make me sleepy."

Stephen was about to reply when suddenly a scream and a loud crash came from above.

◆ ◆ ◆ ◆ ◆

John was at the beach. Not just any ordinary beach but one of the most beautiful tropical Caribbean beaches he had ever seen. The stunning blue sky was clear and endless. The water was an unbelievable turquoise and the sand beneath his feet felt as soft as baby powder. He sat in a beach chair with a cold beer in his hand as he looked toward the two figures coming out of the water. They were exquisite. The first was Ariana Grande wearing a hot pink thong and nothing else. Water droplets covered her body, and she squeezed the water from her long ponytail as she walked next to the other figure.

The other figure was equally as stunning. Her dark hair was plastered back against her head from the water that she had just emerged from like a goddess of the sea. Her tan body was barely covered by the tiny black bikini she wore. As the two neared him he realized that the other person with Ariana was Evelynn.

John was beyond happy as they approached him and sat down upon the white sand near him. A faint groan came from behind him, but he ignored it as he looked upon Ariana's form.

"The water is so warm. You should join us, John," Ariana said, toweling off her nearly naked body.

John lifted the martini that had appeared in his hands to his lips, wondering where his beer had gone. He sipped it and enjoyed it despite having never had one before. Another groan or more like a moan, louder this time, came from behind him, but again John ignored it, focusing on Evelynn as she spoke to him.

"Ariana's right, John. The water is perfect," Evelynn said, turning her back to him and undoing her top. She removed it and tossed it aside as she lay upon a towel on her stomach.

"Ariana, can you put some lotion on my back? I would hate to burn," Evelynn said.

"Sure," Ariana said, getting up and moving over to Evelynn. John watched as Ariana applied lotion to Evelynn's back, rubbing it in and moving down toward her perfect buttock. A moaning noise louder than before sounded right behind John.

"What's that?" Ariana said, looking past John.

"Yeah, what is that?" Evelynn said as she turned, lifting and exposing her bare torso.

The moaning was very loud, and even though he did not wish to remove his gaze from Evelynn and Ariana, he turned and opened his eyes.

Less than five feet away was the face of nightmares. Two eyelid-less orbs of inky darkness stared at John. The gray semi-scaly skin was devoid of features except for two large, pointed ears and a mouthful of sharp teeth. It moaned and reached for John in his chair.

John screamed and struck out without thinking, hitting the creature with the computer keyboard. He was surprised when he heard it crack against the creature's head causing it to fall over a chair and crash to the floor.

◆ ◆ ◆ ◆ ◆

"Holy crap! Was that John?" Evelynn said, standing up. Stephen got up too, but his stiff leg and numb butt made him slower than Evelynn as she preceded him up the stairs and into the hallway.

29

After making impact with the keyboard, John almost accomplished an inhuman feat, jumping up and backwards as if he were a spooked cat. Unfortunately for him gravity and the table prevented him from accomplishing a Matrix-like move. He struck the table and fell to the floor in sync with the "thing" he had struck with the keyboard.

"Oh shit, dude!" the "thing" said as it peeled its face off. Underneath the grotesque mask was Robb rubbing the side of his face where the keyboard had struck him.

John blinked once, blinked twice. He was doubly mad at Robb for scaring the crap out of him and for interrupting the incredible dream that he had been having. John looked at Robb, who was on the floor rubbing the side of his head, and started to laugh. Evelynn came running into the dining room.

"What happened?" Evelynn asked, searching the room for hostiles. Stephen followed her into the room a moment later.

John was still chuckling as he stood up. Robb slowly pushed the mask behind a nearby box.

"Sorry, Evelynn, Professor. I got freaked out and tripped into Robb. I'm just clumsy," John said, standing the chair that had been knocked over upright.

Stephen looked at Robb, who seemed to be unusually quiet. "You okay?" Stephen asked.

Robb stood up and likewise started straightening up some of the furniture.

"Yeah. I'm good," Robb said, not looking at Stephen.

Not sure of what had really gone down but knowing that something had, Stephen decided that he was too tired to try and figure out what Heckle and Jeckle had been doing and dropped the subject.

After having no success in the basement, the group decided to give it one more try upstairs. Robb remained behind while the rest of them went up the stairs to go over their plans. In the hallway Stephen noticed that the covering that they had taped to the broken window was upon the floor several feet from the window.

"What the heck?" Stephen said, walking toward the material. "When did this happen?"

Nobody knew. It was suggested that maybe the wind had blown it down, but nobody could recall any strong wind that night. Another thought was that the tape just wasn't that sticky anymore and gave way. They seemed to settle on this idea. Some of them, however, didn't think that was the case.

Stephen picked up the covering and walked over to the window. He was noticeably limping now. The pain was not terrible, but it was constant. Once at the window Stephen looked out and to the side of the manor. It was a cool brisk cloudless night. The moon lit the entire area as it cast a shadow upon the ground from the barn. *What are we missing?*

◆ ◆ ◆ ◆ ◆

Robb's face was hurting, but even though it was, he began to chuckle softly to himself. It was funny seeing John do that leap straight up and crash to the ground, and he had to admit he deserved the part when he got hit. He was impressed that John hadn't told the professor the truth as to what had happened; he would have to let him know that later.

He sat in the chair and looked at the monitors. Watching video was not exciting when nothing was going on. He looked at the basement first; boring. The fact that the camera didn't even move made it even more boring. The picture displayed most of the basement and included the well. Robb looked at the well in the monitor, really looked at it and then remembered that damn movie *The Ring*. He shivered and looked at the other monitor. Again, boring. Nothing was happening in Elizabeth's room either. He could hear Evelynn and John talking out in the hallway but couldn't really make out what was being said. *God my face hurts. John really did whack me good*, he thought.

Getting up, he moved over to one of the two coolers they had brought to keep the subs, drinks and snacks cold. They sat in the corner out of the way near the shuttered window. Opening one of them up and picking past the water bottles, Robb removed some of the larger pieces of ice and placed them in a towel that he had brought. The sound of a board creaking somewhere made him freeze in place.

◆ ◆ ◆ ◆ ◆

Stephen finished taping the covering back over the window and walked to where Evelynn and John were. They had been standing near the banister discussing what Evelynn had experienced over the past few hours. Neither of them were probably thinking about it, but where they were standing was most likely the last spot Elizabeth Crimshaw stood before going over the railing and ending her life.

"Stephen," Evelynn said, turning toward him as he came down the hallway. "How's your leg?"

"It's stiff and it hurts," Stephen replied.

They spoke more about what had happened and figured that their best method to get answers was going to be either using the Ovilus or doing an EVP session. Evelynn's *Spiritus Viatorem* technique had produced great results, but it was an unpredictable way of obtaining information and was up to the individual performing the technique to interpret what was seen. Equally unpredictable and documentable was the dream state. Evelynn, for all her abilities, was not a device that could be turned on and off. The spirit box had not yielded any results lately and, due to Evelynn's distaste for it, was out. The plan was to slow things down, use scientific reviewable methods and try and get some answers.

◆ ◆ ◆ ◆ ◆

The hair on the back of Robb's neck stood up. The sound of the creaking board was near him, but Robb didn't see anyone in the dining room. He knew it did not come from above. He remained still and slowly scanned the area. The dining room was dark except for the glow coming from the monitor. He could see into the kitchen, and even though there were no lights on, the space was well lit from the moonlight coming in through the two windows. Nothing was in that area that he could see.

Robb continued his slow scan like a mechanical camera panning to the left. The foyer was likewise lighter due to the light of the moon coming through from upstairs, but the living room and the dining room were dark because of the shutters blocking the windows. Something caught Robb's attention that he had not noticed before probably because it was dark outside. He noticed a sliver of light between the two shutters that was slipping into the dark room. The moon must have been on this side of the manor for the light to shine through. As he investigated the room, he heard the floorboards creak once more and saw a shadow pass by outside blocking the sliver of light. Something was moving around outside on the porch.

◆ ◆ ◆ ◆ ◆

Stephen and Evelynn went into Elizabeth's room with the Ovilus and a digital recorder. John was about to go downstairs to the command post, but before he left Stephen pulled him aside.

"John, I need you and Robb to take this seriously. Can you guys work together without screwing around?" Stephen asked him.

"Yes, Professor, we can. It's been a long night; we were just getting a little punchy," John replied.

Stephen patted him on the shoulder and went back into the room. Evelynn had sat down on the edge of the bed where she'd had the experience with Elizabeth earlier. The mantle looked like a great place to put the Ovilus and Stephen did so before taking a seat near the door.

"What are you thinking, Evie?" Stephen asked.

Evelynn had been looking through her notes and looked up at Stephen. "A lot has happened since we have been here. I'm just wondering if this level of activity is always present or if this is because of something we have done."

"Well," Stephen began. "I don't think anyone is normally in Crimshaw Manor after dark. We are the first paranormal investigators I have ever heard of doing anything here."

"True, but I'm still thinking that more of an effort is being made to contact us, to give us a message."

"Evie, you need to approach this as a scientist. I'm sensing you are getting emotionally connected to Elizabeth and Jonathan Crimshaw."

"Perhaps, but it doesn't change anything. The truth is what we are after…isn't it?"

"Of course," Stephen replied.

"Then maybe a little bit of emotional connection is needed to find that truth."

"Perhaps." Stephen grinned at her.

"What is that look? What are you thinking of now, Stephen?" Evelynn asked, not sure if she should have.

"I was thinking about how you got banned from the hospital." Stephen chuckled.

"Oh God," Evelynn said, turning a bit red.

◆ ◆ ◆ ◆ ◆

Robb was now focused like a predator after its prey. He was certain the noise of the creaking floorboard was coming from the porch outside. The shadow that had crossed past the window was moving from left to right. More silent than the average person, Robb moved stealthily out into the foyer going toward the living room. John was coming down the steps and was about to say something when Robb signaled him to be silent. John must have known Robb wasn't playing around this time, so he stopped on the steps and watched Robb slink into the living room.

The living room was very dark, and Robb was a shadow within the shadows. He looked at the shuttered window and, like the one in the dining room, he could make out a sliver of moonlight between the two shutters. He crept up to the window and paused to listen. He waited for a brief moment, straining his ears but didn't hear anything. It would have been strange for a floorboard to be loose and creaky in front of the very window he was waiting by, but he figured he would have heard something, some type of weight upon that old porch.

Robb decided to look through the narrow space to see if anything could actually be seen. He moved over to the window and slowly placed his right eye up to the space between the shutters. It was odd at first. He instantly felt the coldness of the night air coming through the single pane of glass. Getting used to the angle and closing his other eye, he could see much better. A thought of peeking into the girl's locker room came to his mind, but he pushed that memory away for now.

Robb could see the front porch, the pillar, and part of the steps. He couldn't really see much to either side but could make out the yard and part of the Jeep parked out front. He started to adjust his head to see if he could get a better angle when suddenly the sliver of moonlight was blocked, and to his horror a malevolent yellow eye was staring back at him.

30

"Oh crap!" was what Robb was going to say before a hand from behind covered his mouth and moved his face away from the tiny opening. John motioned with his other hand for Robb to be quiet.

The two of them could not see what was peering in, but Robb knew what it was. They both stood motionless as the creature pressed against the window and frame. Robb could now identify the noises he heard previously. These sounds were not creaking floorboards but sniffing, grunting and the smacking of lips.

Robb and John stood still and waited. They waited till they felt that the creature had stopped peering through the window.

"The door!" Robb said excitedly. Both ran to the foyer and skidded to a stop. They stared at the large front door as the doorknob began to turn.

◆ ◆ ◆ ◆ ◆

Stephen heard a noise from the hallway.

"What was that?" He slowly stood up.

"What? What did you hear?" Evelynn said, getting off the bed and walking toward him.

Stephen looked out and down the hallway. There upon the floor several feet away from the window was the covering he had just taped up thirty minutes ago. It hadn't simply come unstuck and dropped to the floor; it was too far from the window for that to be the case.

"What is going on?" he said and started walking toward the object on the floor. As he neared the banister the REM pod chirped and flashed briefly. It drew his attention away from the covering and toward the banister. Looking in the direction of the foyer Stephen saw Robb and John doing an impersonation of Tom Cruise in *Risky Business.*

"What are you doing?" Stephen called down.

Like foxes caught in the henhouse the two of them turned with a look of alarm on their faces and scattered. Robb bolted left into the dining room; John dashed up the stairs toward Stephen shouting, "Red alert! Red alert! It's trying to get in!"

Stephen wasn't sure what was going on as John came running toward him in a state of panic saying something about "it" coming in.

"Stop! John, stop! What are you yelling about?"

John made it to the top of the stairs and stopped, seeming unsure of which direction to go.

"John. Calm down. What are you talking about?" Stephen said again, meeting John's eyes.

John stopped and tried to calm down but still was bouncing around like a five-year-old about to pee his pants.

"The creature—the skunk ape—is outside trying to come through the front door."

Stephen turned in time to see Robb emerging from the dining room, sword in hand.

"Oh shit," Stephen said with a moan.

◆ ◆ ◆ ◆ ◆

Evelynn was following Stephen into the hallway and heard the REM pod go off at the same time she heard from behind her a *tap, tap...tap, tap.* The noise was not an accidental sound but a deliberate noise coming from within the room. Turning around she went back toward the fireplace as the Ovilus said, "*You.*"

Evelynn heard this but the commotion in the hallway was distracting. She was curious, however, and walked closer toward the fireplace where the Ovilus sat. The feeling in the room had changed quickly; something was here.

"Hello?" Evelynn said, "Are you here, Elizabeth?"

Evelynn only heard Stephen and John talking loudly about something in the hallway. She couldn't focus any longer, so she turned and exited the room. She did not see the small ball of light appear near the fireplace nor hear the Ovilus say "*Help me.*"

◆ ◆ ◆ ◆ ◆

"Whoa. Whoa. Whoa!" Stephen exclaimed, starting to come down the stairs. Robb had his ninja sword out in a two-handed grip before him as he faced the door. He prepared himself as he watched the doorknob slowly turn to the right, stop and then slowly turn to the left. Thankfully, the door had been locked.

"Robb. Robb…chill out. Put that thing away," Stephen said, stepping into the foyer where Robb was. "I don't want another accidental injury caused by—" Stephen's words were cut short by a tremendous slamming of something against the front door that seemed to shake the entire house.

Robb glanced over at Stephen who was now standing next to him.

"I thought you said you didn't bring any weapons with you?" Stephen whispered out of the side of his mouth, not taking his eyes off the door.

Robb whispered back, "I said I didn't bring my crossbow with me." The door slammed again.

"Okay then," Stephen replied. "Stay here. I'll be right back."

Stephen slowly sidestepped past Robb all the while keeping his eyes on the large front door. He went into the dining room and found his backpack. Opening it up he grabbed Gruncle Mike's service revolver, opened the cylinder and placed six .45 caliber bullets into the chambers. He then returned to the foyer.

◆ ◆ ◆ ◆ ◆

Evelynn joined John at the top of the stairs near the banister where he was looking down into the foyer at Stephen and Robb.

"What is going on?" she asked.

John hadn't noticed her and jumped before replying, "That skunk ape thing is outside, and it is trying to get in here."

Evelynn looked down into the foyer and saw Robb with a sword in his hands and Stephen with a pistol.

◆ ◆ ◆ ◆ ◆

Robb glanced at Stephen when he returned to the foyer with a pistol in his hand.

"That's not a crossbow either, Professor," Robb said.

"No, no it is not. How's the door standing up?" Stephen asked.

"It's fine, solid. Haven't heard anything since that last bit of banging. Should we go check to see if it's still here?"

"No!" came the reply in unison from Stephen and Evelynn, who was coming downstairs and to the foyer.

"A gun, Stephen? You brought a gun on an investigation?" Evelynn asked incredulously.

"Evie. Now is not the time to have this discussion," Stephen said, already knowing her position on firearms. It wasn't a huge point between them. Stephen believed in the right to protect oneself with a firearm; Evelynn believed them to be dangerous and not necessary.

Stephen placed the revolver into his waistband, believing the threat to have gone. He turned toward Evelynn and Robb and said, "Look. I'm not a fan of any type of violence, but I honestly believe that creature is dangerous, and I will not allow any harm to come to anyone if I can prevent it. I didn't believe it would still be here after falling out of the window—"

"Being kicked through the window," Robb corrected him.

"But the fact is that it *is* still here, and we will all be safe as long as the doors are locked. We will be leaving when the sun comes up," Stephen said and then looked at Robb with his sword still out.

"What? It's my ninjato," Robb said, flinging the short straight-bladed sword about in a fanciful way almost hitting Evelynn before sheathing it. Stephen had no leg to stand on regarding bringing a weapon on an investigation. Robb was doing what he thought would protect him and the others.

"Don't hurt anybody with that, please," Stephen said.

◆ ◆ ◆ ◆ ◆

John was a spectator from the second floor looking down at Stephen, Robb and Evelynn. When he heard a noise from his right, he turned in time to see the door to Benjamin's room closing shut.

"No, no, no," John said quickly as he started down the stairs and stopped halfway down, not sure if he wanted to go any further.

"What now?" Stephen said, looking at John.

"The door up there just closed on its own," John said, pointing upstairs.

As if on command each door that had been opened during Evelynn's spirit walk technique closed. Each one closed with more force than the one before it, with the final door to Elizabeth's room slamming shut with a bang.

31

"I'm guessing that was Elizabeth," Stephen said.

"I think so. Right before all this stuff happened down here there was activity in her room," Evelynn replied.

"What kind?" Robb joined in.

"I was alone. Stephen had just left, and I was following him. I then heard a tapping sound."

"A tapping sound?" Robb said, looking like he wanted to make a joke.

"Yes, a tapping sound." Evelynn continued, "I think there were multiple taps. Also the Ovilus said '*You.*'"

"We should review the camera." John said, "It should have captured it."

"Excellent idea, John. You okay now?" Stephen asked.

"Yeah. Just not used to this ghost thing yet."

All of them moved into the command post to review the video and audio of Elizabeth's room. The video captured Evelynn perfectly, but Stephen was off-screen. The mic was of great quality, able to pick up everything easily in the room and some of the noise from the hallway.

John went backward through the video up to when Evelynn and Stephen entered the room. Fast-forwarding a little to the point where Stephen expressed hearing something, John paused the tape at the request of Evelynn.

"What was it you heard?" Evelynn asked, "Was it Robb?"

Stephen thought for a second and replied, "No. I heard a noise that was odd. Knowing what I know now, I assume it was the covering over the window coming down."

John continued the video. They watched as Evelynn got off the bed, headed to the door and turned back. When they heard *tap, tap… tap, tap* on the video, John hit pause.

"Play that again, John," Stephen said.

He did and then paused it again, waiting for further instructions. Stephen had a thoughtful look on his face. "That is a specific noise," Stephen said.

"That's what I thought," Evelynn said.

"What? The tapping sound?" Robb stated.

"Yeah." Stephen said, "I mean we know it's a tapping sound as opposed to a knock."

"Uh…Okay," John said softly.

"No, there is a difference. A knock is usually a single noise event. Sort of letting a person know you're there. A tap on the other hand is more specific," Stephen said.

"In what way? It's a noise, isn't it?" Robb commented.

"Yes, Robb, but some tapping has a purpose—"

Robb and John snickered.

Stephen ignored them and continued, "Three taps in a row sometimes may be interpreted as a mocking of the Holy Trinity. This is seen in places that have a demonic presence in it."

"But that was four taps," Evelynn said.

"Yes, but more than that it was four patterned taps. John, play it again," said Stephen.

John did. All eyes were on the monitor as Evelynn got off the bed, walked toward the door and stopped. *Tap, tap…tap, tap.*

"Four taps," Robb said.

"No, Robb. The pattern is two taps, a pause and then two taps," said Stephen.

"What like Morse code?" John said, already doing a search on the laptop. "As far as I can tell it means *i i*. What does that mean?"

Evelynn shook her head and said, "No. I don't think Elizabeth is trying to send a message from beyond using Morse code. It may be nothing more than a random tapping sound or it could represent something similar to the three taps Stephen mentioned."

Everyone pondered this and continued with the video. The video showed Evelynn turn and go toward the fireplace.

"Pause, please." Stephen said, "Eve. Why did you go toward the fireplace? Is that where the tapping was coming from?"

"I don't know why. I really couldn't tell you where the tapping noise was coming from. I just walked in that direction."

"Interesting. Please continue," said Stephen.

They saw Evelynn standing near the fireplace when the Ovilus said "*you*."

"Pause," Stephen said to John, who was now understanding how this review process worked and anticipating Stephen's commands.

"*U*? Like for union, U2, united?" Robb said.

"Really, Robb? You as in 'hey you!'" Evelynn replied.

"Evelynn." Stephen said, "Elizabeth is aware of you. This is huge. Having a spirit make cognizant recognition of a living person demonstrates it can react."

"Lucky you," John quietly said.

"Please continue John," Stephen said.

John played the video. They heard Evelynn ask if it was Elizabeth and then heard the commotion of John running upstairs yelling, "Red alert!" John and Robb giggled at that. Evelynn is then seen, obviously not able to concentrate, going out in the hallway. As the video continues, they hear the Ovilus say, "Help me." Then a small orb appears, coming from the area of the fireplace and going to the right.

"Whoa," Robb said.

"I didn't hear that," Evelynn commented, still looking at the screen. A chill went through everyone as they all thought the same thing. The orb could have been Elizabeth's spirit asking Evelynn to help her.

◆ ◆ ◆ ◆ ◆

It was decided that Evelynn would have better results contacting Elizabeth if she was alone. So, Evelynn went up to the bedroom with the Ovilus and, after being talked into it, the spirit box. She entered the room and closed the door behind her.

Evelynn placed the Ovilus on the mantel of the fireplace like before and sat on the edge of the bed. With only moonlight available through the window, the room was dark. Evelynn sat quietly and waited.

Evelynn was starting to get tired. The constant adrenaline dump was exhausting. She had tried for the past thirty minutes to contact Elizabeth but to no avail.

She was going over everything that had happened in her mind. It had been an exhausting forty-eight hours, and although she had slept maybe six hours, she felt drained. *Come on, Elizabeth. Where are you?* Evelynn thought.

◆ ◆ ◆ ◆ ◆

"Yes, it's true. Look it up on YouTube," John said to Robb.

"You're telling me that a squad of army rangers was taken out by a giant in Kandahar?" Robb replied.

"Yeah, and when another squad went in to look for the first one, they ended up killing it. After reporting it back to their command post, a black ops helicopter came in and took the giant out in a large cargo net."

"You're on crack," Robb said with a laugh.

"I'm just saying that there are documented giants in the world like this thing outside," John said.

This argument about real giants in the world had been going on for the last ten minutes. Stephen placed his head into his hands and said, "Can you two please be quiet?"

John and Robb sunk into their chairs. John occasionally looked at the monitor; Robb was fidgety again. Stephen was even starting to feel the doldrums of an investigation and was beginning to nod off. If it wasn't for his belief that all of this would be shut down or at the very least extremely curtailed, he would have closed it down for the night.

The issue of the creature still perplexed him. There was no doubt that it did not want people either around here or in the house. Robb still clung to the idea of a skunk ape. Even pointing out the fact that it had spoken didn't seem to persuade him. *It had said "No! Leave her alone!"* Stephen remembered. *Leave Evelynn alone?* A lightning bolt of thought hit his tired mind and he sat up quickly. No, it wanted them to leave Elizabeth alone. Was it protecting her?

Stephen reached for the radio to tell Evelynn his thought and noticed that there were two radios; she had forgotten to take one with her. Looking over at Robb, who was doing crunches, Stephen asked him if he could take the radio up to Evelynn. Robb agreed, slung his ninjato onto his back and proceeded out of the dining room. Stephen watched him go and then said, "Should I be concerned about that?"

"What? Robb?" John replied.

"Well yes, but more about the sword," Stephen said, turning toward him.

"No. He is really good with it; practices a lot in the dorm room," John said. "Uh, Professor? I'm hearing something in the basement again."

❖ ❖ ❖ ❖ ❖

Robb made it up the steps and to the bedroom with no issues. He knocked on the door out of habit, scaring Evelynn by accident and then entered. It was dark and seeing Evelynn's form only outlined by the moonlight from the window made him ask, "Evelynn?" The dark figure stood still, raising the hair on Robb's arms.

"Evelynn?" he asked again, unsure.

"Yes," she replied.

"Professor wanted you to have this radio." He handed it to her. "You okay, E?"

Evelynn took the radio and placed it next to her on the bed. "Tired. Just feeling very tired now, like I'm drained."

"I think everyone is. It's almost four thirty. I think as soon as the sun comes up the professor is going to want to leave."

"Yeah, that's what I think too. Thanks Robb, but I'm good."

◆ ◆ ◆ ◆ ◆

John handed the headphones to Stephen and said, "Listen to this." Stephen placed the headphones snugly upon his head and listened. He heard a noise come across that was not some random anomaly. It was the loud and distinct sound of something being dragged across the floor.

He looked at John, then the monitor and asked, "Nothing showing on the camera?"

John shook his head. Stephen listened again and now thought the noise sounded like something large and metal being dragged. Robb entered the dining room right as Stephen was standing up.

"Robb. You're with me," Stephen said, noting he wouldn't have a radio for this exploration.

"Cool. Where to?"

"The basement."

"Oh man." Robb moaned.

◆ ◆ ◆ ◆ ◆

Evelynn had conducted an EVP session but had no responses that she could tell. The REM pod was silent even after having moved it into the bedroom, and even the Ovilus was not active. She figured that any spirits that had been here were now down for the night. She was thinking about this while sitting in the quiet darkness, when her ears picked up on the sound of something from the doorway. It wasn't a knock, tap or footsteps but the sound of a shifting of weight as if someone had been or was standing there. Whatever tiredness she had felt was now gone.

"Hello." She said, "Is anyone there?"

The sound of someone exhaling or breathing came followed by a sudden chill in the air, making Evelynn become very alert. It felt as if someone had literally opened a door allowing a cold draft to enter the room. The absence of light was giving Evelynn a bit of anxiety. The moonlight only allowed her to see some of the larger objects as shadows; she could not make out any details. She strained her eyes looking toward the door but could not penetrate the darkness.

She heard the sound of shifting weight again. As Evelynn looked toward the door, she noticed that the LED light indicator on the video camera was getting dimmer by the second till it went out, indicating that the battery had been drained.

◆ ◆ ◆ ◆ ◆

Robb had no desire to go back to the creepy basement and was going to suggest that John go with Stephen but figured it was pointless. Stephen told him about the noise they had heard, and that he simply wanted to see if there was a rational explanation for the sound of some sort of metal object sliding across the floor. They went to the door with flashlights in hand and, like before, made a dynamic entry down the steps and into the basement.

Even though they both knew of the phenomenon of the mist coming up from the well, it still momentarily freaked them out. They used the flashlights to examine the room, but to no one's surprise they did not discover anything.

"Robb, do me a favor and see if there are any signs on the floor of something being dragged."

They proceeded to examine the floor. Robb conveniently started at the point farthest from the well. After a few minutes Robb looked up and said, "Do you smell something?"

Stephen looked at Robb skeptically. *He probably thinks I'm trying to tell a fart joke or something*, Robb thought. Cautiously, Stephen inhaled slightly. "I do. What is that? A burning smell? Like a campfire?" Stephen said.

Robb came near him, sniffing the air. "Yeah, but something else. It smells like wood burning, but something mixed with it. Is that bacon?"

The door at the top of the stairs suddenly burst open and the sound of John's excited voice came down the steps. "The camera went out in Elizabeth's room!" The door then slammed shut, followed by a horrifying bloodcurdling scream that seemed to come from nowhere and everywhere.

◆ ◆ ◆ ◆ ◆

Evelynn was now standing, sure that something else was present with her. She continued to stare into the darkness toward where she had heard the shifting of weight. As she did, she heard tapping again, off to her right and behind her. *Tap, tap…tap, tap.*

"Is that you?" She asked, "What do you want?" She was becoming frustrated. The Ovilus suddenly came alive and said, "*Look.*"

"Look at what? What do you want? Tell me, Elizabeth. Tell me!" Evelynn exclaimed into the darkness.

A sudden chill ran down her spine, and as Evelynn investigated the dark room, something changed. A shadow of something began to rise from the floor near the door by the camera stand. Evelynn watched as this shadow form rose from the floor to take on the shape of a person. A person with long hair well past her shoulders, a long dress and her hands clasped together in front of her.

Evelynn was frightened but at the same time exhilarated. She took in every detail, wondering for the slightest of moments if she was dreaming. It had to be Elizabeth standing less than eight feet away. Evelynn could feel waves of coldness flowing from Elizabeth as she looked at her. Elizabeth's features were masked in shadows, but the long hair, the tight haggardness of her face gave Evelynn the impression of someone worn down, so tired, so grief-stricken.

"Elizabeth?" Evelynn said to the unmoving figure. There was no response, no movement.

"How can I help you?" Evelynn asked. Again, the figure, a shadow darker than those around her, stood still, not moving nor responding. Suddenly, scaring Evelynn, the Ovilus spoke saying, "*Read.*" Evelynn was getting frustrated; she had been over this before.

"Read what? What do you want me to read?" she said to the specter.

A noise from behind was her answer. *Tap, tap…tap, tap.* Evelynn's patience was spent. Ghost or no ghost it became very evident when she again addressed Elizabeth. "I don't understand what you want. Damn it, Elizabeth! Tell me what you want!"

A blast of angry cold air hit Evelynn's face causing her to shy back slightly. The shadow figure moved or more precisely glided at an unnatural speed toward Evelynn, stopping a foot from her. Startled, Evelynn stepped backward quickly. She stepped right into the bed, which caused Evelynn to do a strange backward-sitting maneuver, followed by tumbling off the end of the bed.

Evelynn hit the floor with a thud and looked up to see Elizabeth staring down at her. "*Find,*" the Ovilus said, and then Elizabeth opened her mouth. She opened it wider and wider, more than any human mouth could possibly open and then uttered a scream. A scream so painful, so angry, so pitiful that it made Evelynn close her eyes and cry.

The silence that followed was such a relief that Evelynn lay upon the floor thankful that the sound of Elizabeth's pain was gone. The thundering noise of footsteps could be heard coming toward the bedroom. Rather than being afraid, Evelynn waited. She knew that Stephen and the others would be on their way.

The door opened in a burst and light flooded the room.

"Eve! Eve! Are you okay?" Stephen yelled, coming into the room and scanning for her.

"Yes, I'm over here. I'm fine," she said.

As she began to get up Evelynn looked toward the wall barely a foot away from where she had landed. Light from the flashlights illuminated the space well. Evelynn's heart began to beat rapidly. During the fall she must have struck the baseboard where the wall and the floorboards met. Four worn nails had held a portion of it in place, but now it was askew, revealing a small binder of aged papers.

32

Evelynn's hand trembled from exhaustion and excitement as she reached over and grasped the binder. Dust and plaster covered it, and as she pulled it out, she couldn't help but feel the connection with Elizabeth after having seen her last moments.

"Evie. Are you okay? What happened?" Stephen asked as he came near and assisted her up off the floor.

"Stephen! This is it!" Evelynn said, getting to her feet. She held the binder with both hands in front of her. Stephen looked at her, then to the binder and then back to her. A smile spread across his face.

"You did it, Eve. You found Elizabeth's journal," he said, embracing her. John moved over to the two of them and likewise in a moment of excitement joined the embrace, hugging Evelynn as well.

"You're amazing, Evelynn," John said.

Evelynn laughed from the center of the hug sandwich but then pushed them both off her. "Get off," she said jokingly. "We have to read this."

◆ ◆ ◆ ◆ ◆

The group returned to the command post and turned on some portable lights. Robb took a position outside the illuminated area, suggesting that it was not wise to announce their position to the skunk ape. Evelynn placed the journal down on the table in front of her. Excitement and trepidation entered her thoughts. On the one hand she was excited to read Elizabeth's own words as to what had happened. On the other hand, the journal held Elizabeth's private experiences, her thoughts; Evelynn felt like she was invading her privacy.

"What's wrong, Eve?" Stephen asked, sensing her hesitation.

"I'm not sure." She remarked, "I don't feel right opening it."

"Evie, look at me," Stephen said softly. "This has survived for over a hundred years. It has been waiting...no, *Elizabeth* has been waiting for the right person to find it. To hear her story. She won't be silent anymore. She chose you to know the truth."

Evelynn's eyes began to tear up. "I'm not sure I can handle it," she said quietly.

"You can. We'll leave you alone while you read it," Stephen said.

Evelynn nodded, wiped her eyes dry, swept the dust and debris off, opened the cover and began to read.

The journal was mostly a collection of papers and letters stuffed into a binding of some sort. The paper was old with strong, elegant writing upon each page. Evelynn was extremely careful handling the manuscript, realizing its importance and age. The papers were arranged in order with the first few dealing with the affairs of the estate. From a historian's point of view, the papers provided great insight into the daily operations of the Strathmore Estate and the thoughts of a person in the late 1800s.

Evelynn skimmed most of the business papers, leaving their review to someone who would be more interested in them. When she came upon what was obviously more of a diary-type entry, she slowed down and read with purpose.

Sometime three years prior to the historic snowstorm, Elizabeth first mentioned the details of her marriage to Benjamin Crimshaw. She admitted that it was more of a marriage in name only and that while she did not truly love Benjamin, she would try to make the best of it and hopefully, in time, would develop deeper feelings for him. The age issue was a problem, but in those days it was not an uncommon practice to marry someone older and more established. The larger issue was Benjamin's increasing jealousy of Elizabeth's sense for business, her success and popularity.

Elizabeth described Benjamin as a brooding man who was harsh with others. The townsfolk dealt with the Crimshaws but did not associate with them until Elizabeth began to do more outreach between the estate and the town. On the surface the Crimshaws seemed to be happy. A happy marriage, a perfect family, but according to Elizabeth's writing it was far from that.

With the birth of Jonathan, things obviously changed greatly. Elizabeth, who had previously devoted herself to civil causes, now devoted her entire being to her son. For about a year the Crimshaws seemed to be the quintessential family, prospering in business and enjoying the benefits of family life.

Several more of the papers spoke of mundane things but always had an underlying sense of a strained marriage. Several months prior to the snowstorm, an interesting entry caught Evelynn's eye. It read:

It is late spring, and the excitement of the warmer months has been evident in town. While in town this past week I witnessed a strange occurrence that I am still perplexed about. I was doing some shopping and had Jonathan with me. Having finished our tasks, I sought out Benjamin, whom I believed was near the Jones' property (they have several common business ventures together). As I entered their property, I noticed two figures conversing in the tree line of the property. One was Benjamin and I assumed the other was Robert Jones. I waved and proceeded to walk toward them at which point they quickly finished talking. Benjamin hastily walked toward me, and the tall, dark man stepped back into the woods. When Benjamin came to me, he seemed upset and when I asked who he had been talking to, he simply said, "Nobody you need to concern yourself with." I am not sure what that sort of business was about, but it has concerned me since Benjamin apparently doesn't wish to talk about it.

Evelynn made a note and continued to read. It became evident to her that this "tall, dark man" was more than a chance encounter. Elizabeth was at first intrigued as to why Benjamin did not wish to even discuss this person with her. On two more occasions Elizabeth saw Benjamin speaking to him, but she had learned that it was a subject she was not to ask about.

The first of the two sightings was again in town. Elizabeth had been visiting with friends, discussing upcoming events at the university. Benjamin had stayed home, claiming to have work that needed to be done.

While traveling from the fabric shop to the university, Elizabeth saw Benjamin walking out of town. Not wishing to upset him again, she decided to follow him at a discreet distance. At the edge of town Elizabeth had stopped, not wishing to give up the cover of the buildings that obscured her presence. She watched Benjamin walk up a hill to the edge of the forest. The same tall, dark man exited the woods, greeted Benjamin and then they entered the woods together. Elizabeth stated that her intrigue had now been replaced by concern, and that she did not know what this all meant.

I am now concerned with whatever Benjamin is doing with this tall, dark man. I can only assume that they are engaged in some illegal business venture. How terrible am I? I make assumptions without any evidence, but alas I cannot even question Benjamin for fear of his wrath. He has become more distant and quicker to violent outbursts. He has been speaking of procuring our future for eternity. How strange of him to speak so since I know he has no knowledge or respect for the Lord. While I am concerned, I do not believe Benjamin to be a foolish man. Why does he not confide in me, his wife?

Evelynn stopped and stood up, taking a break from the manuscript. She was so tired. She had never been so tired before in her life. The words were becoming harder and harder to read. They twisted and blurred upon the pages, but she had to know what happened. *Perhaps I should go straight to the final pages,* she thought. She smiled to herself. No, she couldn't do that, and she knew it. There was an order to doing everything, and this story had to be read properly in order to fully understand it.

Standing and stretching, she looked around and realized that only John was still at the command post.

"Where is everyone?" she asked.

John looked at her with sleep in his eyes. "They went back down to the basement. Something about bacon?"

◆ ◆ ◆ ◆ ◆

Stephen and Robb had gone back to the basement. They had tried to tell Evelynn that they had smelled wood burning and bacon down there earlier, but she hadn't responded. So they left, realizing she was so engrossed with reading Elizabeth's journal that it was useless to try to get Evelynn's attention.

Robb had wanted to come with Stephen, saying he was feeling antsy not doing anything. He had brought the spirit box and camcorder with him, while Stephen had decided to try one final EVP session with the digital recorder. Robb turned on the spirit box and placed it upon the floor.

The noise the spirit box made was always a bit disturbing. Robb told Stephen about the white noise and the scene from the old movie *Poltergeist*, and how after he'd watched that movie, he always made sure to turn the TV off when going to bed.

Stephen walked about, asking questions in a low tone. He asked standard questions pertaining to if anyone was here, what was their name and how could they help. Stephen was at the far end of the room when he stopped and stretched his neck. While doing so he noticed a strange anomaly in the wall in the far corner.

"Robb. What is this?" he asked.

Robb walked over and looked at where Stephen was pointing. The wall here was like much of the rest of the basement. Dug out from the ground, it rose to a foundation made of brick. What was odd, however, was a circular hole in the wall that had been filled in with concrete.

"I'm not sure, Professor," Robb said, looking at it. "It looks like a hole that had been filled in."

Stephen looked at Robb, wondering if he made these types of statements on purpose. "Yes, I figured that much out. What do you think it was for?"

"Don't know. Maybe plumbing?" Robb replied.

◆ ◆ ◆ ◆ ◆

Evelynn viewed Stephen and Robb on the monitor and saw that they were not engaged in anything interesting, so she went back to her chair and continued to read the journal. The summer at Crimshaw Manor continued to be busy. Elizabeth was ever the socialite and devoted mother. Events, fundraisers and planning an expansion for the university did not stop her from spending time with her son Jonathan. While many women of Elizabeth's stature would have had a nanny and other domestic help, Elizabeth chose to have none of that.

I am so excited about the upcoming Fourth of July celebration in town. Apparently, a grand display of fireworks is planned. I will take Jonathan by myself, of course. Ben does not wish to be around crowds of people. It's strange how he is becoming more of a recluse with each passing month. Jonathan, on the other hand, is thriving more and more. With the warm cheerful weather finally upon us, he has decided to explore more and more of the grounds. Oh, how he loves animals! He has no fear of them, which is both a marvel and a terror to be sure. I so love that boy. He is the reason for my existence.

Evelynn was reading faster now, wishing to understand what had happened. Elizabeth's intense desire to be a devoted mother and benefactor of the university hid her unhappiness with her marriage and growing distrust of Benjamin.

There was a notable change in the writing of Elizabeth in early August, followed by a long gap in entries till mid-September. Evelynn was no psychologist, but she could interpret what might have been on Elizabeth's mind underneath the words on the pages. An entry in late September boiled Evelynn's blood as she read.

I am confused and uncertain with Benjamin's actions. While I am ashamed of what happened, I believed him when he said he was sorry. It was foolish of me, and to some extent I deserved it. Jonathan was playing and while I was making dinner, I failed to keep track of him. He wandered into Benjamin's study and accidentally knocked a bottle of ink over onto some papers on his desk. Nothing important but Jonathan had made a mess, and his inked fingerprints left their mark upon the desk legs. Benjamin was in the basement, doing research as he says, and upon hearing the commotion came into the study. Such anger in his eyes! He stomped toward poor little Jonathan and grabbed him so roughly. I had just come in and screamed at Benjamin to let go of him. He did but his wrath then fell upon me. He struck me but once, and I do honestly believe he did not realize what he had done. The anger left him when he viewed me on the floor, shielding Jonathan. He apologized and then returned to the basement. I am not sure what he does down there but know that I am not to go down there ever.

◆ ◆ ◆ ◆ ◆

"What kind of plumbing would be about eight inches in diameter and placed here?" Stephen asked Robb.

"I don't know. Just a thought."

The spirit box had been on during the entire time they had been in the basement. It had become simply background noise, both used to it, till a voice came through saying, "*No!*"

"What was that?" Robb said, turning around and looking for the source of the voice.

"It was the spirit box." Stephen moved toward it.

"*No. Stop!*" a female voice hauntingly echoed over the speaker.

Stephen and Robb were now standing to either side of the spirit box in the middle of the room.

"What now?" Robb whispered.

Stephen looked at the device and asked, "Stop what? What do you want to stop?"

The static white noise was unnerving in its rhythm until a female voice said, "*Pain.*"

◆ ◆ ◆ ◆ ◆

Evelynn was furious. She had thought that Elizabeth had been physically abused, but this was confirmation. Was this the cause of Jonathan's death? The EVP had said, "*He killed our son.*" Did Benjamin lose control over something the boy had done and kill him in a fit of rage? Evelynn continued to read the entries.

Winter has come early this year. It is cold, always cold. Benjamin doesn't seem to care about much anymore. I am now fearful and think I should take Jonathan and leave, at least for a while. Benjamin is doing something in the basement and now locks it to prevent me from going down there. I am not losing my mind, but I know whatever he does in the basement has to do with the tall, dark man. While washing dishes I saw him again. He was standing at the edge of the forest looking...watching. I was frightened but looked at this figure to try and understand who he was. He was tall, dressed in a black overcoat with black pants and boots. Upon his head he wore a tall hat, not particularly something worn by someone traveling through the woods. Try as I might, I could not make out the stranger's face but knew he was not from town. As I gazed on, I do believe he saw me looking at him from the window, because it was not much longer that he stepped back among the shadows of the trees.

Another entry.

It has been snowing for several days. I do not believe we are prepared for such an early winter. I am so cold. Whatever firewood we had is taken down to the basement. Our supplies are beginning to run very low. I regret that I did not leave when we were able to. I have heard Benjamin in the basement, and I wonder what he's doing. He has either lost his mind or is talking to the darkness. I have heard him say it is almost time. Time for what I do not know. The animals I

fear are dead due to neglect. I am going to try to leave with Jonathan
tonight. Perhaps we can make it to town. All I know is that to stay here
means we will starve.

"Evelynn," John said, bringing her out of the story.

"Yes, John."

"The professor and Robb are staring at the box thing in the basement, and I'm not sure but I think I am seeing things on the camera
upstairs."

Evelynn moved over to look at the screens. One camera was in
Elizabeth's room. After finding the journal, Evelynn had explained
all that had happened when she had been confronted by Elizabeth's
spirit. Wishing to review the video to see if any of the ghost was visible, they discovered that the battery had been fully drained. A replace-
ment was put in place, and currently the camera was showing what
appeared to be an orb of light floating through the room.

"What is it doing?" Evelynn asked in awe.

John was transfixed by the image. "It seems to go in one direction toward the door, stop, then go in the opposite direction toward
the window. It's been doing this for the past few minutes. It seems
like it's—"

"Pacing," Evelynn said, interrupting.

◆ ◆ ◆ ◆ ◆

"Are you in pain?" Stephen asked, "Is this Elizabeth?" The questions had continued, but the female voice gave no further responses.

"I'm thinking she's gone," Robb said.

"What pain do you think she was speaking of? Us inflicting
pain?"

"Don't know, but E said that Elizabeth was grief-stricken. I'm
guessing the pain of losing her son."

◆ ◆ ◆ ◆ ◆

Evelynn sensed that something was indeed beginning to happen.
She went back to the journal, desiring to finish reading.

I am now lost. Since my last writing Benjamin has become angry and upset. He knew, how I don't know, that I had planned to take Jonathan and leave. His rage was intense. He said he needed the boy. The boy? Not our boy, not his son? Benjamin is now keeping me locked within this room. I have thought about trying to escape but not without my son.

Final entry.

Jonathan is lost. He has taken my son to the basement, and I could not stop him. He said that this must be done. I am so scared for Jonathan, my sweet Jonathan. If he does anything to him, I shall not wish to live another moment in this accursed house.

Evelynn looked for any further writings or papers and found none. What had happened? It was inferred that Benjamin killed Jonathan in the basement, but there was nothing further. Upset by the story of events and the disappointment of not fully understanding what had taken place, Evelynn got up and stretched her legs. She had been sitting and reading for so long that parts of her body had gone numb. Walking about in the dining room, she realized that she was very tired. To stop now would mean sleep; keeping her eyes open actually hurt, and she couldn't focus on anything.

As Evelynn walked out of the dining room, she could hear Robb and Stephen below in the basement. Wandering aimlessly through the hallway, she entered the room across from the kitchen that was attached to the parlor. It had been obviously a study at one time. There was a large wooden desk and chair against the wall and a few other chairs in the middle of the room.

Evelynn went to the desk and sat in the large, smooth chair. It was solid and comfortable, and after only a few moments Evelynn felt the pull of rest. Closing her eyes and placing her head down upon her arms on the desk, she drifted and then fell asleep.

33

Evelynn knew it was a mistake to place her head down upon the desk. But she was so tired. Maybe a moment would have been okay, but when her body relaxed upon the cool smoothness of the desk, Evelynn quickly began to drift into the dreamworld over which she had little control.

As if in a gray fog Evelynn spiraled, not sure where she was going, not sure if she cared. Flashes of light in the thick haze made her think of lightning in the clouds as she began to hear a multitude of voices from a distance, low and muffled.

"We shall always be together," a voice said. "I will always love you." A child giggled. Then the voices came, flowing like memories. Trickling at first, then slow and even. They spoke of happiness, of devotion and of love. Evelynn was confused at first and then realized that the voice that stood out among the grayness, that spoke about love and devotion, was Benjamin Crimshaw's. She had not expected Benjamin capable of either.

The voices started coming quicker, and Evelynn realized it wasn't the voices coming to her, but she was going to them. She was traveling, falling, flowing toward the cacophony of sounds. The flashes became larger, and as she seemed to rush through the grayness, the sound of one voice carried through and dominated over all others.

Evelynn was conscious of her movement through the gray veil. A lighter area was fast approaching, and shapes began to form. She also began to smell things: the moist earth, the pine trees, the crisp air of a forest.

Stepping out of the fog, Evelynn found herself in a large forest at the edge of a clearing. Two figures stood facing each other. One man was tall and wore a black overcoat, trousers, boots and a tall black hat upon his head. The other, Evelynn realized, was Benjamin Crimshaw. Not sure if her presence would interrupt this vision, she hid herself behind a large pine tree as she listened to a conversation between the two.

"I do not know if I can do that!" Benjamin responds to the figure in a state of distress. "I love her, but to do what you ask would destroy her, destroy me."

The dark figure does not move and his features are hidden from Evelynn's view due to the shadows of the hat and the overcoat. If he speaks Evelynn is unable to tell or hear, but Benjamin is visibly upset as he falls to his knees and pleads with the dark man.

"You have been generous. You have been wise with your counsel and advice, but this sacrifice is too much...too much..." Benjamin stammers the words through his sobs. The figure reaches into his overcoat and withdraws a black book. With a strikingly pale hand he holds it out to Benjamin; the stranger's long white fingers look odd against the black leather binding.

Benjamin Crimshaw, the abusive husband, the hulking figure of Evelynn's past visions, now lays in a weeping mess at the foot of this mysterious stranger holding forth an unholy book of some sort. Evelynn strains her ears as the stranger speaks to Benjamin in a low, deep voice. "I have given you wealth; I have given you prosperity, I have even given you love itself. Would you rather the woman takes his place?"

Benjamin sobs brokenly as he shakes his head no.

"I now offer you and the woman immortality. Do as I instruct, and it shall be. If you fail, death will come for you and your love."

Raising his hand slowly, Benjamin accepts the black book. Evelynn, wishing to hear more, moves slightly, cracking a small branch lying upon the forest floor. Holding her breath, Evelynn looks back toward the two figures as they stop and look in her direction. As if struck with a blast of cold air, Evelynn is physically pushed back when the gaze of the dark man falls upon her. As she moves her leg it strikes something sharp and pointed.

Evelynn opened her eyes, realizing that she had fallen asleep. *Too much reading of Elizabeth's journal*, she thought. Suddenly she realized that her leg, more specifically her thigh, was hurting for some unknown reason. Looking down to examine the cause of her pain, Evelynn noticed the desk drawer was now open and deduced that her leg must have struck it during her nap. More annoyed than frightened at the unexplained open drawer, a chill ran up her spine as she noticed a tiny impression on the side of the drawer in old ink. A tiny handprint from a tiny child.

Evelynn pulled her flashlight out with a sudden burst of energy and examined the side of the drawer. It was difficult to see but on the side of the drawer was a small handprint in what appeared to be old black ink. Standing up quickly, she still wasn't sure if she had accidently opened the drawer or if someone else had. Was it Jonathan's? Was the tiny handprint the one from long ago that had thrown Benjamin into a rage?

Looking closer she could make out smudges and tiny fingerprints along the edge of the desk and along one of the legs. Evelynn took a step back, not sure what to make of the dream about Benjamin or of the desk drawer. It was late which meant it was probably early morning by now... Evelynn couldn't recall. She wanted to find Stephen and inform him of the journal, the dream and the drawer.

Evelynn came down the stairs to the basement rubbing her eyes, head and neck. She had never stayed awake for this long, not even for exams. Stephen and Robb were standing near the center of the room looking as if they were expecting something to happen.

"Hey. What's going on?" Evelynn asked.

"Just trying to see if any more responses come through," Stephen said. "How's the journal reading go?"

"Good, to some extent." Evelynn said, "Pretty sure Elizabeth became a victim of abuse, pretty sure Benjamin killed Jonathan, pretty sure Elizabeth killed herself...other than that, I'm not sure."

"All righty then," Robb said.

"It did mention something about a tall dark man. I'll have to read it again, but it is strange. It almost seems like this tall dark man had something over Benjamin. I had a dream as well that is really challenging me. I will have to write it all down in detail while it is still fresh in my mind, but it showed Benjamin making a deal with the tall dark man in exchange for immortality. The journal alludes to it, but I will need to go back over all of it with fresh eyes. I'm just starting to get burned out, really drained."

Stephen came closer to Evelynn. "You know we need to give that journal to the historical society."

"Yeah, I know. Boy, they are going to be pissed about how their ideas of Benjamin Crimshaw line up with reality. I will take photos of it all before we do that...just saying," Evelynn said.

Stephen gave Evelynn a breakdown of what he and Robb had heard and then looked at his watch. The sun would be coming up soon and at that point they would wrap things up and go. Evelynn reluctantly agreed. A lot had happened and a lot of evidence still needed to be analyzed. The team had experienced something unlike anything they had before or anything they believed possible. While it was not out of the question that they could come back, it seemed unlikely they would have the freedom that they had this weekend.

Stephen went to check on something upstairs, and Robb was about to leave as well when he asked Evelynn, "You coming?"

"Yeah, in a moment. Since I now know Jonathan was most likely killed down here, I want to try to make contact one last time. I'll be up shortly."

Robb nodded and walked up the stairs and out of the basement. Evelynn walked around the basement, trying to imagine what had happened. Benjamin was into something, something weird. Elizabeth had called it "research." Research into what? The whole business of the mysterious tall dark man was equally bizarre. It was apparently strange enough to Elizabeth that she commented on it several times.

Evelynn began to feel a chill as she walked about the basement, thinking. *It's probably just the damp air from the well,* she thought. But she consciously kept her distance from the well. Running through everything in her mind, Evelynn walked and thought; this was her way of working through a puzzle. Elizabeth had said in her journal something about Benjamin stating that this must be done. Why? For what reason? Evelynn was so deep in thought that she did not notice the slight dimming of the portable light or hear the quiet scraping noises.

The chill became more intense and as Evelynn came back toward where the camera and light were, she noticed that it seemed less bright than it was a moment ago. She wondered if it was something as simple as a bulb needing to be replaced. That was her initial thought, but when a sudden chill penetrated her body and ran from the base of her skull all the way down her spine, she knew it was not the case. Evelynn froze in place as a dark shadowed form descended from the ceiling. The light went out as if drained, and the form stood in front of Evelynn.

"Hello?" Evelynn tentatively said as a coldness suddenly gripped her, and an outstretched hand grasped her left arm.

◆ ◆ ◆ ◆ ◆

Robb and Stephen had started taking down and packing up the equipment. They were in Elizabeth's room dismantling the camera and tripod and coiling up the cables.

"I'm not sure about that," Stephen said in response to Robb asking about the smell in the basement. They both had smelled it. It smelled of campfire and bacon, but different. Trying to determine whether there was a natural cause for the smell, such as a camper, seemed hopeless. They likely would never know.

They headed down the stairs and into the dining room where John had started packing up equipment himself. Stephen looked about and asked, "Where's Evelynn?"

John nodded toward the monitor and replied, "Still in the basement."

Stephen walked over to the monitor and looked at the screen. It was dark, the light having gone out, but he could make out Evelynn standing in the corner motionless from her flashlight upon the floor. At first Stephen thought the picture had frozen but then realized three things. He could hear a slight moaning noise coming from Evelynn, her feet were about six inches off the floor and a dark huge figure was crouching behind her.

"Oh shit!" Stephen yelled and ran toward the basement.

◆ ◆ ◆ ◆ ◆

Evelynn had seen the shadow form descend from the ceiling and stand before her. Similar to when she encountered it upstairs, an intense coldness emitted from the figure as it became more than a shadow. Evelynn began to see the hair and the dress, and when she started to say hello to this spirit that she believed was Elizabeth, a hand shot out at a surprisingly fast speed. The spirit grasped Evelynn's upper left bicep with an iron grip, then came the sensation, the pain, the visions and the word: *remember.*

The sensation felt like an intense injection of cold liquid iron that bit into her bicep and spread from there. The cold surge went up her arm like frozen water through her veins. It then flowed into her chest and down to her feet. The pain came next. It could only be described as plugging into someone else's emotional psyche, so intense the emotions were. When the pain and sensations hit the base of her skull, her vision left her. She felt as if she was floating, and then began to see what she believed were shadows of the past.

Elizabeth sits in her room with Jonathan upon her lap. Unlike the pleasant vision Evelynn had experienced previously, this one ached with despair. Jonathan sits, crying softly, as Elizabeth strokes his hair saying comforting things into his ear. A waiting, an anticipation hangs in the air. The moment is broken by the sound of heavy boots coming down the hall and stopping before the door. A key is placed in the lock, and with a slow metallic click the lock is released and the door opens.

Benjamin enters and, without so much a word, strides toward the mother and son, reaching for and grabbing the young boy's arm roughly.

"NO!" shrieks Elizabeth as the young boy is pulled from his mother's grasp, all the while crying and calling for his mother. Elizabeth tries in vain to stop Benjamin from taking her son, but a swift, hard blow sends Elizabeth reeling to the floor, stunned and dazed.

Benjamin, with Jonathan in hand, leaves the room, locking the door behind him. Cries intermixed with heavy footfalls fade down the hallway, down the stairs.

Coldness unlike anything Evelynn has ever experienced before enters her chest, and for a brief moment, she truly believes that her heart is breaking slowly apart. Despite wishing for it to stop, Evelynn's vision continues. The memories of long ago finally have a canvas upon which to play.

Benjamin easily takes the young crying child to the basement. A metal cauldron sits atop a blazing inferno of coal and wood. What smoke that doesn't escape through the chimney in the wall fills the room with an acrid haze that burns her eyes and throat. This is hell, she thinks.

Benjamin walks with purpose toward a table where a clutter of objects are placed in a haphazard fashion. Centered in the middle of this jumble of tools and objects is a book, which Benjamin glances at as if to make sure that what he is doing is correct. Then without a word or hesitation Benjamin picks up a length of cord and encircles his young son's throat, lifting his tiny kicking body upwards till the legs and arms become still.

A wail, a scream and a piercing of Evelynn's soul rips into her as she witnesses Benjamin Crimshaw strangle his young son to death. Unable to stop the vision or to wake from this horrific cinema, Evelynn cries as she believes she is actually dying.

As if the murder of Jonathan was not enough, the vision continues, unwilling to release Evelynn. Benjamin again consults the book and, with knife and cleaver in hand, begins to dismember Jonathan and place the various parts into the boiling cauldron.

◆ ◆ ◆ ◆ ◆

Stephen ran without explanation, knocking over chairs, equipment and anything else in his path as he flew toward the basement door. Robb, not knowing what had happened, was up and running as well several yards behind Stephen. As Stephen flung the door open and disappeared down the steps, Robb witnessed something he could not explain. It seemed as if a black mass rushed out of the basement, slamming the door shut as it rose up and exited through the ceiling. When Robb reached the door, he tried the knob which was ice-cold to the touch. It would not turn, barring him entrance to the basement.

◆ ◆ ◆ ◆ ◆

Evelynn feels very weak from exhaustion and is disgusted as she is forced to watch Benjamin remove the small bones from the boiled flesh. Finally, with great ceremony and ritualistic movements, he consumes the horrific stew. He stands but for a moment before falling to the floor. Wishing him dead Evelynn watches as his body jerks and convulses upon the hard-packed dirt floor. She is beyond caring at this point for herself, her sanity; she only wishes for the peaceful sleep of nonexistence. Benjamin, however, as he twitches about and begins to change all the while vomiting and coughing up bits of bile and flesh, does not die. He suddenly stops moving, and with an exhalation of breath he screams as his life force leaves him to be replaced by something else. Lying still, his eyes suddenly snap open, and with yellow hatred he looks

about the room as if searching for something. Those eyes then stop and
focus. They focus on Evelynn, and he begins to advance in her direction.
Somewhere in the distance she hears her name, distant at first but then
becoming louder till a release of sorts is upon her.

Falling to the floor, Evelynn was free of the specter's grip, free
of the visions. She vomited, expelling anything and everything she
could, as if to purge her body of the filth, the disgust and the emotions
she had just experienced. Raising her head, she thought she saw
Stephen near the steps, but what drew her full attention was the thing
coming toward her slowly. What had been Benjamin Crimshaw,
murderer in life and whatever monster he had become in death, was
now slowly advancing toward her. Yellow hate-filled eyes glared at
her as he opened his foul mouth and said slowly and clearly in a deep
voice, "*Now you die.*"

◆ ◆ ◆ ◆ ◆

Stephen had opened the door to the basement and had gone
about halfway down the stairs when he momentarily stopped and
tried to process what he was seeing. Evelynn was in the far corner
near the camera and fuse box. She was being lifted off the ground by
a dark shadow form that as he looked on became clearer in detail.
The figure was that of a woman with long unkempt hair wearing
a long dress. Her hair obscured her face, but Stephen knew it was
Elizabeth.

What was more frightening than that was the other figure near
the well slowly, cautiously moving toward Evelynn and Elizabeth.
It was Robb's skunk ape, but this time Stephen was prepared. He
pulled from his waistband Gruncle Mike's revolver and yelled, "Elizabeth, stop!"

The command had its desired effect. Elizabeth released Evelynn,
who fell to the floor like a rag doll. The creature momentarily stopped,
and the spectral image of Elizabeth changed to a black mist that sped
past Stephen on the steps and out of the basement, slamming the
door behind it.

Stephen didn't have time to think as he turned his attention back to the basement floor. The creature looked at Evelynn and spoke in a harsh forced way. "*Now you die,*" it said as it advanced upon her.

◆ ◆ ◆ ◆ ◆

Robb pulled and pounded upon the basement door, unable to force his way in. He ran back to the command post where John was looking at the screen with alarm.

"Oh shit, is that the skunk ape?" John asked.

Robb looked at the screen as it flickered once, flickered twice and then went blank.

◆ ◆ ◆ ◆ ◆

Benjamin Crimshaw slowly walked toward Evelynn, who had managed to bring herself to a semi-sitting position. He seemed to either not notice Stephen or did not care. "*I told you to leave her alone,*" Benjamin said through clenched teeth. He was getting closer, but if Evelynn had any sense of the danger she was in, it didn't seem to register with her.

A thunderous explosion occurred from the stairs, followed by a loud impact on the far wall to the left of her. Evelynn and Benjamin turned toward the stairs and saw Stephen come deeper into the basement with the revolver held up toward Benjamin.

"Get away from her," Stephen said, aiming the revolver at the creature.

Benjamin turned and begun to walk toward Stephen. "*Do you know who I am? Did she tell you?*"

"Stop," Stephen said, following Benjamin's movements with the pistol.

Benjamin continued walking toward Stephen, opening and closing his clenched fists.

"Stop!" Stephen yelled, pulling the hammer back on the revolver. Benjamin chuckled and continued to approach. When he was approximately six feet away, Stephen squeezed the trigger, firing the weapon.

Another explosion of light and flame erupted from the barrel, and with a solid thump the bullet struck Benjamin in the chest. He stopped, doubled over and then—while Stephen held his breath—he stood up again with a hole in his chest.

With insane speed Benjamin swung his massive hand out, knocking the pistol from Stephen's hand and sending it sailing toward the wall. Benjamin's hand then swung back, striking Stephen in the head and sending him tumbling toward the center of the room.

He felt the hard floor as he hit it, not sure how he had gotten there. Trying to regain some sort of focus, Stephen soon realized that he was being lifted off the floor and into the air by powerful hands.

Stephen blinked rapidly in order to clear his vision and saw that he was above Benjamin. He quickly surmised that Benjamin had picked him up and was intent on throwing him into the well. Willing his body to react, he began to strike at Benjamin's arms that were gripping him tightly. His efforts had no effect, so Stephen braced himself for the throw, thinking that perhaps Benjamin would miss the hole. An explosion shattered the basement's air, and another bullet struck Benjamin, this time in his back. Stephen fell, dropped and bounced off the wall of the well, then looked in the direction of the shot.

Evelynn, now standing, held the revolver with both hands and was pointing it at Benjamin. He appeared to be in some sort of discomfort, but other than that the second bullet still did not have the desired effect. Evelynn fired another shot, this one going wide to Benjamin's right and hitting the well, causing Stephen to roll out of the line of fire.

"Die you son of a bitch!" Evelynn yelled, squeezing the trigger rapidly.

One bullet struck Benjamin again in the chest; the next one hit his yellow right eye with a sickening crack, forcefully pushing his head back. The impact was so forceful, Benjamin turned back toward her. The right side of his face had been deformed by the bullet. With his good yellow eye trained on her, he said with a smile, *"Not likely."*

Evelynn pulled the trigger several more times with only a hollow click, indicating no more rounds remained in the revolver. Wondering what to do now, Evelynn didn't see much hope and assumed they were going to meet the same fate as Jonathan did in this cursed basement some hundred years ago. She collapsed to her knees, too weak to stand.

A sudden noticeable chill entered the basement as if someone had turned on an air-conditioning unit. Chills ran through Evelynn's body as a shadow figure floated down through the ceiling and wrapped its arms around Benjamin's body. The shadow figure became more solid and distinct as Benjamin, try as he may, could not break the grip of the specter.

The ghost of Elizabeth was no longer unkempt, dark and indistinct. Elizabeth Crimshaw was now a full apparition of a strong young woman in her prime. She was fully Elizabeth, who she was and who she was supposed to be. Squeezing her unbreakable embrace tighter around Benjamin, she opened her mouth. Instead of the soul-breaking scream Evelynn and Stephen both had experienced earlier, she simply said, *"Your sins are remembered."*

Benjamin howled in pain as something began to happen. A light began to spread from where Elizabeth's arms encircled Benjamin and grew in intensity as it spread through his body. Stephen and Evelynn watched in horrified fascination as the energy of Elizabeth slowly dissolved Benjamin's body from within. Howls of pain, of defeat, of damnation bellowed from Benjamin's ruined mouth as he, in no uncertain terms, melted.

Stephen had rolled away from the well when one of Evelynn's stray shots had struck it. He now crawled toward Evelynn, away from the ungodly dance happening before his eyes. With a final scream of triumph from Elizabeth and howl of defeat from Benjamin, the two tumbled over the edge of the well and fell within.

Evelynn was sobbing when Stephen finally made it to her; she quickly entered his embrace where all would be made whole again.

Where the world of pain, suffering and grief were pushed into the shadowed corners, and where love, joy and hope basked in the light. The last of the screams drifted away into darkness and Stephen said in a calm whisper, "It's okay. Everything is fine now."

Evelynn nodded between silent sobs and just sat there with Stephen in the darkness of the damp basement. Stephen was content at the moment just holding Evelynn. He was in pain but having her safe in his arms was worth any amount of pain.

Trying to make out anything in the darkness was difficult. His flashlight lay near the stairs providing some light although it was facing the wall. It was enough to make out some shapes in the darkness: the stairs, the well, the camera and the tripod. It was during this time of insignificant scanning that Stephen noticed something over at the well, something shining within it.

Looking at the well, Stephen could see that a light of some sort was growing brighter from within it. Then he heard a scraping noise from that direction.

"What is that?" Evelynn asked, having noticed the light and noise from the well.

"I don't know." Stephen gazed at the phenomenon.

The light grew brighter and the scraping noise louder. Too tired and fascinated to move, Stephen and Evelynn watched as a hand emerged from the well, grasped the edge and was quickly followed by another hand. The light came out of the well, momentarily blinding the two figures huddled together against the wall. A figure emerged and said, "What the hell was that?"

Robb Winchester, student and ninja, exited the depths of the well in the basement of the creepy house.

34

"Robb?" they both said in surprise and in unison.

"Yep. Everyone okay?" Robb asked.

"Yeah, sort of…" Stephen started to say.

"How did you…" Evelynn began.

"Hold on," Robb said, turning around and looking into the well. Grunts and noises preceded John as he too came out of the dark hole with Robb helping him. Once over the edge and on the floor, he fell to a sitting position, leaning against the stonework.

"That's messed up," John said, a little shaky.

"I don't understand," Stephen stated.

"Well, once the basement door slammed shut, I couldn't get in. I went back to the monitor, and we saw the skunk ape in the basement; then the screen went blank. When I heard the gunshot, I had to do something," Robb said.

Robb went on to explain that both he and John could not figure out how the skunk ape had gotten into the basement until John rewound the video and saw the creature coming up out of the well.

"It then made sense to me how that thing was getting in here. I grabbed John, and we ran to the barn—"

"The root cellar," Stephen said.

"Bingo. I knew something was off with that hole—"

"Oh man, that was messed up," John interrupted. "You don't want to know what's in that hole."

"Yeah, but it's not just a hole. It opens up a little way back and becomes a friggin' chamber. That's where it has been living!" Robb excitedly said.

"But wait. There's more," John added.

Evelynn and Stephen sat on the cold floor like school children listening to Robb the storyteller. Robb said that the chamber contained all kinds of junk, bones, and stuff probably from past victims but also had a weird shrine thing set up in the wall. Knowing they didn't have a lot of time to explore, they had headed down a tunnel that got tighter and tighter, but they could feel damp air and continued.

"I was having issues at this point and thought about turning around, but then we heard more gunshots, screaming and yelling so I figured we were going in the right direction," Robb said. "We came to what seemed to be an opening, and that's when we saw *something*, bright and angry, fly past the opening. Come to find out that the opening is along the side of the well about fifteen yards down."

Amazed and grateful, Evelynn and Stephen explained all that had happened and that Elizabeth had finally obtained some sort of justice on Benjamin.

"So, it wasn't a skunk ape after all?" Robb asked, a bit disappointed.

"Sorry, Robb, but no. It was Benjamin Crimshaw or some part of him," Stephen said.

"Can we get out of here?" John asked.

"Sure, but I'm not sure if Evelynn or I can go down the well."

"John, try the basement door. I have a feeling it's fine now," Evelynn said, slowly getting up.

John walked up the steps and to his, not Evelynn's, surprise the doorknob turned easily, allowing the door to be swung open. Stephen believed one of his ribs had been fractured or at least seriously bruised from hitting the side of the well. His leg was aflame with pain, and Evelynn was about as weak as he had ever seen her. They slowly worked their way up the stairs and as they did, they heard a knock.

"What now?" Robb said.

The knock sounded again followed by another louder knock, both coming from the direction of the foyer. Once in the hallway it was surmised that the sound was coming from the front door. Robb withdrew his ninjato and nodded to John to slowly open the door. Stephen was about to tell them to wait, but John flung the door open while Robb let out a yell and advanced on the figure outside.

Robb stopped suddenly and started laughing. Standing on the porch was a figure wearing blue coveralls and holding a clipboard. He looked at Robb and the others, then without so much as an inflection in his voice asked, "You have a broken window?"

The sun had risen by now and the morning fog quickly retreated toward the forest. They were all tired, bruised and a little dazed after experiencing all the events from the past two days. Taking Evelynn to the Jeep, which incredibly had not suffered any further damage, Stephen placed her in the front seat and grabbed a blanket from the back. She fell asleep before Stephen could place it upon her. Locking the doors, he then returned to the house.

The equipment was packed up and set near the Jeep. While the window guy worked, the other three cleaned up the house as best as they could. Stephen was sure to place the journal in a protective cover, and that all photos, audio and video were protected and saved. A lot of follow-up would need to be done in the following days.

When the window guy had finished and left, Stephen pulled Robb and John aside.

"I need you guys to do one more thing," Stephen said.

John and Robb looked puzzled but had a feeling about what "the one more thing" might be.

◆ ◆ ◆ ◆ ◆

"Why me?" John asked nervously.

"Because you're small, wiry—" Stephen began.

"Please don't say like all Asians," John interrupted.

Stephen continued through clenched teeth, "I was going to say because I simply can't." He was sure that another trip to the hospital was in his future. Was he on Strathmore's health plan yet?

"What about Robb?" John protested.

Robb had been grinning at John's discomfort but became serious and responded, "I can't. Not again. That was an emergency situation."

The three of them were in the root cellar next to the hole in the wall. Stephen had a strange hunch and needed to confirm it prior to leaving Crimshaw Manor for good.

"John, it's okay. Ben is gone; Elizabeth is gone. There is nothing here that can hurt you." Stephen continued, "Just go in there, send back video to my cell phone and scan the area."

John reluctantly agreed, looked at Robb and said, "You owe me." Then he grabbed the flashlight and went through the hole in the cellar wall.

The examination of the chamber took a little longer than expected. Stephen's hunch was right. What Robb and John had initially described as a "weird shrine thing" was exactly that—a weird shrine set up by Benjamin containing some candles and a box of small bones. Scrawled across the lid was the word *Jonathan*.

The chamber contained an assortment of bones, some animal and some possibly human. Old moldy backpacks and other personal items led Stephen to believe that they had once belonged to hikers, hunters or would-be investigators who had crossed paths with Benjamin. Stephen got the general impression that Benjamin had hibernated for long stretches of time down here and would emerge when needed or when he felt threatened.

Stephen instructed John to take plenty of photographs and to leave everything but the box of bones. Loading all the equipment into the Jeep and securing the manor, Stephen, Evelynn, Robb and John left Crimshaw Manor.

As they drove down the dirt road away from the iron gate Robb asked, "So, what now?"

Stephen looked into the rearview mirror, smiled and said, "I'm taking Evie to Red Lobster."

35

The rest of the day was spent in sleep. Evelynn rescheduled the first club meeting to the following Sunday, and they all agreed to meet Monday at the Student Center. As predicted, first thing Monday morning Evelynn received a phone call from Miss Strydecker stating that there had been a great misunderstanding regarding access to Crimshaw Manor and that future visits would be with a historical society escort. Evelynn was to return the key to Miss Strydecker as soon as possible.

Evelynn could care less about what Miss Strydecker wanted. She would get her key back but not today. Evelynn told her that they had gone into the house and done a little investigation, stressing the fact that they had been given a key. She stated that she would drop the key off as soon as she could. She did not feel the need to explain anything further about what had happened.

Evelynn had slept the sleep of the dead, and when she awoke she discovered that she had experienced burns similar to frostbite on both arms where Elizabeth had held her and lifted her into the air. Other than strange finger-shaped scars and intense exhaustion, Evelynn seemed to have recovered from her ordeal.

◆ ◆ ◆ ◆ ◆

Stephen felt better after a good day and night's sleep. He opted to not go to the hospital in lieu of a lot of Advil and taking it easy. Robb and John acted as if nothing had happened.

After teaching class on Monday, Stephen decided to stop by Dr. Marcus's office to let him know of the weekend's investigation. Dr. Marcus was surprised by the amount of activity that Stephen and his team had documented. Stephen elected to not fully describe everything that had transpired but did mention the EVPs, videos, and photographs. Dr. Marcus couldn't wait to read their final report.

"Was this an official club investigation?"

"It was. Something that the president of the club had been working on for some time," Stephen replied, taking the offered seat.

Dr. Marcus poured himself a coffee and brought one over to Stephen. "So you had actual recorded EVPs?"

"Yes, as well as some photos and video/audio." Stephen took the offered coffee.

"Amazing. Where did you get the equipment? I don't recall the club having anything like you described."

"Well, about that. It would be helpful for the school to perhaps put some funding toward equipment that the club could borrow. I could develop a course of study on using equipment in paranormal investigations," Stephen explained.

"That sounds like a great idea. Have you written up your findings yet?"

"No. We need to go over a lot more of the material and analyze it. I hope to have something written up in a few weeks."

"Outstanding. I am very excited by this, Stephen. You have really started off on the right foot. This type of research will boost our standing in the university; it really promotes our studies as professional scientific research and not just a strange hobby. I couldn't be happier. Oh, and how's Ms. Dumavastra? How did she fare during this investigation?"

Stephen had just sipped some of the hot coffee and was taken off guard by Dr. Marcus's comment. "Evelynn? She is fine. She has some very special talents that aided in the investigation." As Stephen said this he could hear Robb's voice in his head making a crude comment about the "special talents" of Evelynn.

"Yes, she does indeed. Please don't let me keep you, Stephen. I am sure you are busy and tired from that full weekend. Please send me a copy of the report as soon as you are done. In fact, plan on giving me a review of findings when you are done. I will look into equipment and how to justify it as needed for one of our courses. Good work, Stephen. Good work."

"Thank you, sir," Stephen said as he gingerly got up from the chair. Dr. Marcus shook Stephen's hand and saw him out. As Stephen was walking away, Dr. Marcus asked him, "Are you limping?"

◆ ◆ ◆ ◆ ◆

So it went for most of Monday. Each of the team members inwardly processed what had happened, what it all meant and what they would do in the future. When the time came for their meeting, the four sat in a far corner of the Student Center well away from others.

Stephen began by saying, "I'm glad to see everyone looking rested and recovered. It was a busy, busy weekend. A lot of things happened that I am proud to have been a part of, although some of it will have to remain just among us."

Robb, of course, broke the awkward silence. "Yeah, I'm sure a lot of our investigation wasn't par for the course, but…I am confused. Are we going back there?"

"No," Evelynn said without hesitation. "Miss Strydecker asked for the key and wants us escorted at all times. I don't see any reason to do that."

"But…" Stephen said, looking at each of them. "There is some unfinished business."

"Like what?" John asked.

"Well, I'll get to that. But before I do, what are your thoughts about this investigation?"

Nobody spoke up. Stephen wondered if they were still tired or if something else was going on. He looked at Robb since he sat opposite of him and asked, "What about you, Robb? Your thoughts?"

Robb sat there, cocked his head like a dog and then replied, "I'm upset about the skunk ape theory. It was fun even though some of us might have 'accidentally' been hurt. It was cool even though I still have yet to see a ghost."

"Yeah, I agree." John said, "I would, however, like to suggest more equipment if we do this again."

"Okay, good. That's the type of feedback I want to hear," Stephen said, jotting down notes. "Eve. What about you?"

Evelynn had been quiet, but said, "I think back to all that happened, and I'm a bit confused on things."

"Like what?" Stephen asked.

"Well…for starters, what about the box?" she whispered. "What about the fact that we uncovered probably a bunch of unsolved murders, but in so doing can't explain that the murderer was some paranormal creature from over a hundred and fifty years ago. What about the real possibility that those running Crimshaw Manor knew about Benjamin and Elizabeth? What about—"

Stephen held his hands up, motioning for her to both slow down and quiet down. Now it was his turn to speak, and he likewise lowered his voice. "I know. There's a lot of things that don't make logical sense. I'm with you, Eve. I have a hard time believing that nobody at the manor ever came across Benjamin's tunnel. It's possible that they are not out there that often, but it just seems strange to me. As for that matter I don't even know what the hell Benjamin was. He wasn't human."

"Ghoul," Robb said, interrupting Stephen's thoughts.

"What?" Stephen said, turning toward him.

"Ghoul. I think the skunk ape was a ghoul."

"How did you arrive at that conclusion?" John asked.

Everyone looked at Robb as he explained. "You saw this thing up close. It had superhuman strength, and you even shot it several times, yet it did not die. It has been 'alive' since the late 1800s, hiding in the tunnel under the house and surviving by eating human flesh. That's a ghoul any way you slice it."

Stephen, Evelynn and John were dumbfounded and didn't know what to say. Like many things Robb said that she didn't have a response for, Evelynn just glossed over it and continued, "So what are you saying, Stephen?"

Stephen returned his gaze to Evelynn and said in a low voice, "I am saying that we need to be on the same page about what happened. I have some ideas but need your help to do them." Stephen looked at everyone who nodded in agreement.

The tunnel under the barn and the chamber that Benjamin had been living in for over a century really bothered all of them. A lot of the stories surrounding Crimshaw Manor revolved around strange disappearances. Seeing the evidence of animal and human bones spread throughout that chamber made it obvious that Benjamin was the cause of a lot of unsolved disappearances. An anonymous tip to the police would most likely start an investigation and in turn clear up any suspicion of whether the historical society knew anything about Benjamin.

The other problem was what to do about the box of Jonathan's bones. Evelynn had at first believed that Elizabeth's spirit had been settled after obtaining justice with the destruction of Benjamin. She surmised that Elizabeth needed her energy to manifest into some sort of corporeal being. The fact was that probably no one was foolish enough to have stayed at Crimshaw Manor after being frightened by Elizabeth or, in the worst case, killed by Benjamin. Finding out that Benjamin had brutally killed and devoured his son in order to have some sort of hellish undead life kind of put a brutal spin on things.

After discussing it further the group believed that to put Elizabeth's and Jonathan's spirits to final rest the best possible course of action would be to reunite them.

"Reunite them how?" John asked.

"Well, that's where you and Robb come in," Stephen replied.

◆ ◆ ◆ ◆ ◆

It was very late Monday night that Stephen and Evelynn sat on the couch in the office at DeMaine's.

"What is taking them so long?" Stephen asked Evelynn, who was sipping on a glass of wine.

"Well, it wasn't like you asked them to go to the Pick and Pack to pick up some milk and a lottery ticket. I'm sure they will be here soon."

Stephen got up, paced a little and then sat in one of the leather wingback chairs across from her. He placed the bourbon he had been nursing down on the table. "Are you okay?" he finally asked her.

"Yes. No. I don't know," Evelynn replied. "I am still a bit exhausted. I think Elizabeth was draining me, either intentionally or accidentally, of my spirit in order to seek revenge on Benjamin. Something changed...in me. It's like she awoke something that had always been there but was unknown."

"I'm not sure I know what you're talking about, Evie."

"I don't either. I'm not making sense even to myself. My arms, however, look like I attempted some strange ritual." She lifted her sleeves up and looked at the marks Elizabeth's ghostly hands had left behind.

Stephen moved over next to her and put his arm around her. "I think they give you character," he said, kissing the wounds.

"Oh really?" Evelynn laughed. "And is character the reason that you're walking around with a limp now?"

"That was Robb's fault."

"Yes, but he probably saved your life." Evelynn placed her hands around his neck.

"Don't tell him that." Stephen leaned in and began kissing her.

Evelynn easily met Stephen's passion, and as they kissed the front door of DeMaine's opened and two figures walked in.

"Really? How long has this been going on?" Robb said in feigned surprise. John was behind him and placed two shovels against the wall. Evelynn laughed and Stephen looked embarrassed.

"All done?" Stephen asked.

"Yes, it is. Nobody saw us place the box into the ground next to Elizabeth's grave. Wow, now I'm a ghoul," Robb said.

"No, just a grave digger," John remarked.

"I think that was the best thing to do." Evelynn said, "It is weird if you think about it. It was her hatred of Benjamin and his possessiveness of her that most likely fettered her to this world. She sought vengeance, he sought forgiveness; thus creating what she had become."

Everyone was quiet, not sure what to say until Robb, caked in dirt, mud and grime from the grave, looked at Evelynn and replied, "Can I have a drink?"

◆ ◆ ◆ ◆ ◆

Stephen gave Robb and John a quick tour of the nightclub, telling them that they would be expected at the grand opening. They spoke more about the investigation in the library, deciding to hold onto Elizabeth's journal for now. They discussed the upcoming club meeting and figured that membership would increase once word got out about the very real research the four of them had done.

They laughed at Robb's expense after he discovered a text from the girl whose name he didn't know. He'd apparently forgotten about a date they had planned. They joked about the crossbow, the flying dropkick, drank and enjoyed each other's company. Evelynn mentioned she would be moving in with Stephen and swore Robb and John to secrecy about it due to her being a student and Stephen a professor. John was excited about getting involved with the club and merging his technical expertise with his interests in the bizarre. Stephen simply sat back and took it all in.

Around midnight the group decided to call it. John and Evelynn had left and were waiting outside. Robb was finishing the last of the complimentary beers Stephen had been supplying him.

"Wow," Robb said as he finished the beer and walked to the door. "You got a cool job, a hot girlfriend and an awesome place to live... You got it made, Professor."

Stephen smiled and responded, "Yes. Yes, I do. Life is good, Robb Winchester. Life is good."

EPILOGUE

Crimshaw Manor stood dark and silent in the night. No lights or sounds disturbed the stillness of the scene. That was soon to change as the sound of heavy booted steps walked from the foyer down the hall and stopped at the basement door.

Even though no light shone on the figure, it was obvious he was tall and darker than the night that surrounded him. His hand extended out and grasped the doorknob. His long fingers encircled it, a silver signet ring upon one of them. The door opened and bootsteps sounded as the figure strode down the steps and into the basement. He then stopped upon the dirt floor and looked about.

A viewer of this scene would be able to make out a tall figure standing in the basement even though it was completely dark. The tall figure stood still, a shadow among the shadows, and surveyed the basement. A coldness, an evilness emitted from this figure in waves as he began to walk over toward the corner of the basement where the fuse box was.

He stopped again, bent down as if to examine something upon the ground and then rose. A white unnatural-looking hand with long fingers and a glint of silver was placed against the dirt wall. The figure withdrew his hand and inhaled deeply. Turning, he then walked toward the well.

Again, the strange dark sleuth seemed to bend down and examine the area around the well and touching the stones. Finally satisfied, he rose and peered into the blackness of the hole itself. Unfamiliar words came from the figure's mouth, sounding of some dark black tongue of long ago. Finally, sensing his purpose was finished, he simply said, "Well done, faithful servant. She is the one."

◆ ◆ ◆ ◆ ◆

Stephen awoke with a start and a yell, cold sweat upon his brow. His hand shot out to the naked form beside him and brought him back to reality, to the present world. The darkness meant it was still night. Evelynn stirred beside him and whispered, "It's only a dream, Stephen. It's okay." She snuggled next to him.

Taking her into his embrace and feeling the heat of her body, he soon began to relax. His heart began to slow its pace back to normal and his breathing calmed as well. "Yes," he said. "It's only a dream."

As Stephen began to drift back to more pleasant thoughts, all the while intertwined with Evelynn, the room seemed to be still. The television, which had been on a timer, clicked off giving the room a definitive stillness. That stillness, however, was interrupted by a shadow that seemed to rise from the chair near the corner of the room and glide toward the door.

No one was aware of it, no one saw it and no one heard the words it spoke as it said, *"Now it begins, lad."*

AUTHOR'S NOTE

Life is a strange and exciting journey. All of your experiences have an impact on your life for good or bad. *The Haunting of Crimshaw Manor* was originally an idea for an adventure for the Chill Role-Playing Game that I ran at Radford University in the late 1980s. It was during this time that I moved into a one-hundred-year-old home and experienced my first contact with the paranormal. Good times.

I am a believer in the paranormal. I can say that without embarrassment or doubt. The many TV shows that have aired since the late 1990s have truly exposed the field of Paranormal Investigations to the entire world. While some of those shows may be entertaining and questionable, most of them are scientific and undeniable. People are quick to rationalize the strange away instead of keeping an open mind. But currently, I think that is beginning to change. By writing this book and, hopefully, future books, I aim to expose readers to the world of the paranormal in an entertaining, suspenseful and at times, humorous way.

A lot of the material within my stories is based upon facts, partial facts, stories, folklore, strange dreams/nightmares and the real-life experiences of myself and my friends. All the characters are fictional, except…Robb. He is a real person, the snow ninja, and he did give me the okay to use his likeness. Thank you, Robb, for bringing a smile to my face when I think back to those college days.

Please visit my website at *MEDrotos.com*. There you will find a lot of additional material, including maps, stories, location information, and music that I felt added to the experience of the story. I do try to respond to questions and comments. Thank you for walking in the dark with me and exploring the unknown.

ACKNOWLEDGMENTS

I can't go without thanking Vern and Joni Firestone at BHC Press. Thank you for taking my story and fulfilling my dream. Likewise, I am grateful to Stephanie Bennett for editing *The Haunting of Crimshaw Manor* and making it better.

I must also thank my brother, Michael, for his strange stories and adventures and my sister, Lisa, for all the great childhood memories. We will continue to make more.

To my friend, Todd Kingrea, who is my advisor in the world of writing and in the process of publishing a book. We have both come a long way from those years at Radford University. Thank you for your advice and friendship.

And finally, to all my friends and family who have supported me in my endeavors and encouraged me to follow my dreams. Thank you always.

ABOUT THE AUTHOR

Mark E. Drotos has always loved the strange and unexplainable. While attending Radford University, he lived in a haunted house off campus which fueled his interest in the paranormal.

After a successful career in law enforcement, it was only natural to blend his interest in the paranormal and his experience as a criminal investigator with his love of writing. *The Haunting of Crimshaw Manor* is his debut novel.

In his spare time, he enjoys boating, fishing, and being with his family. He resides in Alexandria, Virginia where he is currently working on his next ghost adventure.

CPSIA information can be obtained
at www.ICGtesting.com
Printed in the USA
LVHW100111220622
721799LV00014B/92/J